Praise for Marie-Nicole Ryan's
Love on the Run

"...Truly a delight to read."
~ *Barbara Buhrer, The Word Museum*

"LOVE ON THE RUN sprinkles generous humor over a dollop of danger, an adorable boy, a tasty hero, a spunky heroine, and a unique plot. Marie-Nicole Ryan knows how to create atmosphere and charm the reader."
~ *Denise A. Agnew, best-selling author*

"...the characters are strong and the treachery realistic. The author provides nice touches of humor, making the reader truly care about her characters."
~ *Literary Nymph Reviews*

Rating: 5 Angels "I couldn't guess what was in store for David and Miranda from one page to the next. It was fun to travel along with them and see them fight the growing attraction they both felt... I will be looking for more books written by Ms. Ryan."
~ *Kim N., Fallen Angel Reviews*

Rating: 5/5 Stars "Marie-Nicole Ryan grabs you from the first sentence and never lets go!"
~ *Nicole, Manic Readers.*

Rating: 5 Blue Ribbons "LOVE ON THE RUN has everything you could want and more in a romantic suspense."
~ *Jenn L, Romance Junkies*

Praise for Marie-Nicole Ryan's
Too Good to be True

2008 EPPIE Winner in
Erotic Romance Contemp/Suspense/Mystery Category

Rating: 5 Angels and Recommended Read . "Too Good To Be True has it all, death, drugs, sex, lies, suspense and romance."

~ *Fallen Angel Reviews*

Rating: 5 Hearts! "...gripping tale filled with edgy twists and turns... Mac and Rilla smolder when near each other... Erotic scenes are very well-written and intense."

~ *The Romance Studio*

Rating: 4 Cups "This is one steaming novel that will keep you guessing until the very end."

~ *Coffee Time Romance*

Look for these titles by
Marie-Nicole Ryan

Now Available:

Too Good to Be True
One Too Many
Holding Her Own

Love on the Run

Marie-Nicole Ryan

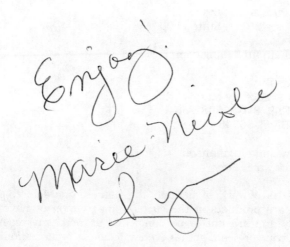

A Samhain Publishing, Ltd. publication.

Samhain Publishing, Ltd.
577 Mulberry Street, Suite 1520
Macon, GA 31201
www.samhainpublishing.com

Editing by Linda Ingmanson
Cover by Dawn Seewer

First Samhain Publishing, Ltd. electronic publication: November 2007
First Samhain Publishing, Ltd. print publication: September 2008

Dedication

To Marti Miller for her friendship and for being my first fan.

To author Carole Buck who encouraged me to follow my dream.

To Karen Doherty who encouraged me to read some fan fiction.

To Debi Potts who proofread the first version of this book and was my good luck charm.

And finally to actor Roy Dupuis whose portrayal of Michael in *La Femme Nikita* made me dream of tragic heroes and inspired me to write their stories.

Prologue

London, 2001

"I'll start the motor and let it warm up, darling." Cassie Wheeler shut the Land Rover's door and turned the key in the ignition.

"Hold on, Cassie," David called over his shoulder. "I'll be right—"

Terribly. Unbelievably. The Land Rover shook itself like a wet dog.

And exploded.

"Cassie!" Her name ripped from his throat. "No!"

Get to her, man.

On legs of overcooked pasta, he sprinted as if in slow motion. Metal fragments rained down on his head. He swiped them away.

Flames erupted from the front window of the Rover and scorched the air in his lungs. He tore at the crumpled door. Heat blistered his face and hands. One thought in mind.

Save her.

From a distance, someone yelled, "Watch it, mate! The petrol's going to blow."

David stared, his brain not believing what his eyes told him. Numbed, he backed away from the devastation—from Cassie.

A lick of flames reached the rear petrol tank. The percussive wave tossed him into the air. The pavement came up and smacked him in the face.

Then nothing.

CB

Randi Raines took a deep breath, opened the door and walked into St. Marylebone Infirmary. Her stomach heaved, as it had too frequently in the last few weeks, threatening to disgrace her right there in front of everybody. She swallowed back the nausea.

She approached the fresh-faced receptionist at the information desk. "The room number for Inspector French?" she asked.

The receptionist keyed David's name into the computer, then looked up at Randi, frowning. "I'm sorry, but he's not allowed any visitors." The young woman's voice dropped to a whisper. "Under police guard, he is."

"Under guard?" David hadn't done anything wrong. Maybe it was for his protection? "May I speak to the officer guarding him? I don't want to cause any trouble. I just want him to know I came by."

"Well, I don't see what harm that could do. I'll just ring the room." The volunteer punched in an extension. "I've a very nice lady down here who wants to see Detective Inspector French. Do you think she could? Looks harmless enough." The young woman listened, then asked, "Your name, please?"

"Miranda Raines."

The volunteer repeated her name into the telephone, then nodded. "You may go right up. Take the lift to the third floor—room three-twelve. The officer outside the door will talk to you. Maybe even pat you down, know what I mean?" she said, grinning.

Randi offered up her best imitation of a smile. "Yeah, thanks." Cringing at the thought of being touched by any man, much less patted down by a police officer, she swallowed hard. More likely she'd throw up all over his shoes.

She stepped off the elevator at the third floor. A convenient sign directed her to the left. Three-twelve was easy enough to find. It was the only room with a police officer sitting by the door.

The officer stood at her approach. "Ma'am?"

"M-Miranda Raines. The receptionist said I could come up."

"Yes, your name's on the list. I'll let D.I. French know you're here."

"I'm on the list?" She gulped. "Th-thank you." If she'd been a betting woman, she would've guessed her name would be on the list of people David *never* wanted to see again.

The officer nodded, gave a quick glance up and down the hall, then entered David's room. She strained, but all she could hear was muffled voices. Maybe David was resting. Maybe she should come back later. Maybe she shouldn't have come at all.

The door opened, cutting off her downward spiraling train of thought. "Go right in, ma'am."

"Thank you."

Put one foot in front of the other. Yes, that's how it's done.

The faint odor of disinfectant hung in the air. David sat in a chair by the window, his hands and head swathed in bandages. Dear heaven, her freedom had a high price tag.

He turned toward her, his normally handsome face distorted by redness and swelling. "Miranda, I'm glad you came."

"I-I didn't know if I should or not." She crossed the room, her hands clenching her purse. "I'm so sorry. Believe me, if I'd had the slightest idea what Stefan would do, I would've stayed with him."

"It's not your fault," he said with obvious difficulty.

She sank down in the chair opposite David's. "But it is." Tears, hot and unwelcome, started streaming down her cheeks. "Cassie's dead. If I hadn't run away from Stefan...if I hadn't moved in with her, n-none of this would've happened."

He turned his gaze on her. Unshed tears glistened in his silver-gray eyes.

Tears for Cassie.

Her own tears fell unabated with the sure knowledge she would never forgive herself. Never.

"You did the right thing."

"But you. Your face and hands—"

"The surgeon says I'll be fine—with a little time."

"B-but nothing is going to bring Cassie back." She broke down, her whole body shaking with sobs. "I'm s-so sorry."

"No, no, please don't cry," he consoled her, his voice hoarse with emotion. "It's *my* fault. You see, I'm the one who underestimated your husband." He paused, swallowed, closed his eyes for a second, then wiped his eyes with the back of a bandaged hand.

David turned away and stared out the window, then hunched his shoulders and continued. "In my arrogance, I thought all I had to do was threaten him a bit, let him know the authorities were watching, and he'd leave you alone...and you could start your life over. I was horribly wrong."

What if Stefan should find her here? What would he do? She glanced over her shoulder. "Have the police found him yet?" She pulled a tissue from her purse and blew her nose.

He turned and faced her again, his eyes soft and kind. Not that she deserved either softness or kindness.

"Don't worry, Miranda. We're certain he's fled the country. His family has contacts all over Europe. It would be a simple matter for any of them to shelter him."

"I know." She nodded. Damn Stefan and his horrible brothers and deadly father.

"What will you do now?" he asked.

"I'm leaving London. Uh—I've filed for divorce. I thought about going back to Nashville. I mean, I can always find plenty of session work, but—" She shrugged, still not sure why she didn't want to go home. Maybe it was a case of not wanting to hear her mother say, "I told you so". Maybe it was something else. It seemed so indifferent—ruin two lives, then cut her losses and run home to mama.

David's swollen mouth quirked up on one side. "You love our British food and can't bear to leave it?"

How like him to make a joke. She attempted a smile. "Something like that. I think I'll just move somewhere quiet, dig in and rethink my life. What about you?"

"I'm a copper for life. They tell me I'll be out of these..." he held up his bandaged hands "...in another week or so. I'll be back on the job in no time."

Tears abating, she sniffed. "I'm glad you're okay. I mean, physically—"

"It's all right. I don't blame you. Stefan Kristoforus killed Cassie. I won't let him get away with it."

"You'll go after him yourself?" Lord, if anything happened to David, too...

"I'll bring him to justice. See that he stands in the dock for his crime. See him rot in prison for the rest of his sorry life. That's what I mean."

"Then get him. Get him good." Clenching her fists to keep her hands from shaking, she stood. God, she had to get out of there. Seeing David was a lot harder than she'd ever imagined it could be. "I-I have to go now."

He even managed to give her a crooked smile. "Thank you for coming. It's good to see you, again."

His kind words fell softly on her ears, but felt like a kick in the stomach. Immediately more tears threatened. She'd already made a big enough fool of herself. She had to get out of there. "You, too," she managed to say, then bolted from the hospital room and made a dash for the elevator.

She punched the down button, once, twice, three times and waited. The indicator light came on, the bell—a half tone flat—dinged and the elevator door slid open.

"Finally." Breathing a sigh of relief, she entered the elevator and pressed her face against its cool metallic surface. Seeing David all wrapped up in bandages, his handsome face burned, made her guilt that much worse. He might be scarred for life. And after all he'd been through, he still tried to reassure her. Even made a joke, for pity's sake!

But no matter what he said, it was her fault. Single-handedly she'd managed to ruin the lives of two wonderful people.

But that wasn't the only reason she felt uncomfortable around him. During the short time she and poor Cassie had shared a flat, Randi had fallen in love with David. He'd been so wonderful to Cassie, so considerate and such a good man...nothing like Stefan. Randi shivered, remembering the cloying, demanding touch of his hands—and worse.

Funny, when Cassie had revealed she was engaged to the son of an earl, Randi thought he'd be stuck-up and pretentious. To her surprise, David was anything but. He went out of his way to be kind and included her in some of their plans. Of course, she hadn't intruded on their relationship. It had taken all of her willpower, but she kept to herself most of the time.

But then one terrible night, Stefan found her and David came to her rescue and warned Stefan to leave her alone. What happened after that was a matter of public record.

Heaven help her—she still cared about David, carried a torch for him...along with her soon-to-be ex-husband's baby.

Chapter One

Oxford, England, 2007

All day Randi worried and waited. But why? And for what?

Wandering from room to room, she peered out the windows into the night. All she could see was the rain. "Rain, rain, go away," she muttered. "Hell, maybe it's just PMS."

But all day she'd felt like something was about to happen. She rubbed her arms, trying to banish the army-of-ants sensation that had plagued her since morning.

Satisfied all was as it should be in her world, she walked back into the living room. "So what the hell's the matter with me?" she asked the empty room. "Relax. I know exactly what I need. Some hot chocolate and a book."

Ten minutes later, a warm mug of hot chocolate in hand, Randi settled into her favorite chair, placed the mug beside her and picked up the latest Victorian mystery. She rolled her head from side to side, trying to ease the tension in her shoulders and neck, then tried to focus on the story.

All day long everything had been a little off-key from the moment she'd awakened from a nightmare. For the first time in ages, she'd actually dreamt of Stefan. Stefan in a rage. Demanding sex. The excruciating pain that followed. And being powerless to stop his depredations on her body.

Not that she believed in ESP or anything in that realm. Her dreams never foretold the future, and her Gran Perkins hadn't made a detour on her way to the hereafter—even though Randi wouldn't have minded if Gran had found her way from Tennessee to Oxford, England. Gran had been a great listener.

I just wish you were here. Now more than ever she missed grandmother's no-nonsense advice—and her chocolate meringue pie.

The nightmare had only been the start of her bad day. To make matters worse, the clerk at the greengrocer's had been rude beyond belief. "You're in the wrong queue, Mrs. Peyton. Ten items only."

Randi looked up at the aisle marker in confusion. The clerk was right; she was in the wrong lane at the checkout with a basket full of groceries. "Sorry." She looked behind her. "There's no one behind me. Can't you just—"

"No! The sign says ten items only. You must get in the other queue."

Randi gritted her teeth. The other lanes had at least three customers each. "But—oh, never mind." Reluctantly she backed out of the express lane and wheeled her basket to the next aisle.

Her day got worse. Waiting in line for twenty minutes made her late to pick up Jamie at his private day school. She found him sitting on the curb, his backpack at his side and a concerned expression on his little face. His teacher stood beside him wearing a frank frown of displeasure.

"Students are supposed to be picked up by three-thirty sharp, Mrs. Peyton." She tapped her watch. "You're ten minutes late."

"I'm sorry. I was at the greengrocer's and—"

"Your tardiness mustn't be repeated," the teacher said with a sniff, then turned to leave. "You're setting a bad example for the boy."

"I'm sorry. I really am. It won't happen again. I promise."

"I thought you weren't coming," Jamie said with a worried whine. "Teacher was very angry."

"Of course I was coming. I'm here. I just got in the wrong line at the... Never mind."

At that moment a raindrop hit her nose. "Uh-oh. Forgot my umbrella."

"Your *brolly*, Mum. You forgot your *brolly*."

"You say brolly, I say umbrella," she sang.

"You're a silly mum."

The raindrops fell harder. "Better a silly one than a wet one. Come on. Let's run."

And run they had, but the sudden downpour soaked them both to the skin.

After changing out of their wet clothes, she prepared Jamie's dinner—she'd been too edgy to eat—then put him to bed at his usual time and read him a chapter of the latest *Harry Potter*. She closed the book, wishing she could capture the moment for all time.

Jamie held up his face for a goodnight kiss. "Just one more chapter, please."

In spite of her edginess, she'd given in. "All right. Just one more."

"Wizard!" he exclaimed and rewarded her with a beaming smile and a contented wiggle as he snuggled against her. When she finished, Jamie tugged on her sleeve. "Drink of water?"

"Okay." She gave him the water. It was all part of their evening routine.

"Mm." He wiped his hand across his mouth. "I was so thirsty. Thank you."

"You're welcome." English children were nothing if not well-mannered. She put her hands on her hips and gave him the time-to-go-to-sleep stare. "Are you ready for your hug?"

"Yes!" Holding up his arms, he wrapped them around her neck and squeezed. "I'm your only boy, aren't I?"

"You certainly are my only boy," she said, hugging him back and then planted a kiss on his sweet little forehead. "G'night, son."

"Night, Mummy. I love you."

Her heart clutched as it always did when he said those magic words. "I love you, too."

Yet all things considered, it hadn't been that bad a day, she tried to convince herself.

She was just a worry wart. Everybody had days that didn't go like they should. Today was just one of those.

CЗ

Not long afterward, she found herself still staring at the first page of the book, and there was a nasty skim on top of the hot chocolate. She glanced at the long case clock. "Thirty minutes? Damn. Might as well go to bed."

At that moment, a knock sounded at her front door. She jumped and dropped her book. Making a valiant grab for it, she knocked over the mug of hot chocolate.

"Damn it." She tried to extricate herself from the yawning maw of the recliner. Whoever was knocking on her door had piss for brains or he wouldn't be out in the middle of a downpour, banging on her door, now would he?

"Hold on!" She stood and promptly tripped over a foot-high stack of as-yet-unread mysteries. "I'm coming. Don't get your panties in a wad." Finally making it to her feet, she jammed her big toe on the coffee table. "Damn!"

Her caller knocked again, this time louder. "I'm coming!"

She limped to the front door, regrettably still swearing. She flicked on the porch light, but naturally, it was burned out and all she could see through the glass panel was the tall figure of a man. "Wh-who is it?"

Frankly, she liked her mysteries on the printed page—not at her front door.

Oxford, England, the City of Spires, might be a wonderful place to live, but she wasn't about to open her door in the middle of a god-awful storm to just anybody.

"Miranda, please open the door. It's a beastly night."

Miranda? Only two people ever called her by her given name. And unless her mother's voice had deepened by an octave or two, the only other person who did was a certain Scotland Yard detective. And it had been...how long?

Six years. "David?"

As she opened the door a cautious inch, a bolt of lightning flashed nearby and a crash of thunder rent the night. She jumped back, then quipped, "I should've known you'd bring your own sound effects. What'll you do for an encore?" Okay, so she was babbling, as usual, when her nerves were on edge. Now that she knew who her mysterious visitor was, her heart revved up. What did he want? Somehow she knew it wasn't a cup of cocoa.

Detective Inspector David French strolled into her house, his rain-slicked auburn hair waving back from his forehead. His six-feet, two-inch frame made her living room seem a lot smaller than it had only moments before. She'd forgotten how tall he was. She took another step back and looked up into his cool gray eyes. "What's wrong? Why're you here?" Her voice wavered. She hadn't seen him since that day in the hospital.

Relief washed through her. Thank God he wasn't permanently scarred. In fact, he hadn't changed much at all. Always lean and angular, he was still handsome enough to play a detective on the BBC. True, he had a few tiny lines at the corners of his eyes, but they didn't detract. They just made him seem a shade more human.

Six years since the horrible business with Cassie and Stefan.

One step away from a full-blown panic attack, she blurted, "What's going on? Something has happened, hasn't it? You might as well tell me"

David scanned her living room, as if taking in every item. "You've made a nice little home for yourself. I'd no idea you were still in the U.K., until the call came from MI5. Are you alone?"

She looked over her shoulder and down the hall. "Not exactly."

His body appeared to go on alert. His shoulders straightened. His jaw clenched. "Who else is here?" He paced around the living room. "You're living with someone? That wasn't in my briefing."

Randi swallowed, wishing she could keep her secret a little longer. "My son."

His eyes widened, his thick dark brows arched in surprise. "Your son?"

She nodded. "Stefan's."

"I never knew." His eyes turned to slate.

"I managed to keep it a secret during the trial. Then MI5 relocated me to Oxford and changed my name to Peyton. They knew about the baby, but there was no reason to tell anyone else.

"This rather complicates matters," he said, staring at the ceiling as if he might find a solution written there.

"Please, tell me what's happened? Why're you here?" Her stomach lurched into a *Danse Macabre*, keeping counter-time to the staccato jittering of her knees.

David looked down, placed his hands on her shoulders and gazed into her eyes. "Your ex has escaped from prison. I'm here to take you to a safe house."

"Omigod. No, not again." Stefan couldn't possibly know where she was. Not this time. She shook her head. "No, I'm not running. I have this house and my work. My son. He's in school. He needs stability. I just can't up and—"

Grasping her shoulders, David stopped her rush of words with a gentle, but firm, shake. "Listen to me, Miranda. Stefan's already killed once. You and your child are in danger. What if he discovers he has a son? He'll try to take him, and he won't care who gets in his way."

Reality settled, crushing her, followed by a thin veil of resignation. "How long do I have? What can we take?"

"Fifteen minutes. One bag for the two of you. That's it. Sorry."

"Fifteen minutes," she repeated, her voice dull. She fought back her fear. No time for self-indulgence. She had to think about Jamie, not herself. She could put up with anything if it meant keeping her son away from Stefan and the rest of his family. "Where?"

"There's a safe house on the outskirts of London, about an hour from here. After that, it'll be up to MI5."

"MI5, hmph! Not a very cheerful lot." She gave him an appraising glance. "You're working for them now?"

He shook his head. "No, they sent me because they knew you'd trust me and not quibble over the details."

"Yeah, right." That wasn't what she'd meant to say. The blood rushed to her face. No point in getting mad at David. After all, he was here to help. Just like he'd tried to help six years ago.

Oh, God.

"Not that I don't trust you. Of course, I do. I just—hell,

never mind." Waving her hands in the air in a gesture of surrender, she sighed. "I give up. Guess I'd better get busy."

He brushed a stray lock of hair back from her forehead. "I'm afraid so."

She jerked away instinctively as she tried to convince herself that David, of all people, meant her no harm. Yet his gentle touch startled her as much as if he'd been Stefan. And Stefan had never been gentle.

Somehow she found the strength to muster a casual tone. "Well, have a seat while I get our things together. Only one?"

"Only one."

Looking around the living room of her cozy cottage, she saw all the things she loved. Her books, her plants, her violin, her life—everything shot to hell with one knock on the door. Would it be as simple as he said? *Just until Stefan was captured.*

"I'm sorry, Miranda, truly."

She shrugged and gave another small sigh. "It's just temporary, right?"

"Right," he said in an obvious attempt to reassure her. The grave expression on his long face told her more than his words. But she couldn't help wondering why nature had seen fit to place such a frivolous dimple in the middle of his chin. Not a deep pit, but a sweet, barely-there dimple. She wondered, too, how long it had been since David had smiled. He looked out of practice. And the way things were shaping up, she doubted she'd see the wonderful smile she remembered from before.

So long ago, it seemed like another life.

Without saying another word, she turned and walked down the hall.

Time to get the show on the road. And stop thinking about the dimple in David's strong chin.

Cଞ

David shoved his hands in his pockets and leaned back against the book-lined shelves in Miranda's sitting room. Memories flooded his mind. Images of another snug sitting room, of laughter and easy conversation. Cassie, her dark eyes glowing as she related the latest anecdote from the bookstore. Memories, too, of Miranda, always ready with a laugh, but with an unspoken sadness in her green eyes.

Damn it all! The last thing in the world he needed—or wanted—was an assignment that reminded him of the worst day of his life.

The sound of drawers being opened and closed reached him. He glanced down at his watch: nine-thirty. He'd wasted too much time already. The pouring rain had slowed the traffic on the M40 from London to Oxford, doubling the drive time and tripling his level of frustration. He watched her emerge from one room and shuffle across the hall to another, dragging a large piece of soft-sided luggage.

From where he stood, he heard her soft murmuring to her son. Who would the boy would resemble? Would he have dark hair and eyes like his wretched father or be fair like his mother? He hadn't counted on the boy. MI5 had known about her son. Surely his superiors had known, as well.

Bloody hell, but they could have warned him! A minor detail and one he damn well should've known about in advance. Bad enough he had to play bodyguard to Miranda, much less protect the child of the man responsible for killing Cassie. Leading the manhunt for Stefan Kristoforus—now that was the assignment he wanted.

છ

Randi's tears blinded her while she packed everything she thought she might need—for how long? Damn it—just when everything in their lives had come together. The neat little cottage she'd just bought and Jamie enrolled in a private day school, all thanks to the inheritance from her grandmother.

Why now? What a fool she'd been, thinking she had everything under control. Stefan had ruined her life once. And now, sitting in her living room was a reminder of the other lives her ex had destroyed.

"Stop it," she told herself, then wiped her eyes. Jamie was the important one. She had to protect him, no matter what it cost.

Securing the last zipper, she hauled the suitcase off the bed. She'd pack Jamie's stuff next, then wake him. How would he react to being dragged out of bed in the middle of a thunderstorm? Heaven only knew.

She stole into her son's bedroom and started packing his clothes. She even packed a few small toys, doubting a government safe house would come equipped to meet the needs of a bored five year old. Finally the suitcase was stuffed full. She couldn't put off waking him any longer.

Leaning over, she kissed his forehead. "Sweetie, you have to wake up now."

He opened his eyes and stared around the room. "Is it morning?" he asked, stretching and yawning. "Sleepy."

"No, it's still night, but an old friend of mine has come by, and we're all going on a little trip."

He frowned and rubbed his eyes. "But I'm sleepy."

"You can sleep in the car." Without waiting for more objections, she slipped a shirt and a pair of pants over his pajamas. Once she had him dressed, she picked him up and hugged him to her chest. Her sweet little boy—what would her life be without him?

"I love you, Mummy," he whispered, still groggy with sleep.

"I love you, too, darlin'."

ﾂ

David watched Miranda emerge from her son's room, carrying the child on her right hip and dragging their worldly goods with her left hand. Motherhood had wrought changes in the small woman in front of him. Five years earlier she'd had a boyish figure, but now she possessed a woman's rounded curves. He estimated one stone, perhaps a bit less, had made the difference. Her thick, dark-blonde hair, cut in a simple, shoulder-length style, was brushed back from her heart-shaped face, revealing clear green eyes, more troubled than sad.

She cleared her throat, a quizzical expression on her face. "We're ready."

"Sorry, I guess I was wool-gathering."

"Jamie, this is my friend, Detective Inspector French."

"Actually, it's Detective Chief Inspector now," he corrected gently.

"Of course, I read about your promotion when you captured—uh—" She broke off, obviously not wanting to say too much in front of the boy. "We're going with DCI French on a little trip."

"He's a copper?" the boy asked, yawning and rubbing his eyes.

"Yes, Jamie, I am." The boy had his father's dark complexion, hair and eyes, but it wasn't the child's fault, he forced himself to remember. "Would you like to come with your mum and me?"

The boy nodded and gave another big yawn.

Miranda flashed a feeble smile. "I guess we'd better get this over with."

She hadn't lost her soft Tennessee drawl either, he thought. Guessing she'd prefer carrying her son, he reached for her bag. "Allow me. Have everything you need?"

"In one bag?" Her askance look at her bag, not to mention her rolled-back eyes, told him she doubted his common sense.

"Not by half, but I have changes of clothes for both of us and stuff."

"Stuff?" Sometimes, American slang bewildered David.

"Toothpaste, deodorant. Do I have to draw you a picture?"

"No, of course not." What a dolt she must think him. First staring like he'd never seen her before and now questioning her choice of *personal* items.

She gave a worried glance around the room. "How long? Before we can come back, I mean?"

He shrugged. "Depends on how long it takes the authorities to recover—uh, you know whom."

"The authorities? Will you be involved again?"

He shook his head. "No, I'm very much afraid you're stuck with me. I'm your guardian until this situation is resolved satisfactorily."

"Seems like you're the one who's stuck with us."

"Not at all. I'm delighted to see to your safety, as well as your son's."

"Delighted? Odd choice of words." She stopped at the hall tree and grabbed rain gear for herself and the child. "Here," she said, handing her son to David while she dragged on her raincoat.

"I guess it is. I'm not sure myself. It's my duty, as an officer—"

"And a gentleman?" she completed for him with a wry half smile.

"I suppose there is an element of duty and honor in how I feel. Besides, you were Cassie's friend. How could I not help you?"

Not to mention I was ordered here.

He poked the boy's limp arms into his anorak and pulled the hood over his head, then handed him back to his mother.

She gazed up at him, her crystal green eyes still troubled. "You should hate me. This is all my fault."

He shut his eyes, trying to blot out the sudden onslaught of fiery images. Struggling for control, he took a deep breath before answering, "This isn't the time. What I mean to say is we may discuss it later, but please be assured I do *not* blame you in any way for Cassie's death. We need to leave—now."

"Right." She glanced around her cottage once more, uncertainty clearly written across her face.

"This is just a precaution, you know. I'm sure it won't be long before you're back home."

CB

Across the street from Randi's cottage, Stefan Kristoforus stood hidden in the shadow cast by a large yew. He'd found her. Better yet, he'd found his son—the son he had known nothing about until a week ago. His older brothers' wives were useless when it came to ensuring the family name wouldn't die. Xander's wife was barren and Theo's only produced girls. Stefan smiled. *He* had produced the only male heir. Only a son could be expected to deal arms and broker terrorist activities. But not one who remained with his wimp of a mother who would rear him soft and good for nothing. He'd rescue his son and give him the life for which he was destined—one of power, money and privilege.

Damn Randi for changing her name and keeping the boy a secret. Once he had his son, he *would* pay her back. Pay her back for leaving him in the first place. Pay her back for the years he'd spent in prison away from his family and his heir. He smiled. Yes, she would definitely pay.

Money in the right hands had engineered his escape, but only fate could've granted him an unexpected bonus in the guise of one Scotland Yard detective. Yes, indeed. Who should appear at the front door of his ex-wife's house but that implacable hound of the law—the one responsible for tracking him all over Europe and sending him to rot in prison? Detective Chief Inspector French—how Stefan despised him, even more than his miserable, little ex-wife.

He watched the three of them leave the house, run through the rain and climb into the detective's car. He smiled, placing the garrote back in his pocket. He could wait.

After all, patience was touted as a virtue, wasn't it?

Chapter Two

Miserable and wet, Randi followed David up the sidewalk to a townhouse. Traffic had been terrible. Who would've thought so many people would be out on a night fit only for fish? If she weren't so afraid of Stefan, she never would've agreed to leave her comfortable little cottage, and for what? An anonymous safe house in a nondescript neighborhood? She looked up at the large, brick detached house towering in front of her. In spite of the dark night, the house, with its tall arched windows, appeared in excellent condition.

David opened the door and flicked the light switch in the wide entry hall. He turned and held out his arms. "Here let me take him upstairs. He's almost as big as you are."

She hefted her son into David's strong arms. "Thanks. I think he's going to be tall."

He raised his eyebrows, the corner of his mouth crooking up. "Like his father."

"Yeah. And I hope his height is the only way he takes after that miserable..." She stopped. No point in waking up her son and having him hear her true opinion of his father. She looked around at the hand-painted French wallpaper, the gleaming dark oak paneling and the antique Persian carpet. "This is a government safe house?"

David gave her a wry smile. "Not exactly government issue, is it?"

Still puzzled, she glanced at the ornate crown moldings and shook her head. "Not unless the queen uses it when she's slumming."

"It belonged to my father. He bought it in a fit of civic duty and had it refurbished from the ground up."

"It's beautiful." She looked about the foyer, noting the fine antiques—an Empire center table with a base of three ormolu dolphins, a tall breakfront topped with matching chinoiserie vases—Ming dynasty, probably. Not that she knew for sure. Her antique dealer-mother was the real expert.

David glanced toward the stairway then at the sleeping child in his arms. "I'll put him in the same room with you, if that's agreeable?"

She nodded. "Thanks." He turned and started up the steps. She hid a yawn and followed, her hand brushing along the satin-finished oak banister. "Someone must live here. There's not a speck of dust." Unlike her own little place, where the occasional dust bunny lived side by side quite comfortably with stuffed toys and model cars.

He stopped at the top of the stairs and peered down at her with a sheepish expression. "I live here. It's mine now."

"Oh. But I thought—"

"You'll be quite safe here and certainly more comfortable than at a government-issue safe house," he told her with a lopsided grin that did serious damage to the functioning of her heart.

If only things could've been different. If only *she* could've been different.

Cʒ

"Sleep well, little one," Randi murmured, kissing her son's soft cheek. She brushed back a lock of dark brown hair from his forehead. Pulling the satin coverlet over her son, she marveled at how much she loved him. Only someone who'd had a child could ever understand the workings of a mother's heart. So much love, all expended on the behalf of one sweet, sturdy little boy, now safe and asleep.

David cleared his throat. "He's a handsome young fellow. I believe I see some resemblance to you."

"You really think so? I think he's his father made over. His hair, his eyes."

"True, he has his father's coloring, but I'm sure that's all."

She heaved a sigh. "I certainly *hope* that's all." She straightened and gazed into his unreadable gray eyes. "Thank you. It's very nice of you, putting us up in your own home like this.

"Once I learned you had a son—let's just say the safe house didn't seem like the best place. Government safe houses tend to be spartan at best."

"What happens next? I mean, where do we go from here?"

"You don't have to go anywhere. Just stay here."

Confused, she glanced about the luxurious bedroom. "Surely you don't mean for us to stay here all the time? That's a lot of trouble. After all, we don't want to interfere with your life." She gave a helpless shrug.

"Why not? You'll be safe. My security system is topnotch. Besides, you're not interfering with anything. In fact, you're my assignment. I'm *supposed* to keep an eye on you."

"Right, it slipped my mind." Again she yawned. It was way past her usual bedtime, too. "Sorry."

"You look exhausted. Would you like some tea or warm milk?"

She frowned and wrinkled her nose. "Warm milk—hmm. Tea would be great."

"I'm not much of a cook, but I'm a pretty good hand at tea."

She giggled. "Isn't that genetic? Aren't all Brits born knowing how to fix tea?"

Once more, his smile appeared, showing even, white teeth. "I suppose that's true."

"A cuppa would be perfect." For some reason tea provided just enough stimulation to perk her up, but never kept her awake—as long as she only had one cup.

He nodded. "Right. I'll bring it up as soon as it's ready." He turned and strode from the room, a man with a mission. She watched his tall, broad-shouldered figure, then gave a soft sigh. She had no business thinking about his broad shoulders or his trim waist. He'd made it perfectly clear: she was his assignment.

CB

Down in the kitchen, he bumbled around, opening and closing cabinets until he found the tea things. While he hadn't lied about his ability to prepare tea, the truth was he hadn't spent much time in his own kitchen.

Once he had the kettle on, he paced about the kitchen, waiting for the water to boil. It was quite uncharacteristic, his being nervous around Miranda. Watching her put her son to bed had nearly undone him. Miranda bending over her son, tucking him into bed...a painting by Cassatt.

Unbidden, an image of Cassie came to his mind's eye. Her waterfall of silken, black hair spilling over her shoulders as she leaned over the child they might've had. The intensity of the image astonished him. He shook his head, trying to clear the image.

The life he'd planned would never be.

The kettle whistled. He whirled around to take it off and knocked over the milk pitcher. "Bugger!" He'd made a fine mess—of pretty much everything—now that he thought about it. He snatched up a paper towel and mopped up the spillage.

Take a deep breath, old man.

He spent the next five minutes preparing a tea tray for two. After all, she might think him rude if he didn't join her, but on the other hand, she might prefer a bit of solitude with her cuppa. Bloody hell, he was worse than a dithering schoolgirl.

He squared his shoulders, then picked up the tray. Time to be hospitable to his guest.

He found the bedroom door closed, so he knocked softly, in case she'd fallen asleep. "Cassie," he called, then cursed himself for a fool. What was he thinking?

"Miranda."

She opened the door, a sorrowful expression across her pretty face. Attired in her robe and a very curious pair of slippers, she took the tray from him and carried it over to the small settee.

"You still think about her, don't you?" she said, setting the tray on the tea table. She patted the place beside her on the settee.

"Yes." He sat and watched her pour two cups of steaming tea.

She looked up, giving him a shy smile. "Sugar, cream or lemon? I'm afraid I've forgotten how you take yours."

"One sugar. If you'd rather turn in, I'll understand."

She emitted a small sigh. "Maybe it would help if you talked about her?"

He shook his head. "No. I mean, I don't see what it would accomplish except keep you awake."

"She's still on your mind. I don't mean to pry, but I'm a good listener."

He looked about the room and shrugged. She was merely trying to be kind. "I'd already made arrangements to purchase this townhouse from my father right before Cassie died." He took a swallow of tea. "Afterwards, I didn't want the place. My father..." He gave a harsh bark of laugher. "He insisted on my going through with the purchase, so..." he continued with a shrug, "...here I am, rattling around."

"It's a lovely place. You'll—"

"Please, no platitudes about falling in love again." He jumped up, unable to stand any more baring of his pain. "I think I'll let you get some rest. I've interrupted your life as it is."

Her face flushed, but she reached out and touched his arm. "I'm sorry, David, I have a bad habit of sticking my foot in my mouth. All I want to say is I miss Cassie, too. She was my best friend, and every day I have to face the fact that if it weren't for me, she'd still be alive."

The pain she felt was obvious in her face. "You mustn't blame yourself. I never did. If anyone was to blame, I was—"

The room went black. The blaring scream of the security system cut off the rest of his response. "Get down!"

Adrenaline propelled him into overdrive. He dropped into a crouch and eased toward the door. He heard, rather than saw, the muffled thump of Miranda pulling her son onto the floor behind the bed.

He strained, listening for the slightest sound.

Squeak.

Second step from the bottom. David reached back and jerked his weapon from its holster. His status in the Criminal Intelligence Division as an authorized firearms officer on one of the Specialist Crime Directorate's' armed surveillance teams permitted him to carry a firearm, and he was damned glad. In the dark he ejected and checked the magazine by touch, then jammed it back into the gun butt. Assured the M9 Beretta was fully loaded, he pulled back on the slide and heard the click of the chambered round.

Still listening. Whimpering... Jamie.

How many were there? Single intruder? Too much to hope for. He crept around the bottom of the door frame. Head low, he inched into the hallway.

CR

Randi hugged her son to her chest, her hand clapped over his mouth. "Shh. It's all right. Mummy's here."

Jamie stopped struggling, but trembled in her arms. She forced herself to quiet her ragged breathing. In all her life, she'd never been so frightened.

Was it Stefan? Who else could it be? How could he have found them so quickly? The Kristoforus family prized their children, especially the males. That was the reason she'd moved away and kept her pregnancy a secret from his family.

Yet somehow, he must've found out about her son.

Her cell phone! Damn! Dragging Jamie with her, she scooted over to her bag—the only one David had allowed her—then unzipped it. She dug around, feeling for the small rectangular object that could be nothing other than her cell phone. Now if the damn battery was charged—it was! Her trembling fingers punched nine-nine-nine. She held her breath.

"Emergency Service, how may I be of assistance?"

"Home invasion," she whispered. Oh hell, what was David's address?

"Address, please."

She shut her eyes and tried to visualize the house number. "Fairway Crescent, one-thirty-nine, I think. DCI French's house. Please hurry."

"Remain calm, madam. Stay on the line."

"I'll t-try."

"Are they in the house? Are they armed?"

"Yes, and I don't know. The electricity's been cut off, but the security is still blaring."

"Yes, the alarm has been called to us. Officers are on the way. Stay on the line."

Randi held the cell so tightly, her fingers must've dented the hard plastic case. "My son is here, too. Please hurry." She bit her lip. Don't panic. David would protect them.

Where was he? From her spot on the floor behind the bed, she couldn't see a damn thing. Her universe had been reduced to her son, David and the voice on the other end of the line. "DCI French is here, too. There are three of us," she cautioned.

She sure as hell didn't want the authorities to injure David, thinking he was the intruder.

CB

Gun drawn, David worked his way down the hall. Hoping there was only one intruder on the stairs, he darted his head around the corner. One shadowy figure stood halfway up the stairway, listening.

He sighted and took aim at the dark figure.

The rasping spit of a silencer! A bullet struck the wall just above his head.

He dropped, rolled and fired off several rounds.

"Ugh!"

One of his shots had hit home.

Then he heard the sound of a body slithering down the stairs, followed by a rush of footsteps.

"Stop!" He fired again and glass shattered.

He peered around the corner in time to see the assailant

diving headlong through one of the front parlor windows.

He jumped up and tore down the stairs, two at a time. By the time he reached the window, the intruder had disappeared. "Blast!" In the distance he heard the familiar dissonant wail of the authorities coming to the rescue.

"Miranda!" he yelled. He backed away from the window, shoved the gun in his holster, then spun and bounded up the stairs. "Come on. We're getting out of here."

As his eyes adjusted to the darkness, he saw Miranda peek around the door frame.

"What? Why?"

"Someone's leaked the intel on your location to your ex. We can't stay here. He got away. He could come back."

She stood, propping a wide-eyed Jamie on her hip. "Do you really think it was Stefan?" she whispered. Then to her son, she crooned, "It's all right, baby. The bad man is gone."

"Same height and build. I don't believe in coincidence. Who else? He must've been watching your house and followed us."

Miranda shook her head, denying the obvious horror of his words. "Already at my house? No. That can't be."

He reached out and ruffled Jamie's tousled hair. "Come on. I have another motor in the alley behind the house. We'll take it."

"What about the police?"

"They'll have made a trip for nothing. Let's go."

"But—"

"I've underestimated him twice. I won't do it again."

Jamie rubbed his eyes and shot a curious gaze in David's direction. "Are we running away? I don't think I like it here."

David's heart clutched. Such a self-contained child. Most his age would be screaming or crying. His behavior said a lot for Miranda's parenting.

C3

David secured the door to their train compartment. "Try to

sleep while you can. We've a couple of hours before we reach Canterbury."

She yawned and nodded. Her son had given up and fallen sound asleep. It had taken them four hours, two taxis and three train changes, but he was certain no one had followed them onto this train.

He stretched out his legs, while watching Miranda through not quite closed eyelids. Lying on the opposite bench seat, even in her sleep, she cradled the boy in her arms.

He kept watch, relieved that she could finally get some rest.

Simple relocation. Move the little woman out of harm's way, just until we nick Kristoforus. That's all the Chief Superintendent had said. Bloody hell, but he should've known something was awry. Naturally, anything involving Miranda couldn't be simple. He hadn't known her very long before Cassie died, but he'd never understood how a musician from Nashville, Tennessee, came to meet and marry an international arms dealer. Like the remainder of his blasted family, Stefan Kristoforus had ties to most of the known terrorist organizations in Europe and Asia.

Why hadn't she simply moved back to the States? If he remembered correctly, she had family there. What had kept her in England?

CB

Stefan winced as the surgeon dressed his left shoulder, packing it with gauze, then wrapping it with an elastic bandage. He attempted to rotate his shoulder, then immediately regretted it. He grunted in pain. Damn thing throbbed like a son of a bitch. Hell, it hurt to breathe.

"It's a shoulder wound. You're lucky you got to me in time. You can bleed out from a wound like this. You'll need to return daily for dressing changes," the surgeon told him. "My nurse can take care of it. It'll take quite some time to heal."

He shook his head. "I'm afraid that won't be possible."

"Of course it will. Just call 'round in the morning. She'll set you up."

"No." With his right hand, he snatched the scalpel from the instrument stand and held it to the surgeon's throat. His face turned as white as one of the exam table linens.

Stefan smiled. "Mind you, you've never seen me and won't ever see me. Or your nurse won't have a job tomorrow. Understand?"

The surgeon nodded in agreement. "Y-yes, I do."

"Thought you would." He snatched the doctor's black leather bag. He opened it and methodically packed an assortment of bandages and tape, along with syringes and a supply of antibiotics. He could manage his own damn dressing.

His days in the prison infirmary hadn't been wasted.

Chapter Three

As they walked across a grassy meadow to the small private plane, David considered his traveling companions. Together, they made an unlikely threesome—Miranda, the mother, attractive and petite, wrenched from her comfortable life and her son, a small, silent ebony-haired child, who clung to his mother's hand as if it were a lifeline and struggled to keep pace with her longer strides. And last of all, he, the protector, a man haunted by his past failure to protect the one he loved.

Miranda kept up her interminable apologies. "I'm so sorry, David."

"None of this your fault," he told her again, "but we have to make the best of it and keep moving." Still baffled, he would discover exactly how Kristoforus had found Miranda and her son so quickly. In the meantime, he walked toward the plane, placing one foot in front of the other.

What else could he do?

"Still, you would've never become involved, if..."

He swallowed the emotions that hung like a clot of regret in his throat. Cassie, so good and gentle. For six years, he'd mourned her. Mourned her still. Now, he was charged with the responsibility of a woman and child he barely knew.

"No guarantees in life, Miranda." He shrugged. Too bitterly he knew the truth of his words.

"It's not that simple. You have to be angry."

He looked down and recognized the willfulness flashing in her clear gaze. Maybe there was hope for her yet. She would need every ounce of spirit she had—and then some.

"Anger is a waste of time and energy. I have to stay focused on the present and the task at hand."

She chewed her full bottom lip, then said, "Okay for now, but you'll have to face it sooner or later."

"Maybe." He stopped. They'd reached the open door of a double-engine Cessna. "Here you go, young man," he said and hoisted the child into the plane.

"Thank you, sir," the child said, speaking for the first time since they'd fled the townhouse. The boy's dark brown eyes, wide with unvoiced questions, gazed up at him, but there was trust in them, too. If only he could live up to that trust.

"You're welcome, Jamie." He turned and extended his hand to Miranda. She placed her graceful, slender fingers into his, her expression wary. No wonder she didn't trust him. After all, he hadn't been able to protect Cassie.

A second failure wasn't an option. He had to protect these two.

How long would they have to run? Stefan Kristoforus was prepared to wipe him—no, them—off the face of the earth. He had to remember there were three of them now, bound together by necessity and honor.

Yes, they made an inconvenient threesome.

⋈

Randi never would've made it into the Cessna if David hadn't given her a no-nonsense boost. After fastening Jamie's seat belt, she sat and attended to her own, her legs still jittering like tree limbs in a tornado. She'd never flown in a small plane, but if she had to bite her bottom lip all the way through, she would—just to keep her son from being scared to death, too. No sense in both of them having the screaming meemies.

"How high are we going, Mr. Pilot?"

Her son's cheerful voice gladdened her heart. So far, so good. It never failed to amaze her how quickly children put trauma behind them.

The pilot, a lanky man in his late twenties, adjusted his goggles, turned around and gave a wide, gap-toothed smile.

"High enough to see everything you ever wanted to see, laddie."

"Super!" Jamie grinned and clapped his hands. "I want to see everything. Will I be able to see Mars?"

"We're not going to be quite that high, but you'll see quite a bit o' the country, never fear."

Randi turned to David who sat across the small aisle from her, staring out the window. "Where are we going?"

He turned, his eyes darkened with an unreadable emotion. Grief? Anger? Damn, he puzzled her.

"France. I thought we'd go there first, regroup and then decide where to go from there."

Horrified, she gasped, "France?"

An expression of irritation passed over his face. "Do you have a better suggestion? We need to get out of the country rather quickly."

She shivered, remembering the horrible flight over the Atlantic when she first came to England. "B-but we'll be flying over the Channel."

"That is the usual route. Flying is less traceable than if we took the Eurostar."

"But don't we have to file a flight plan?"

He gave her a grim smile. "The pilot is an old friend. Shall we say he's been creative with the truth in his flight plan."

The airplane engine roared to life, and she gave a jump.

"What's the matter now?" her protector asked, his tone aggravated.

She rolled her eyes and mouthed, "I'm afraid of flying."

He responded by another blank stare. Only the twitching corner of his mouth told her he was amused. Fine. Just let him be amused. David French was entirely too civilized to be a police detective anyway. She stuck her tongue out at him.

Jamie poked her arm. "Mummy! Why are you sticking your tongue at DCI French? You told me that was very rude."

Honestly, her son was too damned observant. "Uh, well..." The plane had already started to move, taxiing forward across the grass airstrip. She swallowed hard and gripped the arm rest.

"Your mother would never be intentionally rude, Jamie. I'm sure she has a very good reason." David cast her a cheeky grin.

She bit her lip. The instrument of destruction and death picked up speed, hurtling them faster toward oblivion—or at least that's how she felt. She shot David an if-I-could-kill-you-I-would glance and clutched the arm rests until her knuckles turned white.

The Cessna lifted into the air. Airborne. She gasped. Honestly she couldn't hold it back.

"This is super. I love flying, Mummy. Look how high we are already!"

Randi squeezed her eyes shut. No way was she opening them until they were on sweet Mother earth again. "'S all right, Jamie." The plane dipped. Her stomach flipped. She held her breath—and prayed. She could do this for her son. Anything for her son.

C3

David glanced across the aisle at Miranda. Her eyes were tightly shut and her hands gripped the armrests until her knuckles were indeed white. He wondered how in blazes she ever managed to make the trip from Nashville, Tennessee to England. He'd never seen anyone so terrified of flying.

Unfortunately it happened that flying was the best method of transport. With enough money, they could go from one country in Europe to another in an hour or two. She would just have to conquer her fears. If they were all going to stay alive, they would have to stay well ahead of Kristoforus.

Time and distance. David needed both. Time to work out a viable plan to keep Miranda and her son out of her ex's hands. Distance—the farther, the better.

"We're at fourteen-thousand feet," the pilot announced. "The weather is perfect and should hold." The pilot would forget he'd ever seen the three of them.

The plane gained altitude, and the ride evened out. The sky was a bright, clear blue for a change. Miranda opened her eyes, looked over at him and gave him a weak smile. "So, where are we going?"

"Lille. Close to the Belgian border."

She nodded, her shoulders visibly relaxing. "After that?"

David shrugged. "Spain or Italy. It'll be warm and dry."

"Mm, that'll be nice."

"We're not on holiday, you know."

"Duh! Of course not."

"Mummy! Just last week you scolded me for saying 'duh'."

"So I did." She rolled her eyes and grinned. "I can't get anything past you, can I?"

"No, I am very sharp for my age. You said that, too."

David's shoulders shook with suppressed laughter. Somehow, he didn't think the boy's mother would appreciate it if he let loose with a huge guffaw. "I think young Jamie intends keeping the two of us in line."

"Hmph. You might be right."

The youngster piped up again. "I've never been to France. Will we climb the Eiffel Tower? That would be simply wizard, if we could."

David shook his head. "Not this trip. We're going to be moving around rather a lot. Think of it as a grand spy adventure. We'll change our names and our identities and challenge anyone to find us."

A broad smile wreathed the boy's face. "Spies? Super!"

On the other hand, his mother didn't appear quite so pleased. Indeed, her face grew tense, her lips tightened and thinned. Had he said too much in front of the boy? He didn't want to frighten him, merely enlist the boy's cooperation in what would, of necessity, be a group effort to stay alive.

ଔ

The small plane touched ground, but bounced into the air.

Randi's stomach and heart switched places. Somehow she managed to control the scream building in her throat. Instead, she squeaked. And shut her eyes—if she was going to die, she

41

wasn't about to look death in the face.

A hand touched her arm. Her eyes popped open of their own accord. David had reached across the narrow aisle. Warmth rushed from her arm to her cheeks. The plane touched the tarmac again. This time it stayed on sweet Mother Earth.

He grinned, his pale gray eyes shining like two silver dollars. "We're on the ground, and you're still alive. Just imagine."

"I love being patronized. It fairly makes my day." She gave a haughty sniff.

"And it fairly makes my day when you try on your British accent." He arched an eyebrow. "Still needs some work, but it's quite amusing."

"I like the way you talk, Mummy." Jamie's dark brown eyes twinkled, too.

"I didn't know y'all were going to gang up on me. Young man, you'd do well to remember who gave you life, not to mention, who stood in line for hours so you could have Playstation3."

"Playstation3?" David said, his voice filled with awe. "My lad, I would tread carefully. You've a very devoted mum."

Jamie heaved a world-weary sigh or at least as world-weary as a five-year-old boy could manage. "I know. She's forever reminding me. I'm used to it."

Randi folded her arms across her chest and jutted her chin in the air. "I'm not sayin' another word to you two." She turned her head and watched the air strip's blinking blue lights, while the plane taxied, slowed and finally came to a stop at a hangar.

A gray Citroën was parked nearby.

The pilot twisted around in his seat, removed his goggles, and made a sweeping bow. "Lille, France, *Madame et M'sieur.*"

David laughed and, to her amazement, answered the pilot in a rush of French, then turned to her. "Our vehicle awaits, *Madame.*"

"Mercy..."

The pilot sniggered.

She huffed. "I wasn't trying to speak French. I was asking for mercy—as in deliver me from."

David had the grace to look shame-faced. "Two oafs who should know better?"

"Exactly!" She nudged Jamie. "Let's go, hon, before I do something drastic." She managed to keep her laughter in check for about five seconds, then giggled. "Lille, France, huh? Well, let's get off this tin can—no offense to our fine pilot, of course." She gave him her biggest smile. "I'm so thankful to be on the ground, I could kiss you."

The pilot grinned back. "I would say that David has already paid me amply, but," he said, pausing to look first at David then back at her, "if you wish to express your gratitude in a purely physical way, then I would be a right cad if I denied you the opportunity."

"We've no time for foolishness," David blustered.

Tim made a face, pursing his lips. "Sorry, old chap. Didn't mean to poach."

Randi gasped and David's face turned a bright red.

Good grief! The pilot wasn't just on the wrong runway, he was at the wrong airport.

"Not at all. We're in a bit of a hurry. Can't stay to chat," David protested, his face still red.

Jamie piped up. "We're going to be spies."

"Uh-huh." The pilot's expression turned quizzical. "Well, *bon chance* and all that rot."

David leveled a steely glance at the pilot. "Thanks."

Time to take the situation in hand, she decided. "Thank you, Tim." She nudged her son. "Say thank you, Jamie."

A beaming smile still spread across his young face, her son obeyed. "Thank you, sir. I love your airplane."

The pilot nodded and gave them another gap-toothed grin. "You're very welcome. Glad to be of assistance. David, take care. You know how to reach me, if you've further need of my services."

David nodded, then motioned to her and Jamie. "Let's go."

03

Marie-Nicole Ryan

A short ride in the hired Citroën brought them to a small establishment which catered to commercial travelers. David hired the three of them a room while Miranda and Jamie waited in the motorcar.

Room key ready, he stopped at the door and held up his hand, cautioning Miranda to wait. "I know it's bad manners, but I'll go first—just to make certain."

She nodded in agreement, positioning Jamie to the side and slightly behind her body. David inserted the key in the lock, twisted it, then turned the knob. Easing open the door, he surveyed the room, then entered, striding past the twin beds to the window. After drawing the draperies, he inspected the bathroom.

Small, clean, plain, exactly what they required—no more, no less.

He set down Miranda's piece of luggage. His decision to bolt into the night had left him time to do no more than grab his passport and a wad of one-hundred pound notes. He would have to contact someone—someone he could trust—but who?

"David?"

Miranda interrupted his train of thought. He turned and motioned them inside. "All clear."

They scooted inside, closing the door behind them. Miranda walked over to the nearest bed, heaved a great sigh and collapsed. "I am so glad to light somewhere."

The boy plopped down beside his mother, giving her an affectionate hug.

"We won't be here long," David warned. "Unless I'm mistaken, we'll need to keep moving."

"What next?" Miranda asked.

"I need to pick up another change of clothes. We'll work on changing our appearances, and," he paused, "I'll contact an old friend of mine in MI6. He can help with some other issues."

She raised her eyebrows, her attention focused on him. "Like what kind of issues?"

He frowned. "Hmm, contacts here on the continent for identity papers, additional funds, things of that sort."

"I see."

44

"We're going to be spies!" Jamie exclaimed and sprang to his feet, obviously ready to jump up and down on the bed.

"No, you don't, young man. No jumping on the bed."

"Oh, come on. We're on a spy holiday." Jamie whined then looked down at his feet, a guilty expression on his face. "I'm sorry, Mummy. I forgot myself."

David crossed the room and sat on the second bed. "Jamie, the cardinal rule in being a spy is never telling anyone you are one. It is a grievous error if you do. Very dangerous. You must never say the word *spies*."

The boy's dark brown eyes grew wide. He gave a vigorous nod. "Yes, sir. I'll be careful."

"Good."

ᗛ

"Bloody hell!" After being placed on hold for the fourth time, David swore under his breath. Reaching his old friend Brinks from MI6 was proving a bit more difficult than he'd imagined.

Finally! A cautious-sounding Brinks answered, "Hello?"

"Yes, old man, I wondered if I was ever going to reach you."

"What in blazes happened at your place? My source at the Yard says everyone thinks you've done a bunk. Where are you?"

"Never mind that. Is this line secure?"

"It is now."

"Mine's not, but there's no reason to think anyone's listening. I'm in a public lavatory. The water's running."

"Should be sufficient for the time being. What do you need?"

"I need passports for three and an untraceable access to funds, as soon as possible."

"No problem, we have an excellent document man in Paris. Are you anywhere near?"

David ignored the question. "I don't want to use anyone MI6 uses—officially, that is."

"Why not? He's the best."

"We were attacked within minutes after arriving at my house. I don't trust anyone official."

"Present company excluded?"

"Obviously."

"As for funds, I'll give you the account numbers to my..." Brinks paused, lowering his voice, "...Swiss bank account. You may reimburse me when your situation is resolved."

"I would use my own funds, but—"

"Not a problem. If there is a leak, they're sure to have your bank and credit cards flagged. You could be traced in a veritable heartbeat, old friend."

"Exactly."

"I do know an unofficial source or two, but they're damned pricey. Where are you?"

He hesitated. "Tell me where they are, and I'll choose the closest one."

A short bark of laughter came through the phone. "Always the cautious one, aren't you, Davey?"

"Old habits."

"All right, I understand." Brinks read off the two names and addresses, while David scribbled them on a square of T.P. "Thanks, Brinks."

"Keep in touch? It would be reassuring if you checked in on a regular basis."

"I'll try." A sensation of dread slid down his spine. He had to trust Brinks. They'd been friends since boyhood when Brinks's father had managed David's family estate. They'd even gone to university together.

The door slammed open, followed by the entrance of another patron. "Have to ring off."

He severed the connection, then left the loo. He glanced down at his watch. He'd left the hotel thirty minutes earlier. Miranda and the boy would surely be starving, but he couldn't risk taking a direct route.

Ambling along as if he had nowhere in particular to go, he threaded his way through the bistro's morning crowd and out onto the *rue Meloin.* He pulled his cap down across his forehead and strolled down the street, stopping ostensibly to stare at merchandise in shop windows, but in reality checking for anyone who might be following.

After taking a circuitous route back to the hotel, he breathed a sigh of relief when he finally reached the door to their room.

He unlocked it and looked into the small—and very empty—room.

Where the devil? "Miranda?"

Chapter Four

Randi had opened the door of their hotel room and walked part of the way inside when she was grabbed by two strong arms and dragged into the room. Reflex took over. She clung to Jamie with one hand and reached back and clawed at the face of her attacker with the other.

"Where the devil have you been?"

At the sound of David's irate voice, relief flooded through her, quickly followed by a burst of anger. "You just scared the hell out of me." She turned to her son. "Sorry, darlin', Mummy has lost her temper. Cover your ears."

"Lost your temper?" David ground out, his eyes narrowed. "This isn't a game we're playing. I don't want you going anywhere without me. Do you understand?"

Through gritted teeth, she hissed, "Yes."

"Good."

"We were hungry. I could wait, but Jamie couldn't. I remembered there was a small café just down the street from the hotel. We were only gone a few minutes."

"I've been back for over ten minutes and going out of my mind. Don't ever pull anything like this again."

Bemused, she watched her son advance on David. Jamie straightened his small shoulders, pulling up to his full height.

"Sir, I would appreciate if you wouldn't shout at my mummy. I'm afraid this misunderstanding is my fault. I was feeling a trifle peckish."

David opened his mouth, then closed it quickly. He shot a brief, almost amused, glance at her, before nodding his agreement. "My concern for the safety of you and your mother has caused my rash remarks. I do beg your pardon."

"I accept your apology, sir." Jamie looked up at her, his brown eyes sincere. "Mummy?"

She nodded. "Sure." She'd been reckless. "I guess you're right."

"You know bloody well I'm right."

She couldn't resist adding, "And so gracious, too." His upper lip twitched, and if she weren't mistaken, his steely gaze softened for a second before two familiar shutters dropped back in place.

She walked over to one of the twin beds and plopped down. Raising her chin a notch, she challenged him. "Okay, we've had breakfast. What have you accomplished?"

David folded his arms across his chest and announced in the most offhand way, "Merely the names of two document forgers and access to a Swiss bank account."

A little deflated by his achievements, she shrugged. "Oh."

"Oh? Is that all you have to say?"

"Bloody good show, old man?" she quipped in her Tennessee version of his upper-class accent, then flashed him her sauciest smile. She waited. Yes! There it was. His upper lip definitely twitched, at least on the left. His mouth...

He paused before answering, probably composing himself. And she definitely didn't have any business thinking about his mouth.

"We need to move, just in case. I don't think anyone is on our trail, but I don't want to take any chances."

"Where?"

"Dijon."

"Like the mustard? Why there?" She watched as he closed his eyes for a second. She could almost visualize the words form in his mind: Give me strength.

"The closer of the two forgers is in Paris, and that would be the more logical place to start. However, I don't want to do anything which might appear logical. Dijon is farther from Lille, but it has the advantage of being closer to Zurich and the *Banque Nationale Suisse*."

"I love it when you talk—" Honestly she did love his upper class British accent, and when he slipped into a flawless French accent, well...

"Be serious."

"Okay, but maybe this is all a little too much cloak and dagger for me. We've left the country. We haven't taken any of the expected routes. That should be enough, shouldn't it?" She frowned, then paused, not wanting to say any more in front of her son.

David nodded. "I understand how you think, but it's not enough. The more distance we put between ourselves and the one pursuing us, the better."

"Just who *is* after us, Mummy?" Jamie gazed at her intently, his dark eyes questioning.

Her son was too bright for his own good. She gathered him in her arms and wished she could sink through the floor. She swallowed, stalling for time. "Well, son, it's a bad man I used to know. But you don't have anything to worry about. DCI French is with Scotland Yard, and he's protecting us. He won't let anyone hurt us."

He gazed up at her, his expression still puzzled. "The bad man—he almost hurt us last night, didn't he?"

"It's like I said. David protected us, but I don't think he would've hurt you. It's just your mummy he's after."

He frowned for a moment, but then smiled. "I'm glad David is our copper. I feel safe with him."

Randi smiled. "I do, too." Surprisingly she did trust him...more than any man she'd ever known. Not that she'd known many. Her father, her brothers—they'd been her family and they'd loved her. And then there were the males of the Kristoforus clan—a different experience altogether. Old memories, the ones she couldn't quite shake, surfaced and threatened to weaken her nerve.

"He doesn't...?" David asked, arching an eyebrow in her son's direction.

Frowning, she gave a quick shake of her head.

"We may need to discuss this situation further."

"Yeah, just not now, okay?"

David moved about the room in restless jerky movements, piling his belongings on his bed. "We need to make some different arrangements."

Her heart did a little flip "D-different arrangements? What do you mean, *different?*"

What now? Had he decided she and Jamie were too much trouble after all?

"We'll discuss it later."

"Later?" Meaning when Jamie took his afternoon nap.

He nodded. "Yes, later." He gave another knowing look at Jamie. "I don't suppose you stopped at a chemist's shop during your little excursion, did you?"

She pursed her lips, then nodded. "You did say we needed to change our appearance, didn't you?"

An impatient sigh escaped him. "Yes."

Triumphantly, she unzipped her bag and whipped out the contents. "*Voilà!* Scissors and hair color."

"Good. Do you know how to use them—effectively, I mean?"

"Duh!" As if there were a woman alive who didn't.

"May I take your peculiar turn of phrase to mean the affirmative?"

"You can take my peculiar turn of phrase and—"

"Miranda," he cautioned, the bare hint of a grin flitting about his sensual lips. He nodded in Jamie's direction. "Small ears."

Not to be outdone by his playful attitude, Randi waved the scissors at him. "Shall I show you what I can do with these scissors? Would you like to be my first victim—uh, client? After all, that auburn hair of yours is pretty distinctive."

David backed away, his hands raised as if to ward off her tonsorial advances. "Well, I..."

"Well..." She looked him up and down. "And I believe I see you with a spiked do. How does that sound?"

"A spiked *do?*"

"Trust me," she soothed. "Your own mother won't know you when I get through."

"That's what I'm afraid of." He backed away from her

waving scissors. "You take care of your own appearance, and I'll take care of mine. Fair enough?"

"Sure."

⦃

David drummed his fingers on the chair arm. What could possibly be taking her so long? Miranda had been in the lavatory for over an hour. The piercing odor of ammonia wafting underneath the closed door was the only clue to what she was about. Coloring her hair, no telling what else she was up to. Bugger all, but it smelled to high heaven and made one's eyes sting like the very devil. How could she stand it?

Even her son, sitting on his bed, eyelids heavy with sleep, had his nose wrinkled at the smell.

"Here I come, ready or not!" She thrust open the door and treated David and her son to a theatrical movie-queen pose, one hand behind her head, the other on her jutting hip.

He sprang from his chair. "Bloody hell!" he yelped before he could stop himself. Gone was Miranda's chin-length dark blonde hair and in its place, short pale blonde curls barely two inches long—if that. He couldn't believe how different she looked.

"Mummy!" the boy squealed, clapping his hands. "You're beautiful, like a rock star!"

She awarded her son with a beaming smile, then turned to David with a smirk. "See, someone appreciates my skill." She walked over to the boy's bed and gave him a big hug.

"Phew!" Jamie exclaimed. David struggled to keep from laughing when the youngster held his nose between two fingers and pushed away from his mother. "You stink, Mummy."

A puzzled expression crossed Miranda's face. "I do?" She looked to David. "Do I?"

He nodded emphatically. "'Fraid so. Isn't there anything you can do? Tomato juice perhaps."

Her small body drew up in indignation. "That particular remedy, to-MAH-to juice, is for skunks."

"Well, something else, then."

Giving an exasperated sigh, she suggested, "Well, more shampoo and conditioner maybe?"

"Please."

"Men." She stuck her nose in the air and swished back into the lavatory, leaving him slightly bemused. This trip, even with the considered dangers, was proving quite entertaining. Her son was an enchanting child...must take after his mum.

CB

Later, David watched her bending over the boy. "G'night, darlin'."

"Night, Mummy."

Her sweet words were meant for Jamie, but in spite of himself, David enjoyed the sound of her soft Southern accent.

In her nightshirt, she reminded him of his mother tucking him in at night when he was a lad about Jamie's age—his last happy childhood memory. He'd been sent off to boarding school at the age of eight, and not long after that his mother had found consolation in too many of the finest wines in his father's wine cellar.

He tried not to stare at her womanly curves as she hugged her son to her chest. But he failed miserably. He took a deep breath. Gone was the harsh odor of ammonia. The lemon scent of her shampoo drifted toward him...and bath powder. The scent of a woman fresh from her bath—oh God, there was nothing like it in the world. He shifted uncomfortably in his chair across the room.

Good Lord, he'd grown hard. What in blazes was the matter with him? He wasn't a testosterone-crazed adolescent, he was a man—granted, a man who hadn't had a woman in six years.

Thank heavens for the newspaper.

She crawled into the twin bed and snuggled beside her son, stirring David's sensual musings even more. Soft and clean, her skin would be smooth as silk. Her breasts...

"No need for you to double up. I'll sleep on the floor," he

offered, anxious to think about anything but Miranda's desirable body.

She turned around, her expression incredulous. "You won't do any such thing!"

"But—"

"Just hush. Neither one of us takes up much room. You won't get any sleep at all on the floor. It's cold, and it doesn't look all that clean."

He looked down at the tile floor. "Well, I suppose—"

"See here. You need your rest if you're going to be at your best." She challenged him with a casual shrug. "But if you have some macho image to protect—"

"Don't be ridiculous."

"Good, I'm glad you're being reasonable for a change."

"For a change?"

She smirked and batted her eyelashes. "G'night, David," she replied, waggling her fingers in a brief wave.

She turned her back on him and tugged her night shirt down over her softly curved hip.

"Good night." How was he ever going to sleep with her sleeping just two feet away from his bed? And what the hell did she mean by *reasonable for a change?* In his mind, he'd been imminently reasonable. Women, could any man ever understand even what made them tick? The female brain had different wiring. That had to be the answer.

He stood, pulled his shirt from his jeans and unbuttoned it, his fingers hesitating at each button. He crossed the room and sat on the empty twin bed, his back to Miranda. The last thing in the world he wanted was for her to realize how strongly she affected him.

He bent over and pulled off his boots. Reaching for his weapon, he removed it from its holster and placed it under his pillow. He unbuckled the holster and slipped it off. He wouldn't allow himself the luxury of disrobing. He'd remain on guard throughout the night—just in case.

He turned off the light, lay down on top of the spread, then turned over, attempting to find a comfortable position. Sod it! Even in the dark he could see the gentle swell of her hip as she lay cuddled next to her son.

Focus! You're not on your honeymoon, old man. This is deadly serious business.

Worse yet, he still hadn't told her how he planned to safeguard Jamie. Having seen evidence of her strong maternal instincts, he knew she would balk—if she didn't shove his plan down his throat to his navel before he could explain the wisdom of it.

He sat up. "I think I'll take a shower before I turn in."

A cold shower.

∝

Randi tried to sleep. It had been a long night and even a longer day. Her son lay all snuggled and warm in her arms, but he wasn't the reason she couldn't sleep. Maybe the real reason was a man-sized one.

Images of David in the shower danced through her mind. Steamy hot water sluicing down his hard body. Wonder if he needed some help washing his back? She giggled just imagining his shocked expression if she so much as offered.

She gave herself a mental shake, then punched her pillow. Her present line of thought was leading nowhere fast. Why now, when their very lives were at stake, did her hormones have to take a sudden shift into overdrive? She'd done without a man for years—and done quite well, too. As far as she was concerned, sex was a very overrated activity. She'd had a couple of rushed, hormone-ridden romances in college, and then Stefan...

Bad timing. That's all it was. Poor David. Wonder what he thought about being on the run with a little boy and his mother...his *horny* mother?

She heard David turn off the shower.

Need a towel, hon?

Crap. Like she'd ever have the nerve to call David *hon.*

As soon as she heard the doorknob turn, she pretended to be asleep.

The springs squeaked as he sat on the bed. Was he wearing a towel wrapped around his slim hips? Oh, she hoped so. But she shied away from turning over and having a look. After all, the man deserved some privacy, and her imagination was already working overtime. No need to make it worse.

Again she tried to go to sleep, but he was in the other bed, barely two feet away from her. She could tell by listening to his breathing he wasn't asleep either, although she was pretty sure his reason for staying awake had nothing to do with hers. He was on guard, protecting her and Jamie. She, on the other hand, was lusting after her protector in the worst way.

What was wrong with her?

Sure, he was handsome enough to pose for the cover of "GQ", and his body—well, she could only imagine how he must look when dressed in his Adam-and-Eve best. Not counting her son, the male half of the species had held zero interest ever since she'd put her marriage to Stefan behind her. She'd been way too busy raising Jamie and keeping a roof over their heads.

This sudden lust—and there could be no other word for it—had caught her unaware. Still, guilt niggled at her conscience. Cassie was dead, and Randi felt entirely too alive. In spite of the fall chill in the poorly heated room, her body was entirely too warm. Carefully she flipped over her pillow and pressed the cool fresh surface against her face.

"Trouble sleeping?" David asked.

"Not really," she lied. "How 'bout you?"

He chuckled, a merry, low rumbling that only made her lecherous hankerings worse.

"Well, it is a little before my usual bedtime."

A shiver slid down her spine, causing the goose bumps to rise on her upper arms. At least goose bumps were better than being too hot, but if the mere sound of his voice could affect her like that, she was in trouble.

Big trouble.

She swallowed, her throat dry all of a sudden. "Well—uh, g'night. I guess we have to get up pretty early tomorrow?"

"Yeah." He gave another low chuckle. "We have an early flight."

At the word *flight*, she turned and looked over her shoulder. She whispered, "Not another one. Please tell me you're joking."

A look of regret passed over his face. "Sorry. It's the last time."

"Yeah, sure. You say that now, but—"

"No, we'll have new documents by then and we can hire a car without being traced."

"Promise?"

"Promise."

Cʒ

David had almost fallen asleep when a whimpering disturbed him.

Miranda must be dreaming. It quickly became apparent that her dream was a nightmare as she cried and moaned.

He stood and crossed over to the bed where she lay twitching in tortured sleep. Should he awaken her? General wisdom said—to hell with general wisdom. He couldn't bear watching her suffer, even if it was just a dream.

He sat on the bed, touching her shoulder gently, not wanting to frighten her.

She jerked away from him. "No, please don't."

"Miranda, it's David. You're having a nightmare."

"Wh-what?" She shook her head, rubbed her eyes with the back of her hand. "Sorry. Did I wake you?"

"Not really. Do you want to talk about it?"

She glanced down, her face hardened. "No. It's all behind me—except for the nightmares."

"Stefan?"

Her eyes still downcast, she murmured, "Yes."

"I've a good shoulder, if you need it." He wouldn't push, but he wanted her to know she could depend on him for anything.

"Thank you for waking me up. I'll be all right now."

Her brave assurance touched him even more than he could've thought possible. "All the same, don't be afraid. I'll protect you and your son."

"Scout's honor?"

"Scout's honor." Resisting the very real urge to fold her slender body in his arms, he gently flicked the end of her nose with his forefinger. "Sleep, and that's an order."

"Aye, aye, Captain."

He watched her settle back into sleep. What had that bastard done to her? What could still give her nightmares six years later? Through his years on the force, he'd seen the after effects of depravity at its worst. The thought of this gentle woman being at the mercy of a psychopath like Kristoforus sickened him.

He would protect Miranda and her son with his very life. He'd failed Cassie. He wouldn't fail Miranda and Jamie.

Chapter Five

"How in the world you do manage to pick such cheesy planes?" Randi asked, trying not to whine but failing. "This one looks like it was put together with Elmer's Glue." She hated whining, especially since her brothers had always told her how much men hated it.

Too late now.

"Elmer's Glue?" David cast a puzzled glance in her direction.

She shook her head. "Never mind," she said, dismissing his question. She gave the airplane another once over. "Don't tell me. There's a listing for 'no one in their right mind would get on this one', so you automatically rented it?" She looked at David, who, unless she was completely off target, appeared at his wit's end. Her fault, true, but she hated flying. How many times did she have to remind him?

He leaned back in their rental car, not bothering to turn his head, but cut his steel-gray gaze in her direction. "Exactly." He drew on his super spy shades.

"What about a bus or a train? Can't we travel some other way? I—"

"Yes," he interrupted her before she could finish. "I believe you did mention that pertinent fact, about ten times in the last two days. You dislike flying." His tone dripped with sarcasm. "And I've reminded you at least ten times that flying is the most expedient way to put the most distance between us and your ex-husband." He paused, took a breath, and then continued, "And I told you last night, we'll hire a car after we obtain new documents."

"All right, I won't say another word." She rooted around in her purse. "I'm sure I have a paper clip or some bailing wire in here somewhere…" she continued rummaging, "…just in case we need to re-wire a wing or the engine thingy."

Out of the corner of her eye, she watched for his reaction. Aha! He shot her a look over his dark sunglasses. She saw it—a very definite twinkle in those silver eyes of his. Killer eyes. What she wouldn't give to see something else in them.

But a twinkle would do for now.

From his spot in the back seat, Jamie added his two cents. "I like flying."

She rolled her eyes. "Great. Another country heard from."

"It would seem we've outnumbered you again."

Randi glanced from David to Jamie then back again. "That's all right. I'm keeping track."

Touching her forearm, David interrupted. "The pilot just signaled. He's ready."

She groaned and opened the car door.

"This would be easier for all of us if you would restrain your overly dramatic reactions."

Overly dramatic? She winced, then shrugged. "Honestly, I tried. It slipped out. I won't do it again."

Until he makes me get in another damned flying machine, that is.

She watched him swing his long legs out of the small rental car. His snug jeans did everything they were supposed to do. And more.

Distraction, I need a distraction.

Remembering her son was still in the back seat, she spun around and opened the door. "Here you go, kiddo. Time to soar into the wild blue yonder." She held out her hand to her son who grasped it and grinned up at her, his new gap-toothed smile startling her. He'd lost his first tooth that very morning, and only David had been allowed the honor of removing it. Her son was growing up too fast!

Unable to find another excuse for delay, she forced herself to start walking toward the small plane, dragging every step.

David flashed a dazzling, albeit fake, smile in her direction.

"That's the spirit. Think of it as an adventure."

Taking two long strides, he caught up with them. Randi shoved her sunglasses down on her nose so he wouldn't miss her "I'm not buying this crap" expression.

He rewarded her with a casual shrug. "It's for the best. We need to keep moving."

"Yeah, yeah."

David boosted Jamie into the plane first, and then to add insult to injury, he began whistling *Into the Wild Blue Yonder*.

"I owe you for that."

He grinned. "I've a feeling you'll owe me for more than that before this trip of ours is over."

She paused in the open door, turned around and tried to fix him with a frown. "Chief Inspector French, you have a real mean streak," she muttered, half in jest.

He hung his head in mock shame, then gazed at her over his shades. "And you'd do well to remember it."

"I will," she gulped. Her face grew warm under his intense gaze. She tried to glance away, but couldn't. In the bright sunlight, his irises were nearly transparent, like twin reflections of a pale sky. A sensation of uneasiness worried its way up her spine. The man before her could be a formidable foe. Good thing he was on her side and not the other way around.

A spurt of French from the pilot broke the spell.

"*Je suis désolé, monsieur*," David apologized. "Let's move it," he added, giving a not-so-genteel nudge to her behind.

CR

Stefan Kristoforus paced back and forth in his father's technology-heavy war room. He'd never seen so many computer screens and equipment, most of which had been added during his long six-year stint in prison.

"Where is she? Where has the bitch taken my son—she and that bastard detective? I'm going to kill them."

His father, Alexander, leaned back in his chair. "Stefan, you must let my men handle this. It's the computer age. We'll find them. It's only a matter of time. It's imperative you remain in hiding. It's for your own good, you know."

He whirled on his father. "Don't patronize me. I'll determine what's good for me."

"You should have never married an outsider," his father blustered.

"You know why I did it. It seemed like a good idea at the time."

"Yes, but it was your faulty judgment all the same. Marrying her shouldn't have been necessary. Concealing the payoff in an antique desk—what were you thinking? If you'd followed my instructions, you wouldn't have needed to marry the little twit to keep track of the desk she and her mother bought."

"I know that *now*," he shouted back at his old man. "I've only heard you say it for the last six years."

His father jumped up, his face red with anger, his meaty hands drawn into fists. "Don't shout at me in my own house."

Old fool. But Stefan backed down. "Don't treat me like a child. I'm a man, and I'll have my son. And my revenge! Promise me, that when your men find them, I'll be there. I want to see the look of pain and terror on her face when I take my son from her. And the detective—him, I'll kill slowly."

Alexander relaxed his fists and sat, a thoughtful expression replacing the one of anger. Leaning his elbows on the desk, he steepled his fingers. "There may not be time for your revenge," he warned. "You may have to settle for gaining your son. Never fear, the other two are as good as dead. You mustn't risk your freedom for the fleeting pleasure of killing your ex-wife and a mere detective. I won't allow it."

"I want them dead!"

He stalked out into the terrace garden. No matter what his father said or did, he would strangle them both with his two hands.

Chapter Six

Randi stepped from the taxi and admired the weather-aged inn outside Dijon where they would spend their brief time obtaining forged documents. An authentic French country inn with painted blue shutters and front door. Another time, another situation, it would be so romantic.

"Whew!" she gasped. "I thought the flight was bad, but the taxi driver was from you-know-where."

David grinned. "No, just Paris. The driver told me he'd retired to live in Dijon, but he can't stand the peace and quiet."

She giggled. "Well, if that's how they drive in Paris, I'm glad we skipped the City of Light."

David's brow furrowed. "They're even worse in Paris," he told her, his expression one of complete seriousness until the telltale twitch at the corner of his mouth gave him away.

"Hmph!" She placed her hands on her hips. "Then I don't see how Paris has been able to maintain its population."

"It's very simple. They only run over the tourists..." he added with a grin, "...especially Americans."

"No!"

"But of course, *Madame,*" he replied, affecting a quasi-French accent of his own.

Jamie tugged on her sleeve. "David's kidding, Mummy." He looked over at David "Aren't you, sir?"

David grinned and nodded.

Reaching over and ruffling her son's hair, she couldn't keep from laughing. "Sort of."

The driver plopped their bags at their feet with a snort, then returned to his taxi and sped off.

"David, what about our passports? Can't we be traced through them?"

"If *La Porte Bleue* were on computer, we certainly could be. I checked when I made our reservation. They aren't—not yet."

Randi took Jamie's hand and together they walked through the vine-covered arbor to the entrance while David picked up their bags and followed.

The wide rustic door swung open, *"Soyez la bienvenue à La Porte Bleue, Madame et Monsieur. Je m'apelle Gilbèrt."*

"Merci, M'sieur Gilbèrt," David replied, his accent flawless— at least to Randi's ears. *"Nous appellons la famille French."*

"M'sieur French. Enchanté, Madame," he acknowledged, bowing over her hand, a wide smile spread across his weathered face. He continued in English. "We 'ave your reservation. If I may 'ave your passports, I will be 'appy to register you myself."

The proprietor led them to the registration area located in a small alcove. David handed over their passports while Randi held Jamie's hand and her breath.

Gilbèrt perused the three documents, pausing over two of them. He put them down, then smiled. "Everything seems in order, *M'sieur* French. You are recently married, *n'est-ce pas?"*

"Oui, we're on our honeymoon." David hugged Randi to his chest, bestowing the kind of smile only a besotted newlywed could give his new bride.

The wattage of his expression damn near jolted her heart into an electrical frenzy. Stricken speechless by the sudden contact with his hard body, the best she could do was give a feeble nod.

The proprietor looked askance at Jamie. "Honeymoon, *m'sieur?"*

"My new stepson, too young to be left with strangers. I'm sure you understand." David beamed down at Randi again. He still held her close to his side, close enough that she caught the hint of his after-shave mingled with the leather of his jacket.

"Of course, *m'sieur."* The proprietor gave a vigorous nod. "I am sure you will find your accommodations most suitable." He rang the bell. "Pierre, *tout de suite!*"

Ↄ

After tipping the bellboy, David turned to Miranda and Jamie. "Room's nice enough. Better than the one in Lille." He took in the sight of the overstuffed and nearly queen-sized bed. His heart skipped a beat.

Miranda turned and gave him a skeptical look. "Yeah, but—"

"The bellboy said he would bring a cot for Jamie. I'll sleep on that," he offered.

A positively mischievous glint appeared in Miranda's eyes.

"So much for the *honeymoon*," she said, making a visible effort to keep her expression solemn.

"Yes, well, sorry about that. It seemed the best way to explain why your names were different from mine on our passports.

Miranda shrugged. "I should've thought of that. It threw me for a second."

David grabbed his kit, set it on the bed and started unpacking. "On the contrary, I thought you improvised quite well. If I hadn't known better, I would've sworn you were my blushing bride." He waited to see how she would respond.

Her mouth dropped open, but she recovered quickly. Still, her face flushed a gratifying shade of pink.

Interesting response.

Miranda raised her chin a notch. "Well, of course I improvised. That's—uh, what spies do, isn't it, Jamie?"

"Yes, Mummy. Are you and David married now? Is he going to sleep with us?"

Miranda's face passed pink and went straight to scarlet. "We're just pretending, r-remember?"

"That's right, Mummy. I forgot."

Two sharp raps sounded on the door. Instinctively, David reached for his weapon, while motioning them to stay back.

"*Qui?*"

"*Le lit de sangle,* M. French."

David opened the door and allowed the porter to bring in the cot. After he gave a quick explanation of the portable bed's mechanism, David tipped him again.

"*Merci,* M. French."

"*Je vous en prie.*" David closed the door.

When he turned around, he found Miranda staring at him with an expression of pure consternation.

"David, you can't sleep on this—this thing. It's barely five feet long."

Jamie tugged on his mother's sleeve. "But, Mummy, David can't sleep on the floor, can he? May I sleep on the cot?"

"Uh—" Miranda rolled her eyes.

David interrupted with what he hoped was a reassuring grin.

"Not to worry." He nodded toward the corner. "The *chaise longue* looks quite comfortable."

Jamie ran over to the chaise. "What did you call it, sir?" He plopped down on it, giving it a couple of tentative bounces as he did.

"It's a *chaise longue.*"

"I like it better. It's just my size." Jamie jumped up from the chaise and dashed across the room, then leapt onto bed. "But this one is really soft and jumpy." David watched in amusement as the youngster stood and gave an exuberant hop.

"That's enough, young man," Miranda warned in an I-mean-business tone of voice—the one all mothers use at one time or another as a matter of course.

David continued watching Miranda, enjoying her discomfiture. He decided to take pity on her. "I shall sleep on the chaise, and you with your mother."

"I sleep by myself at home," Jamie asserted with a stubborn jut of his chin. "I don't want to sleep with my mummy."

"Of course, you don't, but think how lonesome your mummy will be if you don't sleep with her."

"Mummy's used to sleeping by herself."

David stopped to scratch his forehead. He wasn't used to dealing with children, especially a precocious one like Jamie who apparently had an answer for everything.

"Well…"

"Enough, you two. We can worry about the sleeping accommodations later." She turned to her son. "Go to the bathroom and wash your face and hands, please."

"Yes, ma'am." Jamie jumped off the bed. Landing with a muffled thump on the floor, he hurried off to do his mother's bidding.

Miranda looked over her shoulder, then back at David. "What's next?"

David leaned close and, speaking low, said, "I'll make contact with the forger, then in a day or so, we'll have new passports. Actually, it would be ideal if he'll do more than one set of papers for us. You never know when an extra set might come in handy."

"Yeah," Miranda agreed with a shrug. "That's what I thought."

"We'll have lunch here at the inn, then I'll set up a rendezvous with our friendly forger after lunch. Meantime, we'll keep a low profile until our papers are ready, do a minimal amount of sightseeing, then leave. It's only natural for us to keep to ourselves most of the time. After all, we're supposed to be honeymooners."

"Yeah, 'bout that honeymooner deal."

"What about it?" he asked, raising an eyebrow.

"Oh, nothing. It just—"

"Threw you," he finished for her. "You said that already."

"Yeah, I guess I did."

Miranda busied herself with unpacking her bag, her lips moving. He found the conversation she appeared to be having intriguing.

"I assure you I have no intention of taking advantage."

Her mouth dropped open. She placed her hands on her hips. "Well, I never thought for a single minute that you would."

"Good. After all, I'm here to protect you."

"Then, we understand each other."

"Of course, we do."

Miranda turned toward the lavatory. "James Michael Peyton, you better come out of there. You've had more than enough time to wash your hands and face. Let's go have lunch."

The door opened in an instant. "All clean, Mummy," he said, showing the fronts and back of his hands. He looked up at David. "Don't you have to wash your hands and face, too? Mummy's awfully strict about being clean."

David hid his smile, but nodded. "You know, it's been my experience that all mothers are terribly serious about cleanliness. I'd best get with the program, before she feels it necessary to punish me."

A good-natured "Hmph!" erupted from the lady in question.

"If I'm not mistaken, your mother is only a heartbeat away from taking me in hand." Oh, Lord, he hadn't meant for his words to come out quite like that.

David watched in amusement as Miranda's face flushed a lovely shade of pink again, making his Freudian slip worth it.

Miranda looked down at her watch. "Fellas, time for lunch."

"*Certainement.*" When he thought about it, he wasn't quite sure why Miranda appeared so flustered, but he did like it.

All too quickly, his moment of innocent diversion turned to guilt. Images of Cassie came unbidden, flooding his mind. Her lovely face, her silken hair, her sweet warmth. For a second, his loss overwhelmed him, the memories as fresh as the day she died. How could he allow himself to love another woman, considering the only woman he'd ever loved had died because of his unmitigated arrogance?

He gave himself a mental shake. *Pull yourself together, old man.* It was his duty to protect Miranda and her son. So he would.

Nothing more. Yet Miranda had her own sweet warmth, her own unique beauty, and if he wasn't careful...

Miranda's voice pierced his reverie. "Earth to space ranger, come in, please."

"What?" David responded, the images of both Cassie and Miranda colliding in his mind. "I—uh—"

"Checking out the ozone, were you?"

"Something like that."

An expression of concern crossed Miranda's face. Her brow wrinkled as she chewed on her full bottom lip. "Are you all right, David?"

He waved her away. "It's nothing." *Nothing?* Hardly that, but what could he say? He certainly couldn't tell her what he felt. Not when he wasn't sure himself. "Lunch. I believe you mentioned lunch."

Miranda stepped toward him, invading his personal space.

Her hand extended, she gave him a pat on the shoulder. "It's all right. I miss her, too."

Entirely too perceptive, the woman was! David felt as if Miranda's all-knowing jade eyes could see past all his layers of self-protection. He nodded, unable to speak. Or admit to vulnerability.

"Why is it grownups only talk about lunch? I'm hungry." Jamie pulled on his mother's arm. "Mummy?"

"I would say lunch is in order," David responded, anxious to distract Miranda.

She grinned down at her son. "I suppose we have to feed you, Jamie me-boy." She turned back to David, her expression still thoughtful. "I'm ready if you are."

With conscious effort, he pulled his lips into his best approximation of a smile and offered her his arm. "Ready."

Ready, indeed? Would he ever be ready to give his heart? Risk everything all over again? Not bloody likely!

൫

After a lunch which reminded David of the excesses of French cuisine, he managed to lumber up the stairs to their room. Why had he eaten so much? Now instead of taking an afternoon nap, he had to leave Miranda and Jamie and meet a forger.

"Now this time, if I tell you to remain in this room, will you? That means no sightseeing or trips to the chemist until I return." The last thing he wanted was a repeat of the heart-stopping fear he'd experienced in Lille on return to their small room and finding it empty.

Miranda wrinkled her nose and appeared to be on the verge of sticking out her tongue. "We'll behave."

"That's not what I asked."

"You didn't ask anything. You demanded."

"Will you stay here until I return? I'm not leaving until you give me your word."

Jamie danced about the chamber, his eyes lit with good humor. "I give you my word, sir. I won't go anywhere."

"Miranda?"

"I don't know what you're making such a big deal about. Who would ever expect to find us in a town named after mustard."

"The mustard was named after the—never mind that!" David declared, noticing Miranda's wide grin and mischievous eyes.

"Gotcha!"

"Mummy is teasing. Aren't you?"

"Of course, I am. And you have my word," Miranda paused, then added, "sir. We shall remain sequestered within these walls until you return from your mission."

He managed a grim "Thank you." Confound the woman, how could she retain a sense of humor when her life and the life of her son might be at stake?

Perhaps it was how she coped.

Another thought occurred to him. Damn! He should have considered it before. "Have you ever fired a weapon?"

The smile faded from Miranda's face, replaced by a grave mien. "Yes. My older brothers tried to turn me into a tomboy. I resisted most of it, but I did learn how to handle a gun."

"I'm going to leave one of my weapons with you." He pulled the 9 mil from his back holster. "Ever use one like this?"

Miranda shook her head, but extended her right hand.

"Wait." David ejected the mag and handed it to her. "It holds twelve rounds. Jam it into the handle of the gun, then pull back on the slide. It takes some strength, so pull hard."

Miranda did as he directed, giving a deft backward pull on the slide. "I'm a musician." Her grin returned. "Strong hands."

"Good. Now eject the magazine and repeat the sequence."

David demonstrated the sighting, proper stance and hold. "If you're called on to fire, don't pull the trigger. Squeeze."

She nodded. "I remember that much."

David glanced down at the boy. The youngster had grown silent, his dark brown eyes staring with apparent fascination at the weapon his mother held.

David squatted down to Jamie's level. "Jamie, the gun I gave your mother is a real gun. You mustn't handle it. It isn't a toy. It's very, very real. Do you understand?" Kids and guns and the dangers inherent when the two came together—the very thought gave his stomach an attack of the womblies.

"Yes, sir. It could kill me."

"Exactly."

C8

Stefan hunched over the keyboard in his father's office. According to his father, all his highly vaunted sources hadn't turned up a single trace of the detective or Randi.

Damn it!

She wasn't smart enough to engineer a clean escape. Had to be French's doing.

Or maybe his father had lied. Maybe the old man knew exactly where they were and didn't intend to share the intel with his son. Totally frustrated, he banged his fist on the desk.

If his father did know anything, Stefan couldn't find any evidence of it in the computer.

C8

Brinks swallowed hard, his throat dry beyond belief. He squirmed and shifted—the chair, damned uncomfortable.

71

Bugger all! His balls were on the line, not to mention his career.

"So where *are* they now, Hughes-Brinkley?"

"I'm not certain. I gave him two names. Renault in Paris and Jean-Louis in Dijon. He didn't give me his itinerary. He's far too careful for that."

Deputy Minister of Intelligence Charles Moreland eyed Brinks. "You know DCI French better than anyone. Which one do *you* think he chose?"

Brinks knew bloody well which one Davey would've chosen. It only went to prove, at MI6 some secure lines were more secure than others. He'd known Davey since childhood. He wouldn't betray his friend, even to keep his career viable.

"Paris," he lied. "Bigger city, easier to get lost in the crowd, so to speak."

The Deputy Minister nodded. "I see. Yes, it makes sense. As for your Swiss bank account? I suppose we can let that pass for now. You may go."

Brinks stumbled to his feet and left the Deputy Minister's office, cursing himself. Bugger! What a clumsy fool he'd been.

Now he had to find a way to warn Davey and not tip off his superior.

CB

The Deputy Minister picked up the receiver to his secure line and punched in a number.

"Well?"

"My source here said French will choose Paris, but he was lying. If I were you, I'd cover the document man in Dijon. If you miss them there, then the *Banque Nationale Suisse* in Zurich is where he'll head next."

"Right. Thank you, old friend."

Chapter Seven

Thirty minutes after contacting the forger, known only as Jean-Louis, David paid the taxi driver and stepped out of the cab. As a matter of caution, he'd asked the driver to drop him two blocks beyond the rendezvous point, thereby making his approach from the opposite direction.

No one. At least not yet.

Glancing down both sides of the street, he turned to his left and started off at a brisk pace toward the Church of St-Michel. On occasion, he slowed, then stopped, as if window-shopping, and checked in the reflection for signs of surveillance.

Call it experience, call it intuition, call it extrasensory— didn't matter what one called it—the sensation crawling up and down the back of his neck warned him. He'd felt it before, and he'd learned the hard way to trust it.

Half a block from the church, he stopped at a news kiosk and purchased the latest edition which he folded in half, although his contact had instructed him to roll it up and carry in his left hand. He preferred to scout the meeting site before he made his presence obvious.

He checked the time on his watch. Five minutes early, as planned. Assuming the guise of a tourist, he strolled past the church, a magnificent edifice built during the Renaissance, as he gazed up at the tall campanile.

As soon as he reached the corner, he paused, then turned back. He spotted his contact, a middle-aged, gray-haired man, nondescript save for his bright blue beret and a rolled newspaper carried in his left hand.

David glanced from left to right, then rolled his own newspaper and placed it under his left arm. The contact nodded and motioned toward the church. Unable to detect anyone else worthy of suspicion, he followed.

Once inside the old church, he spied his contact genuflecting before entering a rear pew. Following suit, he entered the same pew, sat and waited.

"*M'sieur French?*" the liaison asked, his tone hushed.

"*Oui.*"

"*Est-ce que vous avez l'argent?*"

"*Oui.*" He removed the wad of pound notes from his jacket pocket, then passed them to the contact. "*Le voici*, half the fee as agreed."

"*Les documents?*"

David hesitated. What would he do if the forger didn't come through? The three of them would be without any passports at all. Basically, it was a case of honor among thieves. Jean-Louis had come highly recommended, and David had no other choice but to trust he would receive what he paid for.

"*Les documents?*" his contact growled and stood as if to leave. "I do not have all day, *m'sieur.*"

David pulled the three passports from his left inside pocket. "When?" he asked, holding the documents just out of reach.

"Twenty-four hours, *m'sieur.*"

"Where?"

The contact gave him a wolfish smile. "Call the same number you called today. You'll be instructed."

David nodded. "*Bien.*" He handed over their passports, breathing a silent prayer he would see them again. He stood, spotted a side door, then walked without hurrying toward it.

When he emerged from the dark interior of the church, he blinked and allowed his eyes a moment to adjust to the light. He stepped into the shadow cast by a buttressed wall, took off his jacket, and removed from it a red bandana, a black beret, and a pair of sunglasses. He jammed the beret down on his head, tied the scarf around his neck, then slipped on the shades.

He strode along the side of the church until he reached the

street. Hailing a taxi, he meant to put as much distance between himself and the forger liaison as quickly as possible.

His interchange with the contact and his slight alteration in appearance had taken less than five minutes. Even so, he could have been observed.

CB

Randi paced around the lovely room which was decorated with wonderful old country French antiques and expensive fabrics. She hated to think how much it all must cost and how this unexpected jaunt would eat into her savings. No matter what it cost, she intended to reimburse David for his expenses.

She and Jamie lived quietly, the majority of her earnings going to pay for his school. She wouldn't have managed to buy a house at all if her grandmother hadn't died two years earlier and left Randi everything. She had always been her grandmother's favorite. Perhaps because she was the only granddaughter, Gran's namesake, and the only grandchild who'd inherited her grandmother's musical talent.

When they went on the run, she never expected to stay in a lovely place like *La Porte Bleue,* but maybe David was right; no one would expect them to stay somewhere as elegant and well-appointed as the inn. Hide in plain sight? Hadn't she heard or read that phrase somewhere? Oh yeah, Poe's *The Purloined Letter.*

Her gaze traveled around the room, from the bed hung with draperies to the matching window treatments. An antique armoire had been converted into an entertainment center and housed a television, DVD player and stereo equipment. In other words, not too shabby.

This very moment, her son sat on the floor with his legs crossed, watching a children's television show in French, of course. Each time he laughed and clapped his hands, she wondered how on earth he understood what was being said.

She certainly didn't.

She glanced down at her watch. David had been gone for two hours, and she was getting more nervous by the minute.

She'd feel a whole lot better when he walked through the door.

Jamie looked up from his television show. "Mummy, are you worried about David?"

"A little." She sat on the floor beside her son. "I'm sure he's all right, because he's taken such good care of us until now."

Her son's brow wrinkled while he seemed to consider her words. "Is David a spy, like on the telly?"

"No, darlin', David is a detective with Scotland Yard. He was sent to take us somewhere safe, but it's—uh, complicated."

"Like when he had to shoot at the bad man? That kind of complicated?"

"Yes, exactly that kind of complicated." Her son was entirely too intelligent to lie to. On the other hand, she didn't quite know how to tell him it was his father who was after them. Sooner or later, she'd have to own up to the truth, but not yet.

She slipped her arms around his shoulders, hugging him to her. "Whose boy are you?"

"Yours."

She pushed aside his black bangs and kissed his forehead. "You're not too big for me to mush on, are you?"

"No, Mummy," he replied, his small face beaming with joy. "Not as long as I'm your boy."

He squirmed in place, turned around, and threw his arms around her neck, pasting a smacking kiss on her cheek.

So much love in the middle of the direst circumstances. If only she could protect him from the hurt which was bound to come when he found out the truth about his father.

The inescapable truth was Stefan Kristoforus had swept her off her feet nearly seven years ago. Even worse, she and her son were still paying the price for her rash, but thankfully brief, marriage.

Yet when she looked at her son who'd inherited his father's black hair and dark brown eyes, she felt nothing but an incredible, overwhelming love. She didn't regret having her son—not for a single second.

"Will I ever have a father like other children?"

"Wh-what?" Startled by the question, she jumped. Had he read her mind? Geez. She took a deep breath, stalling for time.

"Well, I don't know. I would have to get married again."

"You could marry DCI French." He nodded as he spoke, emphasizing each word. "I like him a lot. Don't you think he'd make a good father?"

"He *is* a very good person, but he's protecting us because it's his job."

Dear heaven. Don't let him say anything like that when David's around.

"But he likes us, doesn't he?"

"Of course, he does, but—"

"He really likes *you*, Mummy. He watches you a lot."

"But—"

"You watch him, too."

"Wait a minute. Hold on here, young man. You're moving too fast. DCI French is our protector, and yes, he's our friend, but that's not enough reason to get married."

"What is?"

"Love. You have to be in love to get married. You have to want to spend your entire life with that one person." Dear heaven, his questions would be the death of her yet.

"Is that how you and my—"

"Of course," she interrupted, "we were in love." At least *she* had been or thought she was.

"Do you miss him?"

"Not so much anymore." Whoa, was she the mistress of understatement or what?

"Did—"

The opening of the door stopped whatever Jamie had been prepared to ask next. Thank heavens! Her mouth dropped open at the sight of David standing in the doorway. "David? I wouldn't have known you." Known him? He looked like the latest version of a French tango dancer—beret, bandana and sexy-black shades.

He shut the door behind him, tilted his head to the side and grinned. "That was the point. You two look quite comfortable."

Anxious to distract Jamie from their conversation, she

jumped up. "How did it go?"

"As planned."

"No problems?"

"No." He walked over to the window and drew the draperies.

"Something's wrong. What happened?"

He shrugged. "Nothing. Just being cautious."

"Something *is*..." she insisted.

"I told you. Nothing happened. I met the contact, paid him, gave him our passports."

"Now what?"

"We wait."

"How long?" She glanced at Jamie. Thank God, he'd turned his attention back to the television show and was too absorbed to pay attention to the grownup conversation.

"Twenty-four hours."

"That long?"

"Long enough for two complete identities for the three of us. Passports, birth records and credit cards."

"I don't know, David. Another whole day in one place. I'm uneasy, as it is."

His gaze narrowed. "You feel it, too?"

"Yeah, something isn't right. I thought it was because you'd been gone for two hours, and once you were back, I'd calm down. But if anything, the feeling's worse."

"I'm certain I wasn't followed either to the meet or afterward. We've been careful."

"Then why are we both on edge?"

"Because reality says matters could change at any time."

He sat on the bed, appearing to study his shoes before continuing, "I'm worried about you and Jamie. Stefan has attacked us once. He won't give up. Besides, his family has contacts all over Europe."

"Maybe we should leave?" she suggested softly, then moved toward the closet, ready to pack their gear.

David shook his head. "I don't think so. Leaving the same day we checked in could arouse suspicion. Besides, we have to stay in Dijon for another twenty-four hours." He shrugged. "We might as well be comfortable."

"We can stay in, have room service. That would fit the honeymooner profile, wouldn't it?"

The twinkle returned to his gray gaze, while the left side of his mouth twitched. "Yes, it would."

"Honeymooners?" Jamie piped up, then muted the sound on the television.

David bent down to Jamie's level. "It's part of our cover. Your mummy and I want people to think we're newlyweds."

"Oh, okay." The child shrugged and went back to his program. "May we have pizza tonight?" the boy asked, never once looking in their direction.

"But they have such glorious food," she protested. "Surely you don't want pizza."

"*Au contraire*, I will have you know the chef prepares an absolutely wonderful deep-dish pizza with the most magnificent crust, the most delicious cheeses and the ultimate in sausage, made on site by the lovely Madame Sophie herself."

"How do you know?"

"I've been here before."

"The host didn't recognize you."

"No."

"Oh." It dawned on her. "With Cassie?"

"No, it was the summer I turned eight. We came here on holiday. I've never forgotten. It was the only time my father ever took the entire family anywhere. It was a disaster, of course. My father complained about the weather, the food and all the money he'd spent which he blamed on my mother. I spent the entire two weeks trying to stay out of my father's hair and failed miserably. It was then he decided I should go away to school."

"At eight?"

David nodded. "It's not that uncommon."

"I couldn't bear to send Jamie away like that."

"I hated school, and I hated my father for sending me away from my mother. It—sorry, I don't mean to bore you with my family history. I don't much like talking about it."

"I had no idea, but I'm not bored."

"Well, you must be, because I'm boring myself."

"You're a Chief Inspector for Scotland Yard, and I've read stories all my life about the Yard. You're the second son of an earl, for Pete's sake. What's so boring about that?"

"Being the second son means I'm out of the money and the title. Totally useless, in other words. Being with the Yard..." David paused, then smiled. "All I ever wanted to be was a copper. My friends and I, we played the usual games. I was always the copper. My friend Brinks was always one of the robbers. Kid stuff." The hard planes of his face softened. "Look, what about you? Tell me about Nashville, Tennessee."

She sat on the chaise, tucking her feet underneath her. "Nashville is in the middle of the state. West Tennessee is flat, and the eastern part is mountainous, but Nashville is in-between. Hotter than Hades in the summer, and the roads are a nightmare when it snows, but in the spring, it's wonderful. First the redbuds bloom, then the dogwood. It's green, not quite as green as Ireland, but it's heaven in the spring, just heaven." The thought hit her. "I sound like a travel brochure, don't I?"

"A bit. You sound as if you miss it."

"Sometimes. But I love the U.K. I used to read all the stories about the kings and queens, and I always felt like I belonged there, you know?"

"Knights jousting for the fair maiden's favor. That sort of thing?" he asked with a lopsided grin.

She nodded. "Yeah," she admitted, giving a deep sigh. "Of course I would've been a peasant and way below the salt."

And certainly not worthy of your attention. Anymore than I am now.

"You never know. You might have been a beautiful lady and I a mere court jester, on whom you would never waste a moment's notice." He bowed before her, reaching for her hand.

Reflexes kicked in and she jerked her hand back. "Yeah, right." Geez, what was the matter with him anyway? Resting her chin on her knees, she hugged her legs. "Somehow I think my version is a lot more likely."

Still her stomach gave a giddy lurch. Was it his touch on her hand? Was he really going to kiss it? Dang! Maybe she was just hungry. "Didn't you say something about pizza?" she asked, looking up and favoring him with her most innocent smile.

He straightened. "Guess I'm acting the fool, aren't I?"

To her amazement his face flushed beneath his tan "It's all in fun." What did *he* have to feel embarrassed about? *She* was the one who was ready to—well, what *was* she ready to do—the horizontal mambo? Or just a little down-home Tennessee foreplay on the *chaise longue*?

Yikes! The very thought of foreplay and David made her hotter than a Nashville August afternoon. She reached for a magazine and fanned her cheeks for dear life. And tried not to look at him, who surely thought she'd lost it—her mind, that is.

"Are you all right?"

"It's kinda warm in here, all of a sudden."

"Yes, I would agree. Perhaps I should check the thermostat." He walked over to the thermostat, then tapped it with his forefinger. "Must not be working. It reads twenty-two degrees Celsius. It has to be warmer than that." He tapped it again. "I'll order the pizza, and I'll have the waiter check it."

"Sounds like a plan." Randi glanced at her son. Thank heaven his attention was on the television and not on his flustered mother and a certain DCI who was starting to drive her up the wall with his shimmering, silver eyes and kissable mouth and hard body.

Give me strength.

Chapter Eight

David counted to ten. Would the waiter never leave? After the waiter had served their pizza, he'd assured them the thermostat was functioning properly. He then wished them, "*Bôn appétit!*" with a knowing smirk before leaving the room and giving them a chance to enjoy their dinner.

He counted to ten again. He walked over to the small round table where Miranda and Jamie had already started applying themselves to their meal. Sitting down, he unfolded and placed the linen napkin in his lap.

Miranda was too enraptured with her first bite of Madame Sophie's specialty to notice how insolent the waiter had been.

"Mm, this is so good."

The pink tip of her tongue swept a tenacious string of mozzarella into her mouth. He set his elbow on the table, resting his chin on his fist. He couldn't keep from staring. Her cupid's-bow lips were a lush contrast to the rest of her finely drawn features. While her personality was upbeat and her appearance grew more pleasing every day, her full, lower lip hinted of a sensual nature.

Damn!

He'd done it again. Mooning about things he had no business even thinking about. Losing focus could get them killed. Stefan Kristoforus wouldn't be distracted by a pair of luscious lips.

"Here, have some." She deftly cut a large square of the aromatic concoction and placed it on his plate. "It's wonderful." She turned to the boy. "And you, young sir?"

Jamie gave a vigorous nod, his mouth too full to respond.

"Like mother, like son," David teased.

"Right, just don't ever get between me and a pizza."

"I wouldn't think of it."

"Bodily harm would definitely result."

"Really?" He laid down his fork, his pizza still untried.

"Absolutely." She gave an emphatic nod but, in the process, smeared a dollop of red sauce on her chin.

"Mummy, you have pizza on your face." The boy leaned across the table, aiming at her face with his own pizza-smeared hand.

Miranda dodged the boy's swipe. "Where?" she asked. Wiping at her chin, she smeared it more.

"Allow me." David reached for his napkin. "Just a small smudge of sauce." He dabbed the offending blob from her chin.

A simple touch. His knuckle grazed lightly against the satin smooth skin of her cheek, but it rocked him.

He pulled back, a little dazed by the strength of his response. "Fine now," he added, rather lamely.

"Th-thank you," she murmured, then chewed on her bottom lip.

She appeared uncertain, even to his keen gaze. But why? What was on *her* mind? Certainly nothing like what was on his. He admired her spunk and her devotion to her son. She had to be worried to death, but she still managed to joke and do what needed to be done. "I wish my mother had been more like you," he found himself saying.

"Wh-what?"

"I mean, I wish she'd had the spirit to stand up to my father. I don't love her any less, but I can't see you allowing..." He broke off, remembering the boy's presence. "Sorry, I've said too much."

"I think I know what you mean. It wasn't easy." She shook her head, unwilling to say more.

"Grownups talk too much. I'm going to eat all the pizza," the boy declared and made a grab for a second piece.

☙

Randi bent down over her son where he'd fallen asleep on the floor watching television. She tugged gently on his dead weight.

David stood and then knelt beside to Jamie. "Shall I? He'll be heavy with all the pizza he's eaten."

She giggled. "Thanks. His legs are getting so long. I think he'll be as tall as I am by the time he's ten or eleven." She watched while he picked up her son and laid him on the bed as if hauling a kid around was no big deal.

Strong and gentle—yes, David was a good man. Not like Stefan.

Suddenly shy, she stuttered, "Y-you've really been good to us. I just want to thank you again."

He turned and gave her a quizzical smile. "We're in a difficult situation through no fault of yours. I'm doing my job. You don't have to thank me," he told her, his expression softening, "but it's very sweet that you do."

A hot flush suffused her neck and face. Great. One compliment, left-handed at that, and she was a Fourth-of-July firecracker ready to ignite. All that was missing was the Boston Pops for the soundtrack. "Gee, thanks."

He shot her a sheepish grin. "I admit I didn't phrase that as gracefully as I could've, but it's been an unexpected pleasure, really."

"Oh?" Before her mind could spiral over what he meant by "pleasure", she busied herself with pulling off her son's shoes and socks, then his blue jeans.

"He can sleep in the shirt," she said and pulled the duvet over him.

"Why don't you have a seat? I'll pour you a glass of wine." David stood, ready to make good on his suggestion.

"Aren't you having one?"

"I don't drink."

"Oh, I'm sorry. I didn't know. I don't have to have anything either, if it's difficult for you—because of your mother—I mean."

"Not at all." A frown crossed his sculpted face. "I'm no alcoholic, but they say it's hereditary. I'd rather not risk it."

"All right, just a small glass then." She couldn't resist adding, "They also say it's good for your heart...in moderation."

"They do say that, too." He grinned as he picked up a bottled water and sat. "I think I'll stick with this."

She sat on the chaise and sipped her wine, wondering if she could feel any more uncomfortable.

"Earlier I almost said too much in front of Jamie. I'm sorry."

"I'm just not ready to tell him about his real father. Later, when he's older, maybe he'll understand."

"What I meant to say was that I can't see you putting up with the kind of abuse my mother did. You left your husband."

"It wasn't easy. I was literally a prisoner and *so* afraid of him." She studied her glass of merlot. Somehow she just couldn't face David's pity.

"How did you come to marry him?" he asked softly.

"I was vacationing with my mother. She was on an antiques buying trip. Stefan and I met in a shop on Portobello Road. He sort of swept me off my feet. He was so handsome and oozed European charm, and he had this plummy upper-class British accent. You know, I've a real weakness for British accents." Suddenly her face heated up. Heaven only knew what he thought of that inane confession.

She rushed ahead before he could respond. "Well, anyway, at first he was wonderful, until we were married. He changed. Things got so bad, I couldn't, wouldn't—I mean, I just couldn't go on with the relationship. And his family—don't get me started on them."

"No, please tell me. It might help."

"First of all, Stefan's mother was a witch who scared the hell out of me. She made no bones about how much she abhorred seeing her baby boy marry a washed-out stick of an American. His father was a perfect gentleman..." she paused for effect before continuing, "...with the deadest pair of eyes I've seen outside of a funeral parlor."

"I see. You had in-law problems." His mouth twitched.

"I'm serious."

"Did I imply otherwise?"

"Then there were his two brothers—Theo and Xander—both of them tried to see which one I would sleep with first. They drove Stefan crazy with their innuendos and lies. The night I left, Stefan and I had a terrible fight. He—uh, hit me. It wasn't the first time either."

She swallowed the knot in her throat. Stefan had hit her many times in the course of their short marriage. That wasn't the worst. She stared at the backs of her hands, gathering the courage to admit the awful truth of that night—something she'd never told anyone. "H-he forced me. Jamie must've been conceived that night. I waited until everyone in the family compound was asleep, climbed a tree and dropped over the wall. I ran.

"I had no idea I was pregnant when I moved in with Cassie, until I started getting sick in the mornings. Then Stefan showed up and...well, we both know what happened after that."

David scowled and drew his hands into fists. "I'm so sorry. I had no idea."

"As awful as it was, I don't regret having Jamie, not one minute. I love him so much, the rest just doesn't matter."

"He's a wonderful lad. You've done a bang-up job."

"He's the real reason I didn't keep in touch. I had so much to think about with his birth and all. I had to get away, from Stefan's family and for my sanity as much as anything." Anxious to turn the topic from herself, she asked, "What did *you* do after you left the hospital?"

"Kept to myself, licked my wounds. Almost left the force."

"But you didn't."

"No, I wanted to bring Stefan to trial, but Chief Superintendent didn't want to give me the assignment. Said I was *too involved.*"

"But you brought him in. I read about it in all the papers. They touted you as quite the hero."

"Some hero," he said bitterly, his mouth twisting into a derisive line. "Let my fiancée get blown up."

She felt the tears forming again and brushed them away with the back of her hand. "I'm so s-sorry."

"Don't." He dug a handkerchief from his pocket and handed

it to her. "Here, wipe your nose before it starts to run," he said, his voice husky with emotion.

She accepted it with a sniff. "Th-thank you." His being nice just made her feel worse, but she couldn't let him see. "I think I'll turn in. I guess we're going to have a pretty busy day tomorrow."

"Right." He stood and stretched. "If everything goes well, we'll be on our way to Zurich tomorrow evening." He gestured with his thumb toward the bathroom. "Mind if I shower first?"

"No, of course not." She watched his tall, well-muscled frame. David was a good man, but he was still in love with Cassie. She guessed he always would be.

Randi sighed. Why on earth would he ever look at someone like her?

Enough of the pity party! Wake up and smell the espresso. You can't compete with a ghost.

ଔ

David walked into the lavatory. He reached into the shower and turned on the water until it was as hot as he could stand.

After stepping into the stall, he leaned against the tiled wall. The steaming water cleansed his body, but his mind was another matter.

The more time he spent with Miranda, the more she got to him. More than anything, he'd wanted to gather her in his arms and comfort her and, in turn, comfort himself. They'd both loved Cassie, but she was gone. Yet, her death still caused them both pain. What would be wrong in their comforting each other? But was seeking comfort enough of a reason to turn their lives upside down?

No, it was selfish.

Besides, he couldn't bring himself to make the first move. It wasn't the right time or place. Her child was asleep in the same room with them. And the horrors Miranda had suffered at her husband's hands made him sick. More than anything he wanted to crush the man for hurting her.

Now he knew the reason behind the sadness in her eyes.

℃ℨ

The bathroom door opened; Randi looked up from the map. David walked out wearing a black T-shirt and a pair of athletic shorts, his auburn hair still damp from the shower. She swallowed hard. His lean thighs were firmly muscled. Good Lord, he was a fine-looking man.

"Your turn."

"Save me any hot water?" After all, he'd stayed in the shower a full thirty minutes, just like her brothers did at home.

A fleeting expression of guilt crossed his face. "I think so."

"You *think* so?"

"Maybe." He reached up and finger-combed his hair into a semblance of order.

"So thoughtful. *Not.*"

"I'm sure if you wait a bit, there'll be plenty." He walked over to the chaise and sat.

"You're really not going to sleep on that thing, are you?" she asked. "Your feet will hang off."

"I'll be fine."

"Look, you take the bed. I'm short. I can sleep on the chaise."

"Don't be ridiculous."

"We're both ridiculous. This is a very wide bed." She stifled a giggle when his dark brows nearly met his hair line.

"Miranda, what are you proposing?"

"Well, unless you're just driven wild with passion and can't help yourself, I'm proposing that you sleep on one side, and I'll sleep on the other with Jamie right in the middle."

"But—"

"No buts. It's all settled. Now, I'm going to take my shower." She grabbed her bag, intent on letting him get used to the idea.

"Are you sure that's all you want to happen?" he asked her with a lazy grin that made her heart flip-flop, something akin to doing a double-gainer off the high dive. "What if I *am* driven wild by passion? What would you say to that?"

"W-why would you—I mean—are you?" she asked, more than a little stunned by the sexy aura that seemed to emanate from every pore of his hard body. Was it one of those pheromone deals she'd read about? No, clearly he'd lost his mind sometime while he took his shower. Maybe it was the fine French-milled soap that had affected his senses. And maybe she'd already lost hers, because he had that certain look in his eyes—the one men get just before they're going to kiss you.

"Uh..." She hesitated not knowing what else to say. She had to get away from him.

"Miranda, wait..." he said, catching her by the wrist.

Instinctively she jumped, then glanced down at the sight of his suntanned hand on her wrist, then up into his eyes. "What?"

Her mouth went dry—Sahara Desert dry—she couldn't manage anything else. Confusion reigned. His hand was strong, yet gentle. She hadn't felt a man's touch in six years. Maybe that ought to change.

"Are you afraid of me?" he questioned.

"N-no, of course not. I trust you or we wouldn't be here."

"I didn't ask if you trusted me. I asked if I scared you. That's not the same thing."

"Sure it is," she insisted, trying to cover her confusion. "How could I stay in the same room with you if I were afraid of you? I just suggested we sleep in the same bed—for Pete's sake."

David rolled his eyes. "What I meant was, are you afraid of me as a man? Does my touching you make you uncomfortable?"

"Maybe a little." Her mouth dropped open when she divined his intent. He brought her hand to his mouth and brushed a kiss across the back of it. His lips were tender and warm, and a thrill zapped up her arm and straight down her to lower belly. Warmth pooled between her thighs. Oh, Lord, what would he do next? What did she want him to do next?

No, not *that*—she wasn't any good at *that*.

"Shh, you just haven't been touched by the right man," he

murmured, holding her gaze with his as he continued to hold her wrist. "You have the most wonderful hands."

"I do?" She was afraid to look and see what was so "wonderful" about her hands, but she felt them trembling.

"They're warm, strong and gentle. They know how to love."

Her knees threatened to give out, but she stiffened them. Wouldn't do to crumple at his feet the first time he made a move. Now would it? "Well—uh, they're just everyday, normal hands."

"If you don't hush, I'll be forced to kiss you just to shut you up."

"You will?"

Really great comeback, Randi. Then fortune smiled on her. She didn't have to conjure up any more snappy repartee. David lowered his lips to hers.

Soft, warm and demanding. He kissed her until her knees buckled. Lord, could he ever kiss. Only his strong arms kept her standing. Slipping her arms around his neck, she returned his kiss, still not believing it was real. Her body molded just right with his—small matter he was a foot taller. And then there was the not-so-small matter of his erection pressed against her stomach.

Oh dear.

She couldn't. Not here, not with Jamie asleep on the bed. With more pain than regret, she pulled back. "Not now. I can't."

David leaned his head back, his eyes half-closed. "I know."

"I didn't even know *you* wanted to."

"I know it's crazy, but—"

"Oh, please, flatter me some more."

"No, no. I mean, given our situation. I need to stay focused. But I'm having trouble concentrating on anything but your eyes and your..." He paused, as if afraid of saying more and waved his hands forming a rounded female figure in the air.

"That's better." Lord, was she really standing here in his arms discussing what they *couldn't* do? She must be out of her mind. He couldn't possibly have any feelings for little Randi Raines from Nashville. David and Cassie had been a true love match if she'd ever seen one. No, this wasn't right. Maybe she was hallucinating.

"I guess a cold shower might come in handy, after all."

"I'm not going to apologize."

"You better not!"

"But this is really *not* the time."

She looked over at her sleeping son. "And it sure isn't the place," she said, as a confusing mixture of regret and relief washed over her.

"Agreed." He pulled her against his chest again. His lips found her neck, sending icebergs down her spine. Her hands slid up and down his back, relishing the brawn of his muscles.

"So sweet," he whispered in her ear, his breath warm against her neck. "Now go, before your son awakens and receives an early lesson in the birds and the bees."

A groan escaped her lips. She managed an, "Uh-huh."

Wobbly knees and all, she made it to the bathroom door with the much needed assistance of his strong arms. "I think I can take it from here, big fella," she drawled in her most Southern Belle voice.

A knowing smile played across his mouth. "All right, little lady," he drawled back.

"Was that supposed to be John Wayne?"

"Of course."

She wrinkled her nose, then grinned. "Don't give up detecting."

"You, into the shower," he ordered, aiming a playful swat at her bottom.

"I'm going. I'm going." She escaped, shutting the bathroom door behind her. Leaning against it, she slid down ever so slowly until her butt hit the cold tile floor.

Good Lord, what next? Too much had happened for her to take it all in. Three nights ago she thought she had her life all figured out. Now, nothing was the same, never would be if she wasn't mistaken.

Calm down, girl, she cautioned her runaway emotions.

David's a normal guy. And like any normal guy, he gets horny. And on top of everything else, she'd been right in his face for the last three days. It was proximity—not her sex appeal. Heaven knew Stefan had reminded her too many times of what she lacked.

She really couldn't blame David, now could she?

Slowly, she picked herself up off the floor. Cold shower?

That's what she needed all right. Reaching into the shower she turned on the cold water and stuck her hand into the needle-fine spray.

Chapter Nine

David held his breath until he heard her turn on the shower, then he sank down on the side of the bed. Holding his head in his hands, he groaned. What the bloody hell was the matter with him? Three short days ago, Miranda Raines was so far off his radar she might as well have been in Outer Mongolia, until the Super had called him into his office.

Now, the three of them were on the run from who-knew-how-many of Kristoforus's goons, and he was falling in—no, not love, it couldn't be.

Lust? No, telling himself it was lust didn't solve anything. Miranda wasn't someone with whom he could just scratch an itch. After what she'd been through, she deserved better, much better. But was *he* who she deserved?

Their enforced togetherness had shown him so much about her gentle yet audacious nature. He glanced over at the small boy who was the center of her world. Did she have enough love for anyone else? Unless he was very mistaken, she did.

What would Cassie think? Stupid line of reasoning. Cassie was dead, and if he wasn't careful, the nightmare could happen all over again. Could he run the risk? Of course he couldn't.

Miranda had already become more important than he could've ever imagined. And her son? A wonderfully bright youngster, as yet untouched by all the greed, anger and stupidity in the world, he deserved a father who would love him, guide him and prepare him for a productive adult life.

The sudden cessation of sound snapped him back to the present. She was through with her shower. Without warning, he was assailed by images of her stepping from the shower, her skin beaded with moisture. Rivulets running down her slight, womanly curves. The unique scent of her, fresh and without artifice, filled his mind.

He ached to touch her fair, silken skin and hold her pliant body close to his again. She had a scattering of light freckles across her shoulders which matched the ones dusted like powdered sugar across the bridge of her nose. If only...

How long he sat there, imagining her sliding into bed alongside him, skin soft and fragrant from her bath, he didn't know. In some distant area of his brain, he was aware of the noise of a hair dryer, but the sound of the lavatory door's opening jerked him out of his reverie. He looked about their room, desperate to hide his confused state of mind—not to mention his aroused state.

He grabbed up his newspaper, careful to hold it in front of him. No point in embarrassing the two of them. "You're quite sure you're through?" he asked, even though it was patently obvious she was. Bloody hell, but he was an out-of-control teenager.

She walked by him, and once again, the fresh-from-the-shower scent of her drove him to distraction. He stood in the doorway, watching her scoot Jamie to the middle of the wide bed. Lord, how would he ever manage to get any sleep in the same bed with her?

"You're really set on my taking the other side?" he asked, giving her one more opportunity to come to her senses...and save him from making a total ass of himself.

She looked up at him, her gaze locking with his. A mischievous grin spread across her cupid's-bow lips. "Uh-huh. Jamie will be our bundling board."

"A what?"

"A bundling board. The early American settlers would put a courting couple in the same bed, but would place a board between them to prevent..." she paused, shrugging, "...you know?"

"What about splinters?"

"Splinters?" A puzzled expression swept across her face, quickly followed by one of understanding. "They were careful to pick boards without knotholes. Honestly." She shook her head with apparent disdain, but the jittering movement of her shoulders told him she was struggling to hold back her laughter.

"And this was done for what reason?"

"So they could get to know each other and keep warm at the same time."

"I always knew you Yanks had a weird streak, and now I know it goes back to Colonial times."

She responded to his teasing by drawing up to her full five-feet, two-inches and placing her hands on her hips. "Are you taking *another* shower?"

"Yes, ma'am, I am," he replied, snapping a salute in her direction. He wasted no time seeking refuge in the lavatory.

Closing the door behind him, he considered what he must do next. Breathe. In and out. Yes, that always worked. What a dunce he was to lose control so easily around her.

For the second time that night, he turned on the shower. Just as well there wasn't any hot water.

Ice-cold. That's it. The colder the better.

⊂૩

Randi woke up the next morning, gave a great yawn and stretched. In spite of her misgivings about having David in the same bed, she'd slept like a baby, comfortable and safe. Being with him affected her that way—not to mention the *other* ways he affected her. How *he'd* slept, she didn't know.

Apparently, he'd risen early without waking her and was nowhere to be seen.

Don't be such a worrywart. But she couldn't help it. So many things could go wrong.

⊂૩

David paced around the rear garden which, despite a decided autumn nip in the morning air, remained green and quite pleasant. He would've given anything for a cigarette. He'd quit long ago at Cassie's request and only resumed very briefly after her death.

He'd slept little, keeping to his side of the bed all night; he didn't dare relax for fear his body would seek the warmth of Miranda's, sleeping only two feet away. On the other hand, she'd slept like a rock. Not that he resented her ability to fall asleep and never move all night. No, he rather envied her.

Somewhere around two, he'd finally given up and taken the chaise. He'd fallen asleep, only to awaken at six. Four hours was better than none.

His growing attraction for Miranda aside, he still had her ex-husband and his family to sort out. The uneasiness that had gnawed at him for the last twenty-four hours returned full force.

Stefan was closing in.

And he knew better than to ignore his gut feelings.

He'd told her they should keep a low profile, and so they would. Just a few more hours, and he could pick up their new documents. Then they could bloody well get out of France.

CB

"May I go out and play today?" Jamie asked, tugging at Randi's sleeve.

She sat on the bed and pulled him up in her lap. "Not today. You and I have to pack while DCI French picks up our new passports. Remember our game? We're hiding from someone, and we need to stay out of sight."

"I remember the game, but how could he find us? *I* don't even know where we are."

Stifling a sigh, she hugged her son. "You know how it is on the telly?"

"The bad people use computers, so we have to keep one step ahead of them, right?"

"Exactly."

The door opened. In spite of herself, she jumped.

"David!" Jamie wriggled off Randi's lap and ran to the tall detective, hopping up into his arms. "Mummy says I must help her pack today, but I want to go outside and play."

"You do, do you?"

"Yes, I'm ever so tired of staying inside. I should have some fresh air. It's good for children, you know."

David's shoulders shook with amusement, but he managed to keep a straight face. "I believe I have heard something to that effect."

"Well?"

Heaving a theatrical sigh, David shook his head. "I'm afraid your mum is right. In a couple of days."

"Days?" her son interrupted with an inconsolable whine. "I'll surely turn ill, if I—"

"That's enough, James Michael Peyton, no more," Randi ordered, her tone even, but firm. Deliberately pasting a frown across her face, she stopped him with a glance.

A look of rebellion crossed his small face as if considering just how far he could go; his gaze cut from Randi to David and back to her. Finally, the boy nodded his agreement.

"May I watch telly?" he asked, assuming the most dejected expression she'd ever seen.

Her heart squeezed in her chest. She hated denying her son anything, especially *fresh air*, as he'd put it so concisely.

"Yes, you may."

Amused, she watched Jamie skip over to the armoire, open the door and turn on the television. He settled himself on the chaise and became engrossed in a French cartoon.

Turning to David, she apologized. "I had no idea he would hit you up to go outside."

David gave a quiet bark of laughter. "He saw me as the weak link. Mind you, very shrewd of him. I was ready to cave."

A chill threaded its way down her spine. She hugged her arms to her chest and shivered. "No, you were right to start with. Like you said, we need to keep a low profile, until you're sure we're safe."

He frowned, his thick brows nearly meeting across the bridge of his proud nose. "You feel it, too?"

"I feel something," she admitted. "What do you feel?"

His voice dropped to a whisper. "Stefan."

She nodded, then shivered again. "Yeah, me too."

His expression changed. A curtain dropped in place, shielding all emotion in his usually expressive eyes.

"About last night."

"No problem. I mean you're a man and all," she rushed to say something, anything. God, it was too embarrassing for words.

The curtain lifted; his eyes twinkled, again. "Miranda, stop dithering. It's just this isn't the time or place."

"You think I don't know that? I'm not a love-starved ninny. It was just one of those things... ships that pass in the night," she said, giving a shrug.

He groaned, then stepped closer. "Don't be ridiculous. Our kiss was real. The way I felt holding you in my arms was not a cliché."

Her bottom lip trembled. Biting the inside of her lip, she managed, "It wasn't?"

His eyes softened, a smile played about his lips. "No."

A lump the size of Gibraltar filled her throat. She tried to swallow, but he pulled her to his chest, effectively cutting off her breath. No point in trying to swallow when she couldn't breathe. She gasped for air, knowing she must look like a Big Mouth Bass flopping on a river bank.

He kissed her forehead. "Go on and pack."

Confusion racked her brain. What language was he speaking? "Huh?"

"Weren't you going to pack?" he whispered in her ear, sending a very different sort vibration down her spine to a region of her body long neglected.

She gazed up into his eyes. "Mm."

"I'll take that as an affirmative."

More or less mute, she nodded.

CB

Randi looked up from packing her bag. "Maybe we should go with you to pick up the papers. It would save time, wouldn't it?"

"Yes, it would, but I'm more interested in keeping you and Jamie out of sight. If something should happen—"

"You think it will?"

"No, let me finish. If something should happen...say I don't return within a reasonable time, call a taxi and go straight to the British Embassy. Tell them your passports and money were stolen. They'll take you in. They can sort out the truth later."

"What about you?"

He gave a dismissive wave. "Don't worry about me. I can handle myself. I just want to cover all the bases."

"Okay." Of course, he could handle himself. He'd proved it time and again, but that didn't keep her from worrying about him.

"Promise me."

"All right, I promise."

"Good."

She nodded, keeping her expression grave. "Be careful."

David marveled at the guileless simplicity of her words. "Certainly," he managed to say, trying not to make too much out of a few words. Still, his heart beat a little faster than it had. To his ears, it sounded as if she cared, but it had been so long since anyone had worried about him.

Perhaps, he'd overreacted.

"We'll be ready to leave when you get back."

"Right. If everything goes as planned, I'll hire a car and return for you and Jamie."

She pulled her sweater tighter around her shoulders and shivered. "We'll be ready."

CB

"Let me out at the west entrance of the park."

99

The taxi driver stopped the car. David paid him and stepped from the cab. Pulling up his collar around his neck, he hunched his shoulders, in effect altering his posture and gait so that he appeared shorter and older. He felt for the Beretta in the small of his back. Whether or not he'd need it remained to be seen, but he wouldn't be caught unawares.

He walked past couples holding hands and children on swings. The fall afternoon was warm. The leaves of the hardwood trees were beginning their fall metamorphosis from green to gold and scarlet.

He headed for the center of the park, keeping a constant lookout for his contact and any signs he'd been followed. As it had the day before, the hair on the back of his neck stood at attention.

He glanced about, assessing every person in sight. Each seemed innocuous enough, but that meant nothing. The best of assassins was capable of disguising himself as a pretty young girl. Stefan or his father might be tempted to send a professional rather than risk Stefan's precious hide. Personally, he hoped Stefan himself would come as he had the first night.

At the foot of a statue honoring the French Resistance of WWII, he spotted his contact, the same rat-faced man, except this time he wore a bright red beret. They greeted each other as if they were old friends. The go-between indicated with a jerk of his head that David should follow him.

The contact led him into a less conspicuous area of the park which was well-shaded and less traveled. He stopped and sat on a park bench. "The rest of the money, *m'sieur?*" his contact asked. Patting his pocket, he indicated the presence of the forged papers.

"Give me the originals first," David demanded. He wasn't about to forget those.

"So mistrustful, *m'sieur.*" Rat Face shrugged. "*Mais bien sûr, il est seulement naturel.*" He reached into his jacket and pulled out three passports, then handed them to David who wasted no time examining them. Before giving them up the day before, he'd placed identifying marks on each blue folder. He had no doubts. He held the originals in his hands.

"The others?"

The gray-haired man extended his hand, rubbing his thumb and first two fingers together in the age-old gesture for money. "*L'argent?*"

"I have to inspect the merchandise first. You already have half of the agreed-upon fee. I'm not going to cheat you, and I don't intend to be cheated. Hand them over."

With a show of great reluctance, the go-between produced six more passports, handing them over with a smirk. "*Excellent, non?*"

He scanned them. Excellent, indeed. "*Oui, m'sieur.* They are of superior quality. The credit cards?"

The man pulled two credit cards from his jacket pocket.

David took the plastic cards, checking for the laser-coded inset. "He does good work," he agreed. "They're well worth the price." He handed over the second half of the forger's fee.

"*Merci beaucoup, m'sieur.*"

"*Et vous, m'sieur.*"

While he watched the forger's henchman disappear into the crowd, he scanned for any indication their transaction had been observed. Satisfied it hadn't, he stood and headed for the park entrance opposite the one he'd used earlier.

ॐ

Back and forth, Randi paced. It had been hours since David had left for his meeting with the forger. What was it he'd said? Go to the embassy if he wasn't back in a reasonable time.

Unfortunately, he'd never bothered to define just how long a reasonable time was or had he? Three hours, four, twenty-four? It was already dark outside. What could be taking him so long?

"He'll be all right, Mummy. Don't worry."

"I know," she agreed, just so her son wouldn't worry. Heck, she was worrying enough for both of them.

The sound of a key in the lock, then the door burst open. David rushed into the room, his movements economical and swift as he grabbed for his bag.

"David, I was—"

"We have to leave. Right now," he asserted, his tone measured.

"What's happened?"

"Nothing yet. You said you'd be ready. Let's move."

Jamie jumped to his feet. "I'm ready, sir."

She gave one last glance around the room, then grabbed their suitcase. "Okay." She and Jamie lined up behind David, who paused at the door. He opened the door a couple of inches and peered at the hallway in both direction.

"We'll proceed out the rear exit. The hired car is already parked within a few steps of the door."

"What about the bill?" she asked, unable to keep the practical matters off her mind.

"Done." He stepped into the hallway. "Go in front. I'll cover from the rear. Jamie between us."

She nodded in agreement. What else could she do? What had spooked him? His handsome face had a set, determined look about it, but the telltale muscle in his jaw danced. Maybe he would tell her once they were on their way.

Cʒ

With Miranda leading and David as rear guard, they hurried down the narrow stairway to the first floor of the old inn without incident. He stopped and motioned for them to wait. "Wait. I'll check out things first."

He stepped into the back garden. The temperature had plummeted with the setting of the sun. He looked from side to side, then strode over to the rented Citroën, unlocked the trunk and placed their bags inside. He strolled back to the rear door, where Miranda and the boy waited. Calmly, as if he had all the time in the world, he walked around to the passenger side of the car, unlocked and opened both doors. He gestured for Miranda and her son to come ahead.

"Now."

She left the cover of the inn and walked toward him with

the boy's hand held tightly in her white-knuckled one. She secured him in the back seat while David walked around to the driver's side of the car. "About ready, dear?" he asked, carrying on the pretense of their being newlyweds. "We'll be late for our train if you don't hurry."

"Sorry, darling." She gave him a smile that made him wish it were truly for him alone.

As soon as she was seated beside him and her seat belt safely buckled, he turned the key in the ignition. It took all his willpower not to rev the thing for all it was worth and blast off like the last rocket to Mars.

He eased out of the car park, maneuvering the vehicle smoothly through the narrow alley behind the inn. Turning left onto the street, he threaded his way into the flow of light traffic. He took a deep breath, forcing his hands to relax their death grip on the steering wheel.

"So?"

He shot her a quick glance. Her arms were crossed over her chest. "So, what?" he bluffed.

"So, what happened?"

He'd given the good-old-boy bluff a try, although her scowl told him she wasn't buying. "I told you I'd be in a rush once I returned. You said you'd be ready, and you were."

"You can't pull the wool over my eyes, David French, so don't even try."

"Yes, sir. Mummy always knows when I've told a fib."

"I guess I'm busted," David admitted with a grin. "Since you insist on knowing, after I hired the car, I stopped at the front desk to pay the bill. Gilbèrt told me a man had been asking about a young couple with a small boy. He showed Gilbèrt pictures of the two of us. Gilbèrt told him he hadn't seen us. Besides, he told me, since we were honeymooners, he didn't think we would be expecting any guests."

"Oh my God! Do you think it was..." Randi dropped her voice to a whisper, "...Stefan?"

"No. The description didn't fit *him*, but it could have been one of his brothers or one of his family's thugs."

"So we're safe for now?"

He checked the rearview mirror. "I haven't seen anyone following us." He rounded a corner with a sharp jerk on the steering wheel. "Let's see." He continued on a circuitous route until he was absolutely satisfied no one was shadowing them.

"We're okay for now." He turned onto a heavily trafficked highway. "We'll take the expressway due east to Besançon, then to Mullhouse, Basel and finally Zurich. Seven-hundred kilometers, give or take a few. We'll drive all night and hit the Swiss National Bank as soon as it opens. "

"After that?"

"We'll break in those new passports and credit cards, and we'll fly commercial to Italy. Maybe then we can ease off for a few days."

"Fly?"

"Yes, fly. On a big jet. Surely that meets with your approval?"

"The *size* of the plane doesn't make any difference. I still hate flying."

"How the blazes did you ever cross the Atlantic? A-a native canoe?" he sputtered.

"A canoe? Mummy, did you really come to the U.K. in a canoe?"

"Ever hear of tranquilizers?" Miranda directed to David, then turned around telling the boy, "No, darlin'. Mummy came on a big airplane with your Grandma Raines."

David darted a quick glance in her direction. "You mean to tell me I could've sedated you and I wouldn't have had to listen to your sniveling?"

"Eyes on the road, please."

"I much prefer them in my head," he bantered, hoping to defuse the tension.

"Didn't know you Brits had a sense of humor."

"Oh really? If we don't have a sense of humor, how do you explain *Benny Hill* and *Monty Python?*"

"Or *Ab Fab*?" she suggested, her tone the most dulcet of coos.

"Oh, honestly, you can't compare those two silly women with *Monty Python* or *Blackadder.*"

"And why not? They are just as funny as their male counterparts."

"I can see that your education has been seriously neglected if you think Edwina and Patsy are exemplars of British humor."

"And just *how* do you know their names? You watched them, didn't you?"

"Not *regularly*," he admitted, struggling to keep the smile off his face.

"Hah! I knew it."

CЗ

Stefan paced back and forth in the study while his father listened to his tirade, his craggy face growing redder by the minute. Just once he wished he could shake the old fool out of his complacency.

"What do you mean you haven't found them? How difficult can it be to find a couple with a small child? What good are all your bleeding computers and contacts if you can't find my son?" He rubbed his left shoulder. The wound still ached like the very devil, and with the smallest movement, pain shot through his shoulder like the slash of a knife. He would make the detective pay for that and more.

The old man scowled. "You must be patient, my son. After all, a great deal of money changed hands just to free you from prison."

"And for that I'm grateful. I've no doubt you will remind me of it from now to eternity."

His father smiled. Not a sight calculated to warm the heart of his youngest son. No, indeed.

"You will have your son *and* your vengeance if you're not precipitous. We've discussed this before. I won't repeat my warning again. Plus, the latest intel indicates we just missed them in Dijon."

"Dijon?"

"Yes, and furthermore, my sources suggest that they are headed to Zurich."

Stefan nodded his assent. "All right, I'll do as you wish," he lied. He would not be dictated to by an old man who should have retired to one of the Greek Isles years ago.

Chapter Ten

Randi rubbed her eyes and stifled a yawn. It was nearly three in the morning, and David had driven the entire time, in spite of her offers to help. They'd made good progress, including a stop for dinner at a small inn and several pit stops for her and Jamie. Crossing the Swiss border had gone smoothly, even if she'd held her breath the entire time.

"Are we there yet?" she asked with a giggle, feeling just like a kid again.

"No, but it won't be long."

"So what will we do until the bank opens?"

"Find an all night café, tank up on coffee. I'll check in with Brinks. Then plane reservations and a map."

"A map? I thought we were flying from Zurich to Italy."

"Alternate routes from the bank to the airport...just in case."

Just in case? "You think of everything."

She hesitated, casting a glance at Jamie who dozed in the back seat. "Do you really think they'll trace us this far?"

"It's possible. Stefan won't give up easily," David said, his tone low.

She watched him closely for signs of fatigue. His eyes never left the road, and his hands remained steady on the steering wheel. "Why don't you let me drive? I know you must be tired."

He stretched his neck from side to side. "Okay. Just wait until I find a place to stop."

"Here, let me rub your neck. You must be stiff." She got up with her knees in the seat and, reaching behind him, started massaging his neck and shoulders. "You're tight, like steel bands."

Emitting a soft moan of contentment, David admitted, "That feels super. You're hired."

She smiled. "We'll talk about my salary later," she teased. She had to admit—if only to herself—that she enjoyed touching him.

He flicked on the turn signal and shifted into the right-hand lane. "We'll get off here."

"Then you'll let me drive for a while?"

"Only until we reach the city's perimeter."

C ʒ

Randi decided to stay in the car with Jamie while David went into the truck stop for coffee and to check in with his contact at MI6.

From her vantage point, she watched him hang up the pay phone, shaking his head. He walked back to the car with two large cups of steaming hot coffee. She scooted over in the driver's seat, then reached over and opened the passenger door for him.

"Something's wrong—what happened?"

"He doesn't answer. It's early, but the connection isn't going through."

"Is that bad?"

The muscle in his jaw jumped and his expression grew troubled. "Possibly."

A knot formed in her throat. The thought of Stefan close on their trail scared the bejesus out of her. She swallowed...or tried to.

"We have to be prepared for trouble in Zurich. If someone has gotten to Brinks, Stefan or any of his father's goons could be waiting for us. I can't risk you or Jamie. I'll have to go to the bank alone."

"They're looking for the three of us—a man, woman and a child. What if you're disguised—say as a woman?"

"A woman?" His eyebrows arched in disbelief.

"Well, you are a little on the tall side, but..." she paused and gave him an assessing glance, "...you'd make an attractive one."

"A woman?" His voice rose with disbelief. "How in blazes do you propose to disguise me as a woman? Seriously?"

"Wig, makeup and a nice dress?" she offered, her tone teasing. But it wasn't a bad idea at all.

"I said *seriously*." He took a gulp from his coffee. "Your idea has merit, but how?" he asked, taking the time to give her tiny frame a long, slow perusal. "I don't think your clothes will fit."

She giggled. "We just need to find a shop that caters to the—uh, gender-identity challenged."

"In Zurich?" This time his eyebrows rose nearly to his hairline.

"Sure. Why not? There's more to Switzerland than chocolate and cuckoo clocks. Zurich is just like any other big city. There's bound to be one."

"Might I remind you that time *is* of the essence. We can't shilly-shally around."

"Okay. Here's what we'll do. Find a cyber-café, then go online and find the store we need. Just one outfit now, 'cause we do have to watch the budget, don't we?" Needling him was too much fun, but she was unable to resist.

"You're *not* taking this seriously."

She sobered, then took a sip of her coffee. "Of course, I am. I'm just trying not to think about all the horrible things that *could* happen." She placed her hand on his upper arm, hoping to assure him of her sincerity. "You know, I read somewhere that Bonnie Prince Charlie escaped the British soldiers by masquerading as a woman."

"That settles it. I won't do it."

In pure desperation she suggested, "Then let me disguise myself and go to the bank instead."

"Absolutely not!"

"But my hair is already different. Think about it. They won't be expecting me. I'm already a woman. It makes perfect sense."

"Out of the question."

"Why not?" she asked brusquely, her temper getting the better of her.

"If there's trouble, it'll be at the bank. You're a civilian and you're a woman. I won't run the risk of...of losing you, too."

It dawned on her. "I see what this is about. Cassie. You're letting your guilt cloud your judgment. I'll be fine." At least she hoped she would.

"Partially, but I really don't want to risk losing you...or Jamie," he added.

His "or Jamie" was added a bit hastily. Damn it. Was it *her*, really? Who was actually on his mind? Sometimes she thought he might be starting to care about her. And sometimes she *knew* it was really all about his sense of honor and duty.

She placed her hands on the wheel. "Okay. Make up your mind. We need a plan."

"Well I—"

"That's long enough. I already gave you a plan."

"Now see here, I'm not used to taking orders from American fiddle players. There are contingencies to consider."

"So consider. Either you go or I do. And if you go, you'll need to be disguised, at least so no one will recognize you from a distance."

"A disguise, yes, but—"

"Okay, how's this? You enter the bank dressed as a woman, go to the ladies' room, and change."

"The ladies'? You want me to come out of the ladies' as a man? Have you lost it? That'll bring the authorities down on me."

"Well, find an empty office then and leave the bank as a man. Besides, won't you have to show your passport at the bank?"

"No, with a numbered Swiss Bank account, all I have to do is give them the number."

"That's it?"

"Precisely."

"Then I guess we'd better be finding a cyber-café and finding you a new wardrobe. You'll be heading into the bank as a femme fatale...either that or *I* will."

"Miranda..."

"Make your choice or I'll make it for you." After all traipsing into the bank in disguise couldn't be any scarier than getting onto an airplane, now could it?

"Bloody hell, but you're a stubborn wench."

"What'll it be, Chief Inspector?"

He let out a low groan. "I'll do it. There's no conceivable way I'd risk your life in such a fashion."

"Fine." Truthfully she was relieved. The thought of leaving David and Jamie and sashaying into the bank all alone had her insides doing a ragged cha-cha-cha.

CS

David pulled up in front of *Les Croix* and parked the car. Ten A.M. and the shops were opening. He glanced over at Miranda who, to his displeasure, wore the most annoying and smug expression he'd ever seen. "I hope you're satisfied. I cannot believe I'm going to enter this establishment as man and exit as a woman. Bloody hell!"

He hit the steering wheel in frustration. It might be a good plan, but he didn't have to like it.

"David," she warned, giving a pointed glance toward the rear of the car. "Son, don't you pay any attention to DCI French's language."

"No, Mummy. I won't," he sniggered from the back seat.

"Didn't you ever go out on the beat disguised as a hooker? I've seen them do it on American television shows."

He looked down his nose and gave an indignant sniff. "Apparently, the Metropolitan Police Department has more dignity than their Yank counterparts."

"Don't go pulling your aristocratic airs on me. I'm an American. We're all equal, and you don't impress me one little bit."

She grinned as she made her pronouncement, but there was an underlying truth to her statement. He didn't blame her a bit. All that crap about class had always irritated him as well.

"All right. Let's get this over with."

CB

David eyed the clerk who stood eyeball-to-eyeball with him. He'd seen enough cross-dressers on the job to know her/his flawless makeup and coiffeur were part and parcel of the lifestyle. "I," he began, wishing he could slink out the door with none the wiser. But he might as well brazen it out. He wouldn't be in Zurich again—not for a long time anyway.

"Oh, I'd love to help you choose your new wardrobe. It's so difficult for a big *person* to find the right styles. I've been able to assist so many on their journey toward gender reassignment," the clerk offered, then paused before confiding, "I'm saving for the final surgery myself."

David shivered. His nether regions tightened. Pure reflex.

The very thought of surgery... He shivered again.

"Thank you," Miranda said, making a visible effort to keep her face composed. He'd have to see she paid for that, somehow.

"Now, what look are you going for? Sexy? Well, you certainly are that. Sophisticated career woman?"

"How about something simple?"

"Ah, yes, I just knew you'd prefer an elegant style. I should have suggested that first. I'll be right back with some things I know you'll love."

The clerk turned to the racks of clothing, choosing one garment then another. Shaking her head in displeasure over another, she replaced it. When the clerk had as much as she could carry, she turned toward him. "All right, dear, I have several ensembles for you. Let's take you back and get you undressed."

David resisted the urge—the very strong urge—to growl. He cast a glance over his shoulder at Miranda and the boy. He felt like a lamb on his way to becoming lamb chops. Miranda and her bright ideas.

"But you make a very attractive woman. It is unfortunate your chin is so strong," the clerk said with a slight smile.

"My chin?"

"Perhaps, some judicious surgery could take care of that...and your nose, too, while the surgeon is at it."

"What's wrong with my nose?" he demanded, already tired of being discussed as if he were a side of beef.

"Too manly, *mon chèr*," the clerk replied. "Now which of these lovely frocks will you choose?"

"How about the pantsuit?" he suggested, anxious to get it over with.

The clerk giggled. "Well, if you wear a pantsuit, you won't have to shave your legs, although you should consider it for the overall look."

"Shave my legs? Bloody hell!"

"Right. I really wish we had time to do a real makeover," the clerk told him. "I hate rushing."

Fed up, David declared, "I'm in a hurry. This isn't real. I'm playing a joke on an old school chum."

"Oh, but of course you are, *mon chèr*." The clerk tittered knowingly.

"Now what about your *coiffeur*? Do you have a preference for any certain style?"

"Goldilocks, Goldilocks," squealed Jamie who had followed David into the changing room. The excited boy jumped up and down, clapping his hands.

"No curls, something I don't have to fiddle with."

"Well, you certainly know what you want. I'll say that for you."

"Never mind. Just do it. I have an appointment."

"With your old school chum?" The clerk raised a finely plucked eyebrow.

"Yes." David clenched his jaw.

"Now then, since you've chosen a pants suit and flat-heel boots, we must feminize you with some accessories and a nice frilly blouse, or you won't fool anyone."

"Now, hold on."

Finally after another forty-five minutes of adjustments to the wig and choosing the appropriate accessories, David was ready—makeup and all. If anyone had ever told him he'd be in drag, he would've pronounced them insane.

"I give you Daphne," the clerk announced. "Remember what I told you about your walk. You must swing your hips, just so." The clerk demonstrated with a graceful swaying glide.

"I'm not walking down an eff-ing runway, I'm just..." He stopped.

ᏍᏃ

Randi looked up in surprise. Tall and slender, the new David stomped into view. A long, loose-fitting gray leather coat almost managed to camouflage the breadth of his shoulders. A strawberry blond wig, which complemented his autumn coloring and was styled in a smooth page boy, fell to his shoulders. A gray suede bag hung from his left shoulder. The gray silk suit emphasized his silver gray eyes. A discreet application of pancake makeup hid any sign of beard growth, but didn't hide the frowning scowl of disgust so plainly displayed across his face.

"Isn't she lovely?" the clerk prompted.

"She is—uh, quite tall," she replied, making a sincere attempt to keep from laughing.

"Is that all you have to say? Surely you can come up with something better than *tall?*" David asked, his tone petulant.

"You are unforgettable. Yes, that's what you are."

"I think David's pretty. Do I get to dress up, too?" Jamie asked.

"Oh, how precious," the clerk cooed.

"Not this time, *Precious*," David cooed back.

"Okay, so we're ready." She was more than ready to get the style show over and get back in the car.

When the bill was presented, David gasped.

"It costs to be beautiful," she teased.

He clenched his jaw and paid the clerk, and the fake credit

card went through without a hitch.

"Come on. Let's go, guys." She took her son's hand, then tugged on David's sleeve. "I thought you were never coming out of the changing room."

"Humph!" he said, stretching his neck, obviously uncomfortable in his new getup. "I'll never complain about waiting for a woman to get dressed again. I cannot believe what your gender puts itself through just to get dressed and face the world."

Without warning, her shoulders shook with laughter. "Sorry," she told him, "I've held it in too long."

ᚲᛉ

David started to get in behind the wheel, but hesitated and tugged at the bow at his neck instead. "I detest this thing. It's already rubbing my neck raw."

A decided smirk spread across Miranda's face. "Oh, you poor baby, stop your whining."

"I don't think you are taking this situation seriously."

"Of course I am. Now you look just fine. You'll be in and out of the bank so quickly that nobody's going to pay you any attention whatsoever. Then we can get the hell out of Dodge."

"Grr." He grimaced, showing his teeth. "Easy for you to say."

"Why don't you let me drive? That way I can let you out right in front. Then I'll drive around the block and pick you up on your way out."

He jerked at the bow again. "I feel like a bloody fool wrapped up like a Christmas present."

"Leave the bow alone," she warned. "You've already messed it up."

"I don't know why I agreed to this charade."

"Because you knew it was a good idea. No one will be looking for a tall strawberry-blonde in a gray silk designer suit." She reached over and adjusted his bow, then folded her arms

Marie-Nicole Ryan

across her chest and gave an emphatic nod. "Now, that's better."

Chapter Eleven

Feeling like an absolute ass, David strode into the bank. Looking from side to side, he walked to the first available teller window. "I'd like to make a withdrawal from my account."

The teller gave him an appraising glance, then nodded. "Account number, *Madame*?"

He slid across the paper with the account number written on it.

"One moment." The teller keyed the number into the computer. "Amount? And in what currency?"

"Ten thousand pounds, in Euros."

"*Oui, madame.*" A smile played about the teller's mouth. "You're in luck. The pound sterling is very strong today." The teller read both exchange rates.

David nodded and held his breath, hoping the transaction would go through without any problems.

Quicker than he would've ever thought possible, he was on his way out the door. Relief flooded through him, lifting his spirits and raising his expectations. The fresh infusion of cash would make their escape much easier.

"*Madame?*"

The sound of a vaguely familiar voice brought David to a dead stop. He hesitated a beat, then turned and paused, ready for fight or flight.

Standing directly in front of him was Stefan Kristoforus, his features somewhat hidden by a fedora worn low over his brow and a patently false mustache. "Do you have the correct time?" he asked, tapping his watch. "My watch seems to have stopped." Kristoforus offered an engaging smile. David's stomach lurched. Leave it to this psycho to attempt charming any strange woman he met.

Miraculously, Kristoforus had not recognized him. He struggled with the impulse to strike out and run like hell. "It's eleven-twenty," he replied, doing his best to sound feminine, but ended up sounding more like a castrato.

Stefan's raised eyebrows and open mouth told David he'd failed. Still, he controlled his inclination to knock the hell out of his old enemy. Besides, he'd already spied the two other Kristoforus brothers, one standing at each exit.

David smiled, then ducked his head and sauntered down the steps.

Where was Miranda? Probably on the back side of the block.

Glancing in both directions, he spotted the small Citroën turning the corner to his left. Relief coursed through him. He took a deep breath. All he had to do was keep his cool. He walked to the edge of the street and waited, while the hair the back on his neck stood on end. What was the bloody bastard doing, anyway? Had he stayed behind in the bank?

He managed a casual look toward the bank's entrance. The three brothers had their heads together conferring.

Hurry up.

The gray Citroën pulled up to the curb in front of him.

"Mummy only had to drive around three times," piped Jamie in an excited tone shrill enough to pierce armor. David winced.

"It's them," Stefan yelled.

David ran around to the passenger side, jerked open the door and jumped in. "Drive!"

Miranda threw the car into gear and gunned it. He glanced behind, certain what he'd see. "We have company."

Her eyes widened. "Anyone I know?" Her voice quivered. She had to be scared to death.

"'Fraid so."

"Wh-which way?"

"Straight ahead," David said. "We're two kilometers from

the connector, but we need to get rid of them first."

He angled the mirror, watching. Stefan and his brothers had jumped into a black Mercedes double-parked in front of the bank. In an out-and-out race, there was no way in hell their hired car could outrun a Mercedes.

"How could he trace us here?" Miranda gripped the steering wheel.

"Take a left at the next corner," he ordered, ignoring her question for the moment. But a damn good question it was.

How *had* Stefan traced them to Zurich and to the bank? Had Brinks been compromised? He'd trusted his old friend with their lives, but something had gone wrong.

With horror, he saw her reach for the turn signal. "No, don't use the signal. No sense in telegraphing our moves."

Her hand returned to the steering wheel. "Hold on, son." She jerked the car into a sharp left turn, the tires squealing.

"Next block, left again, then another left. I want to get behind them, if we can."

Two more harrowing turns later, she stopped for a stoplight. David strained and looked ahead, then behind. No sign of the Mercedes. If his ploy had worked, Stefan would be ahead of them. "Go ahead, make another left."

When the light turned green, she whipped the car around the corner into the flow of traffic, her hands still gripping the steering wheel so tightly her knuckles were white.

"Now what?"

He pointed. "I saw a car park on the right. Pull in there."

She followed his instructions, ripping the ticket from the automated attendant and gunning it as soon as the barrier rose.

"Drive to the uppermost level. I'll get out and have a look."

 C3

When she reached the roof of the parking garage, Randi pulled into an empty space. Leaning back, she gasped, "Whew!" Her hands trembled, and her stomach had started jerking in a pretty good imitation of the Twist. If it got any worse, she'd puke.

David reached over and brushed back the hair from her sweaty forehead. "Let's switch places. I'll drive from here on."

"Th-thank you," she managed to say through her chattering teeth. First things first, she turned around to check on her son. "You okay?" She could see he was, but what he thought about the morning's events was another matter. His dark brown eyes were wide, but he had a broad grin spread across his dear, little face.

"It's just like on the telly, Mummy. It's ever so much fun. Will they start shooting at us?"

Randi gave a shiver. "No, of course not," she lied. Let him keep thinking it was a game for as long as possible. No point in his being as scared as she.

David opened the car door and stepped out while she scooted over into the passenger seat. He jerked off the wig and tossed it through the open window to her. "It'll look much better on you," he said, a half-smile crooking up the left corner of his mouth.

"I don't know. I'm not sure I can do it justice," she said, smirking.

She watched him pace in all four directions, holding her breath until he walked back toward her. From his expression, she couldn't tell if he'd seen anything of the Mercedes.

He opened the door on the driver's side and slid inside.

"We're all right, for now."

She let out a sigh of relief. "For now?"

"We need to get to the airport, but I'm afraid they'll anticipate our next move and have the train station and the airport covered."

"We're still going to Italy?"

He nodded. "We need to find a safe house."

"You didn't answer my question earlier. How could they have traced us to Zurich?"

He shrugged and frowned. "There has to be a leak. My friend Brinks is the only one who had any idea where we'd be. And even he didn't know *when*."

"But I thought you could trust him?"

"I do. Something's happened. He didn't answer my last call. I'll try again when we reach Italy."

She shivered. "At least it'll be warmer."

"Are you all right?"

"Yeah," she admitted, but the expression of concern on his face lifted her spirits; it was flattering as all get-out. She gave him a big grin. "I'm cool. In fact, I don't know when I've had a better escape from the bad guys."

His gray eyes twinkled in the bright sunlight, then his expression softened further. "You're either an amazingly good sport, or you're high on adrenaline."

"Me, too?" Jamie asked from the back seat.

"You, too, young fellow."

"Thank you, sir."

She watched her son's expression go from agreeable to glum. "What's wrong, honey?"

"The spy game is fun, but," Jamie paused for a second, then continued, "I still wish I could go out and play."

"I know it's been rough on you, b-but—"

David interrupted, "We'll try to work in some playtime soon. I promise."

Jamie's expression brightened. "Super," he replied, then went back to playing with the Matchbox Cars Randi had shoved into their bag before leaving the cottage.

"If we could get somewhere safe and stay there a while?"

"Italy, perhaps. I've an idea, but..." David's voice faded.

"An idea? What?"

"Later."

"What're you planning?"

"Later, I said."

"That means I'm not going to like it."

"Probably."

"Well, what?" Dammit. Why couldn't he just spit it out?

David glanced toward Jamie in the back seat. Her heart sank. Slowly, she shook her head back and forth. "No, not if you're thinking what I think you're thinking."

"You can't possibly know what…"

"If it has anything to do with…" Randi gestured with a nod toward her son. "…it's not gonna happen." She held her breath. No way was she leaving Jamie with anyone anywhere.

"We'll play it by ear," came his cryptic reply.

"But—"

"I need to change clothes, then we'll head for the airport." He opened the car door, jumped out and started shucking off his expensive designer duds. "Don't watch."

"Don't look! Why on earth would I want to watch?" She let out a little huff.

Why indeed? The very idea!

"I just thought you might." David chuckled knowingly.

Folding her arms across her chest, she declared, "Well, I don't."

The sound of the trunk being opened reached her, along with the sound of his pulling out a change of clothes.

"You're going to change clothes right here in broad daylight?" she yelled, keeping her eyes forward, but watching him in the rearview mirror while he pulled on a pair of snug-fitting jeans.

"We're the only ones up here. I'll only be a minute."

True to his word, in less than a minute he jumped back in the car, dressed in black jeans, T-shirt and leather jacket.

"Did you peek?" he asked her with a wide grin spread across his sassy face.

She rolled her eyes. "No."

"Mummy watched in the mirror. I saw her."

Randi's face grew warm. Busted by her own child. How humiliating.

"I had no idea you were a voyeur," David told her cheekily. "Why don't you wear the wig? We have to assume they had a good look at you just now. It's more your style than mine."

"You changed the subject," she protested as a matter of form, then nodded her agreement. "That's not a bad idea."

"You would rather discuss voyeurism?"

"That's not what I meant, and you know it."

"What's voy-you—?" Jamie asked, stumbling over the unfamiliar word.

"Never mind." Good grief, what was that man thinking?

"But you always tell me to ask if I don't understand a word."

She exhaled heavily. She would get even with a certain Chief Inspector, if it was the last thing she did. "Well, it just means something like being nosy."

"Okay."

From the corner of her eye, she saw David's shoulders shaking with silent laughter. Yes, she would definitely get even with him. Just *how*—that was another matter entirely. Presuming, of course, they lived long enough.

"I thought we were going to the airport," Randi prodded.

"So we are." David reached forward to turn the key in the ignition.

"And do you have any bright ideas 'bout how we're going to avoid, you-know-who?"

"One or two. They're looking for three people. We'll split up. I'll take Jamie, and you'll go ahead—in that lovely wig, of course."

"Of course."

Chapter Twelve

Randi straightened her spine, stood as tall as she possibly could, then tweaked a stray strand of the strawberry-blonde wig. She'd managed to pull it back in a low knot on her neck. Stylish new sunglasses, purchased in one of the airport highway-robbery gift shops, completed her disguise.

She opened the door of the ladies' room and gave a cautious glance up and down the vast halls. She spotted the arrow pointing to her gate and turned left, heading down the concourse to catch her flight. Somewhere behind her were David and Jamie, or at least, that was the plan. They were supposed to wait until she exited the restroom and check for anyone tailing her. She hadn't spotted them, which was a good thing. That meant no one else would either.

After hiking what seemed like miles, she passed through the metal detector at the lounge for Swiss Air. Glancing down at her watch, she was relieved to see she had another thirty minutes to wait. She needn't have worried about missing their flight. Then it hit her. Thirty minutes was a hell of a long time to hang around when she was trying to get out of town without being spotted by her ex.

ᘉ

"There's Mummy coming out of the loo," Jamie whispered, tugging on David's jacket.

"Shh. I know. Now remember what I told you. We're pretending not to know your mum. The bad guys are looking for three people, not two."

"Will Mummy be all right, all by herself?" the boy asked, his eyebrows drawn together in a frown.

"Yes, remember we're watching out for her, too." He knelt down and adjusted the baseball cap on the child's head, pulling the bill forward to conceal his face.

Bloody amazing what one could find in an airport gift shop. He couldn't believe his luck when he found a can of silver spray. He fingered his stiff gray hair. Not that the spray was necessarily meant for hair, but he'd worry about washing the stuff out later. He'd also purchased athletic jackets with football team logos to aid in their disguises.

In addition to his silver hair, he had affected a stoop and a mild limp. "Don't forget, I'm your grandpapa," he reminded.

"I won't, Grandpapa." Jamie beamed, then added in a conspiratorial whisper, "I like this game."

Pray heaven that's all it will be. If anything happened to Miranda or this brave lad, he'd never forgive himself.

CB

Randi set her bag down beside her feet and eased her body into a chair. Now, there were only twenty-nine minutes until the flight would be called. She checked the zippered side of her bag. Yes, her ticket to Torino was right where she'd left it. She opened the paperback book she'd chosen, a romance—how fitting. Maybe the flight wouldn't bother her so much if she were engrossed in a nice, juicy story of passion and intrigue. Come to think of it, passion would be fine, but she'd had enough intrigue to last several lifetimes.

Halfway into the second chapter of *Holding Her Own,* Randi picked up snippets of a nearby conversation. "We can't search the entire airport. We don't have enough men."

"I don't care. I want them found." Stefan! Instinctively she shrank down into her seat and at the same time buried her nose in her novel.

Invisible would be nice. Where was the magician with his hat full of tricks when you needed him? And where were David and Jamie?

Afraid she might turn around and run smack dab into her ex, she sat there like a damn lump on a log. Peeking over the edge of her book, she checked for reflective surfaces. The sound of Stefan's voice came from over her left shoulder—at least she thought it did. She strained, trying to hear more.

Perhaps, he'd had gone to the next gate. Maybe he was waiting for her to make a dash for it. If only she could do something—anything—to warn David.

CB

David rounded the corner and spotted the metal detector. His baggage had been loaded into the hold of the plane. There was no bloody way he could get through the metal detectors of the most secure airport in Europe armed. He'd already stashed his weapons in a trash bin before entering the airport. All he had were his wits and a five-year-old boy clinging to his hand as if his life depended on it...

He and Jamie breezed through the metal detector without any problems. No one bothered to give them a second look. He scanned the waiting area and, with a sense of great relief, spotted the top of Miranda's strawberry-blonde wig. She appeared to be shrinking into her chair. Why? Was it just her way of trying not to attract attention, or was it something else?

His senses slammed into overdrive. "Very important," he whispered into Jamie's ear, "don't say a word to your mum until I give you the signal, all right?"

"Right," Jamie whispered back.

Careful to maintain his stooped posture, he limped over to a seating area across from Miranda, keeping a firm grip on Jamie's hand. His position would enable him to watch her back along with the comings and goings of hundreds of air travelers.

Not for the first time, he regretted the presence of her child. She would be devastated if anything happened to him. *And let's face it,* he reminded himself, *just about anything could happen.*

Still, there was nothing to be done, but—

A broad-backed man strutted into his field of vision. The

arrogant thrust of the shoulders as well as the manner in which he held his head reminded him of Stefan, but the man's height was wrong. Stefan Kristoforus was a beefy man of medium height, five-feet, ten at most. This fellow was closer to David's height. One of Stefan's brothers?

Damn! It was none other than Xander, the eldest brother who would inherit the family business—a mental lightweight, but reputedly every bit as treacherous as the baby of the clan, Stefan.

Bugger it.

Jamie shifted in the seat next to David, who placed a warning hand on the little fellow's shoulder. The boy quieted.

He kept his gaze on her, praying she would hold position and not give away her location. He gave a casual glance at his watch. Twenty minutes until their flight.

⚃

Brinks walked into the Deputy Minister's lair. He'd been summoned again. The grim-faced man sat behind the broad expanse of a mahogany desk, plotting and weaving webs of deception. He looked up, frowning at Brink's entrance.

"Hughes-Brinkley, it seems DCI French has tried to reach you. Why didn't you answer?"

"I-I didn't think you'd want me to."

"We don't want to make him suspicious, do we? We need to keep ahead of him. It's proving very difficult without the intel his calls provide."

Brinks considered his answer carefully. What answer would please the Deputy Minister and still not betray his friend? "I believe he called when I was not here, sir."

"You were instructed to stay *available*."

At the risk of sounding like a wimp, Brinks replied, "I thought I was coming down with something, Sir Charles. I went home for the evening."

The Deputy Minister smiled—a chilling sight at best.

"That eventuality has been remedied. I've arranged for your

secure line to be switched to a mobile phone. Constant communication, you see?"

Brinks stood and gave a brief nod. "Thank you, your Lordship."

"When he contacts you next, you will obtain his current location and his itinerary."

"He'll be suspicious."

"See that he isn't."

"Yes, your Lordship."

"That will be all," the Deputy Minister said, giving a dismissive wave.

Brinks protested, "I'd like to know why MI6 is interfering? What DCI French is doing has nothing to do with national security."

Sir Charles shook his head. "Need to know, Hughes-Brinkley. Need to know."

"I see."

"I'm sure you do."

The Deputy Minister swiveled around to look out his window. Brinks would learn nothing else from the wily bastard. He turned on his heel and started to leave, but was stopped by his superior's admonition, "For your own good, don't warn him."

Brinks control lasted until he reached his office. Bam! He smashed his fist into the plastered wall. Bloody hell! What was MI6 about? If he didn't know better, he'd think MI6 was on Kristoforus's side, not Davey's. Bloody hell, was that it? Was the D.M. channeling intel to the bad guys?

Gingerly he rubbed his knuckles. From the way his hand felt, he'd probably broken a bone. But the pain helped him focus. Someone at MI6 was up to no good; that was only too apparent. How could he warn Davey without tipping off his superiors at MI6?

CB

Wishing she could run for the nearest exit, Randi tried to control her nerves. She counted to ten, then twenty. Across from her were David and her son. And right behind her were two men speaking Greek. She held her breath.

One of them sounded exactly like Xander Kristoforus. She didn't dare turn around and look. Xander had a harsh, gravelly voice that made her cringe, even in good times. He'd always delighted in moving behind her silently and placing one of his meaty hands where it had no business. She'd learned to stay out of his way pretty quickly.

The second brother, Theo, wasn't as bad, but he'd used his gentle manner, trying to seduce her once while Stefan was away on a business trip. When she'd refused him in a huff, he'd told Stefan she'd been unfaithful.

She wasn't sure what they were saying for she remembered only a bit of Greek, but she did make out two words—airport and find. The rest of their conversation was a loss. She glanced over at David and Jamie. She could tell from his alert demeanor that he'd spotted the men, too.

It was bad enough having one of Stefan's brothers standing within five feet. Things couldn't get much worse. But no sooner had the thought crossed her mind than they did get worse. The oily sound of her ex-husband's voice caught her ear.

Her stomach took a nose dive. Revulsion, utter fear and disgust roiled through her in swift succession. She'd forgotten how much she loathed him.

And feared him.

If she just had a gun, she'd shoot him like the dog he was. He didn't deserve to live, not after what he'd done. After the car bomb, there hadn't been enough left of Cassie to recognize the cool, dark beauty. A young woman who'd never harmed anyone. A woman whose death was the result of her kindness to a stranger down on her luck—Randi.

Fighting for self-control and her book forgotten, she tried to slow her breathing, clenched her fists along the arm of her chair to keep from jumping up and attacking Stefan with her bare hands.

Across the waiting area, David crossed one leg over the other and caught her eye. He shook his head, the movement barely perceptible, his eyebrows furrowed in a frown. Yet she could see he was concerned. No wonder, she was within a millisecond of losing it, totally and irrevocably.

She reined in her reckless need for revenge. Instead, she listened.

"I've shown her picture at all the ticket counters. No one has seen her. Eff-ing bitch," Xander muttered.

Stefan spoke. "They probably changed cars and are halfway to Italy by now,"

Xander insisted, "No, the intel said they would fly out of Zurich."

"Ever hear of a change in plans, big brother? This Chief Inspector, he's not a novice, is he?"

"If he was smart enough to find you six years ago, he's smart enough to leave you in the dust," Theo said, his tone dripping with derision.

Stefan cursed.

Overhead the announcement came. "Swiss Air Flight 201 for Torino is now boarding at gate N30. I repeat Swiss Air Flight 201 for Torino is now boarding at gate N30."

Again she heard Stefan's voice. "Watch everyone who gets on that flight. How hard can it be to find a man, a woman, and a small child?"

"We can't stay here all day, Stefan," Xander groused.

"I know they're here."

Closer than you think, dip wad.

She waited until they announced, "Last call for Swiss Air Flight 201," then closed her eyes and took three deep breaths before she could manage to stand up and walk toward the gate. It was the plan. She would go first. David would follow with Jamie, protecting her back.

CB

After the last call was announced, David watched her stand up. *Don't rush,* he urged her silently.

He waited. And held his breath.

Stefan and his two brothers, along with one of their

henchman, hung about the gate, sussing out each passenger who passed. As she walked toward the gate, Stefan's brother nudged him. "What about her?"

"Right height, but that one's got some curves. Randi's straight as a stick."

David exhaled. Giving Jamie a nudge, he whispered, "Now or never."

The boy nodded. Careful to remain in his old man pose, David stood. Taking the boy's small hand in his, he limped toward the gate to the jet way. He showed their boarding passes to the flight attendant and prayed for divine intervention.

ひ

Randi held her breath. The plane was still minutes from takeoff. Her familiar fear of flying already had her in its grip. The walls of the plane were already closing in on her. Her heart started racing. She'd already stowed her bag in the overhead bin and fastened her seat belt when a hand touched her shoulder. She jumped.

"Piece of cake from here on," David whispered in passing.

"You think so?"

He nodded. Jamie tugged at his sleeve. "Jamie and I are four rows forward. See you in Torino."

Chapter Thirteen

Randi had to give David credit. His prediction of an uneventful flight from Zurich to Torino had proved true. No hijackers. No crying babies. No obnoxious, drunk passengers. Compared to the Swiss bank nightmare and the frantic rush for the airport, the flight had been a breeze.

After deplaning and renting another car, he found them a small *pensione* in the older part of the city.

"How do you find these places?" Randi asked, looking at the quaint but clean rooms.

"Spent most of my holidays bumming around Europe." He cleared his throat. "Now, as charming as your accent is, perhaps you should try not to talk too much, when we're around other people, that is. Stefan's people will be looking for a woman with an American accent."

"In other words, keep my mouth shut?" After living in England for seven years, she liked to think she'd lost most of her Southern accent.

"I didn't phrase it quite so impolitely, but since you seem to admire frankness, yes."

"Hmph." While she debated on whether she ought to throw something or stamp her foot—just for the effect, mind you—Jamie tugged on the tail of her sweater. "Do I have an American accent, Mummy?"

She settled on the bed and hugged her son. "No, darlin', you have a very proper British accent."

"But I'd like to have an American accent, *you all.*" Jamie drawled out the last two words.

David ruffled Jamie's hair, then laughed. "I think your mum has been a very bad influence on you. What shall we do to punish her?"

Jamie chewed on his lip and appeared to consider his question very seriously before answering, "Send her to bed without dinner?"

David's mouth twitched. "I'm not sure your mother would appreciate going without her dinner. She's a little bit of a thing. We wouldn't want her to blow away in a hard wind, would we?"

"No! We mustn't let that happen."

"Okay, you two, that's enough!" Grateful that Jamie got along so well with David, she sometimes felt left out of their easy, back-and-forth banter. Maybe she had too many memories generated by his choice of the words "blow your mummy away". He didn't seem to notice what he'd said, but she had. Would she ever be able to forget poor Cassie?

"All right, we'll stop picking on your mother, and I'll check out the local *trattorias*."

Randi nodded her agreement. His routine was well-known by now. Each time they checked into a new place, he would attempt to make contact with his friend Brinks at MI6.

Geoffrey Hughes-Brinkley was their only contact in England. "Back in a few." He pointed to her head. "Weren't you going to do something about your hair?"

She feigned a pout. "And here I was, having so much fun as a blonde." Digging in her bag, she pulled out two cartons of hair coloring and held them up for his approval. "Redhead or brunette?"

The corner of his mouth crooked up. "Surprise me," he said, then winked.

∾

"*Signore, lei progetta su stare sul telefona tutta la notte?*" a drink-roughened voice asked David.

"*Scusi, signore.*" He shrugged, hung up the telephone and walked back to the bar. He'd chosen a small tavern, frequented by the locals, from which to make his call. Even after talking to

Brinks, he couldn't banish the troubling unease he'd had in the back of his mind for the last forty-eight hours.

Something was off in his friend's tone. Brinks had said all the right things, but he'd asked too many questions. So David lied about their location and about where they were headed next. Something wasn't right and he wasn't about to risk Miranda and her son. So far, they'd had three near close calls with Kristoforus. Once might be coincidence. Twice was troubling, but the third was too much to accept.

He nursed his beer, relishing a few minutes alone with his thoughts. What did Kristoforus want? Revenge or his son? Both?

Only two nights ago he'd held Miranda in his arms, however briefly. More than anything, he had to protect her. He refused to lose another woman to that bastard.

Or Jamie—what a fine lad he was—adventurous and brave as only a child of five could be. He would die before giving the child up to his murderous father. Miranda had been Stefan's victim once before. And once was enough.

He intended to make Stefan pay for his crimes, pay with his life, if necessary. He swore under his breath, then left several Euros on the bar.

He'd been gone too long. Assailed by the sudden urge to get back to Miranda and the boy, he stepped out into the crisp night air. High over the Alps, the moon seemed close enough for him to reach out and touch. A slender, silver crescent, it cast faint light on the cobblestone street. Always on the alert, he listened for signs of anyone who might've followed. Even though he detected no one, he took a roundabout route to the *pensione*. The last thing he wanted was to lead Stefan or his brothers back to Miranda and the boy.

A pebble rolled. His only warning, but enough.

He ducked and spun around, lashing out with a downward spiraling back-hand block designed to shatter an assailant's wrist. And it did the job. He heard a satisfying crunch.

"Ugh!" A gun flew from the man's hand and skidded across the cobbles to his right while the gunman writhed on the ground moaning an impressive rash of obscenities.

A second man leapt from the shadows. His knife blade

flashed in a sweeping arc. David jumped back, but too late. A searing pain erupted as the knife ripped across his ribs. "Bloody hell!" he gasped, then feinted to his right and punched the knife wielder in the throat with his fist. Unable to utter a sound, the second assailant collapsed.

David scrambled over the cobbles for the dropped gun. "Got it!" He pulled back on the slide and fired a shot into each attacker. "That should slow you down," he told them.

Overkill?

Maybe, but they hadn't asked for his money. They'd meant to kill him.

Two shots! Too many.

Without waiting, he slid into the shadows and walked away. He took in a deep lungful of chilling night air. He forced the air in and out, trying to still the jackhammer beat of his heart.

Don't run. Too conspicuous. Think, man, think.

Blood, warm and wet, oozed from his side, soaking his shirt. The wound wasn't deep, but it was already bleeding like a son-of-a-bitch.

Behind him, he heard voices shouting, spreading the alarm. Picking up his pace, he clung to the shadows until he could hear nothing behind him. He glanced around, searching for a familiar landmark.

Bloody hell! Nothing like losing one's way in a strange city.

Finally, after ten minutes of wandering, he found himself in front of the small tavern located across from their room. He rounded the corner to his left and spotted the *pensione*, where Miranda had damned well better be ready to leave on a moment's notice.

Chapter Fourteen

Randi bent over the sink and wiped up the splotches of hair color. *Red.* She wondered just how red it would be when her hair dried. Somehow she had a feeling that it wouldn't be the soft strawberry-blonde of the wig. What if it turned green like the girl's in *Anne of Green Gables?*

Jamie walked into the bathroom, wrinkling his small nose and making a terrible face. What else could she do but warn him? "Your face'll freeze like that if you're not careful."

"Mummy!" He stuck out his lower lip in a bona-fide pout. "You know it won't. I've done it before, and my face is still my face."

"Yeah, well, that's just it. It's in the mother's handbook. What the handbook doesn't say is how many times it'll take before your face freezes," she told him in her most earnest tone.

His expression grew pensive. His little black eyebrows furrowed together. He watched her carefully, chewed his bottom lip, then a spark of understanding flashed across his face. "Yes, Mummy."

"I mean it." It was hopeless. Her son had seen right through her teasing. Her face had always been an open book. If she thought it, people around her knew it. Now, even at the ripe old age of twenty-eight, she couldn't fool her five-year-old son. It was downright depressing now that she thought about it.

The door burst open. She jumped, knocking over the plastic bottle of hair color. She grabbed it before it could spill, then turned and saw David holding his side. "Omigod. What happened?" she asked, running toward him.

"We've got to get out of here," he gasped.

"You're hurt!" Suddenly short of breath, she reached for his jacket. "Let me see."

He shrugged off the right side of his jacket. "I think I'd better keep the pressure on this," he said, biting his bottom lip and still holding his left side. "It's not deep, just messy."

"Does it hurt?" Jamie asked, his brown eyes widening at the sight of his blood.

David shook his head. "Not really."

Randi gave an exasperated huff. "Either it hurts or it doesn't. Which is it?"

He darted a glance at her so sharp it could've eviscerated a squirrel before letting out a ragged breath. "It burns, but not badly."

"Big, strong guy. So tough," she muttered as she tried to pull the sticky wet shirt away from his ribs, but he jumped back.

"Hold on. Mind you, we don't have time to quibble over details. We need to hit the road again."

A *"but"* nearly sprang to her lips, but she refrained. "We need to dress that cut," she told him, brooking no nonsense. She opened her bag and started rummaging. "It's in here somewhere."

A wry grin crossed his lips. "I suppose you have something like an extra-large plaster in there for the occasional knife wound?"

"You're in luck. I do have *something* in here that might just work." She gave him an evil grin before adding, "It's super absorbent."

His grin faded, then he shrugged. "Anything else in your bottomless kit? Weapons, ammo?"

Randi shook her head. "Nope. They didn't make it through the metal detector."

"Surely, you didn't attempt—"

"Don't be silly." She pulled out a sanitary napkin.

It pays to be prepared.

Not that she would ever, in her wildest imagination, have thought of putting the pad to this particular use.

"You're going to take the rest of that shirt off." She nudged him toward the bathroom. "I need to clean the wound and put some Neosporin on it."

"Neosporin?"

"It's a good thing I'm the mother, not you. It's an antibiotic ointment—a mainstay in every mother's bag of tricks."

"Anything in there to hold on this...thing?"

"Hm. Maybe." She rummaged again. "This will do the trick..." she paused and pulled a long, white silk scarf from her bag, "...if I wrap it around your chest and tie the ends together. But you really need stitches."

"No time. Can you just get on with it?" he dropped his voice to a whisper. "I took out two men—back there—on the street," he said with a glance over his shoulder at the door.

Randi swallowed the apple-sized knot in her throat. *"Took out? As in—"*

"I'm not sure. Yes, possibly."

"You're not sure?"

"Well, I didn't stop to check for a bloody pulse," he hissed.

A new sense of urgency filled her chest, causing her heart to exceed the speed limit. Surely hearts had them?

She eased away his bloody T-shirt, which was already stuck in places along the wound. "Soap and water, then the ointment, okay?"

"You seem to be in charge."

"I'll take that as a sign of approval."

He twitched as she pulled a loose thread from the wound.

"Hold still. I don't want to make it any worse than it already is."

"Yes, ma'am."

She filled the sink with warm water, then lathered up a clean washcloth with soap. "This might sting a little."

"I'm sure of it," he replied, an apprehensive frown flickering across his face.

She washed the area around the knife wound first, cleaning away the sticky residue of dried blood. With a careful swipe of the washcloth, she wiped the edges of the wound, then slapped the sanitary pad over the five-inch gash. "Here, hold it while I wrap the scarf around you."

He frowned at the white and pink object, but did as he'd been instructed. Of necessity, she stood close to him as she wrapped the long scarf around his chest.

"You do this mother thing quite well," he told her. Brushing the top of her head with his lips, he rested his head on hers for a brief moment before straightening up.

She stopped wrapping and looked up into his silver-gray gaze. Her heart shifted into overdrive. His arms snaked around her waist and pulled her closer. "Excuse me, but you're supposed to be holding the—uh, bandage," she reminded him.

"You're supposed to be tying the bandage," he murmured in her ear.

More than anything, she wanted to melt and lose herself in the awakening of sweet sensations, not the least of which was one enormous ache in the pit of her belly and between her legs.

But she persevered. "I'm tying the bandage now," she muttered, hoping her fingers would cooperate. After a couple of tries, she managed a knot. Miracle of miracles, it held the pad in place. "Raise your arms. See if it'll hold."

He raised his arms. The makeshift dressing remained in position. "Remarkable."

"Not at all. After all, I'm a doctor's daughter." Randi grinned up at him. "Now that we've got you held together, what are we going to do?"

He looked over his shoulder. "As you Yanks would say, we're getting the hell out of Dodge."

CB

With Miranda and Jamie literally on his heels, he hesitated in the doorway. "Let me suss it out." He looked up one side of the narrow street and down the other. Two doors to the left, a rusting motorcar took up half the road. He had no choice. They had taken a cab from the airport. Poor planning on his part. Another sign he was losing focus. And now, he was less than one-hundred percent physically.

"If I weren't so scared, I'd laugh," she whispered into his back.

"I'd much prefer it if you resisted."

She sniffed.

"Cold coming on?" he asked and was rewarded with a nudge in the small of his back.

"Two doors down, see the rusty motor?"

"Yes."

"That's our means of escape."

"You mean *steal* it...if it even runs?"

"I do." Without waiting for another response, he took off at a brisk pace. "Come on."

He reached the car and tried the door. "Good show." It wasn't locked. Opening the rusting door, he reached beneath the dashboard and found the wires he needed. He rubbed them together, then breathed a sigh of relief. The motor cranked, a sound calculated to warm the darkest heart of any would-be car thief.

"Jump in," he ordered.

Cʒ

On a narrow road flanked by steep mountains on one side and a sheer drop on the other, they hurtled along in the stolen car. Randi held her breath. Hell, it seemed like she'd been holding it the last hour.

"That was too close," he said, stating the obvious.

Still trembling, she hugged her sleeping son to her chest and nodded. "I know." She sighed, then added, "What next?"

Keeping his eyes on the road, he told her, "I have a plan. It's not perfect, but I think we need to leave Jamie somewhere safe. As long as Stefan is after us, Jamie's in danger."

"Leave him?" she whispered, to keep from waking her son. "Just where do you suggest we *leave* him? I'm not dumping my child on the side of the road like an inconvenient puppy."

"Calm down. We're not dumping him on the side of the

road. My old nanny is retired and married to a French farmer. They live in a small village in Provençe. We'll go south, toward the Riviera, then to Mina's. We'll leave Jamie with her."

"But if she's an old woman, how do you expect *her* to protect him? And what'll I tell him? So far he thinks this is just one big adventure. I don't want to scare him."

David glanced over at her, "Miranda, be sensible. It can't be helped. Believe me, Mina is very capable. My brother and I are proof of it. But it's been years since she's had any visible contact with our family. Your ex would never think of looking there for Jamie. That way you and I can draw him out into the open. Don't think for a moment that Jamie is all he's after. He wants revenge, and he won't be able to resist going after the two of us."

She considered his suggestion. He had a point, but the thought of leaving her son with a stranger, no matter how capable, went against all her maternal instincts. "He's never been away from me, not even one night."

"And if we get through this alive, he'll never have to be again."

She looked down at Jamie's dark head, the child she'd brought into the world five years earlier, the child she'd carried beneath her heart for nine months. Tears formed and trickled down her cheeks. She let them fall, unchecked. "I-I know you're right. It's just I can't imagine a day without him."

Chapter Fifteen

Another *pensione*, another cramped room. Randi dragged her satchel along while David brought up the rear, carrying a worn-out Jamie. "Good Lord, it's stuffy." She walked to the window and threw it open, then stood back and waited for a breeze to cool her hot cheeks.

"Stay away from the window," he warned.

"Just for a second. I'm suffocating." She fanned her cheeks with her hand.

He pulled back the thin coverlet and lay Jamie down on the bed. Randi moved away from the window. There wasn't a breeze anyway. She sat on the bed and tested its spring.

Great! There wasn't any spring, just lumps of wadded padding. She covered Jamie's bare arms. A small sigh escaped her lips before she could contain it.

David sat beside her. "I know you're tired. It won't be much longer."

"Longer before what?" she spit out, not meaning to be bitchy, but she was exhausted and afraid. "Sorry."

"It's all right. I think we can spend a day or two here in San Remo. Mind you, if nothing else happens."

"Really? You know this place isn't so bad, after all. I could just collapse here on this bed, lumps and all."

A smile played about his lips. "You're a great sport. I know this hasn't been easy for you."

He placed a comforting arm around her shoulders, and she rested her head on his broad chest. She didn't know when she'd ever felt so warm and protected. In some ways she'd be sorry to see their time together end—in a lot of ways, if she admitted the truth.

"I'm afraid for Jamie. I don't know how Stefan found out about him. I never went near any of the family during or after the trial, and I didn't show until I was six months along. His trial was over before I went into maternity clothes." The sudden tension in his body stopped her flow of chatter. "What's wrong? How do *you* think Stefan found out he had a son."

He pulled back and faced her directly. "Don't know for certain, but maybe someone leaked the intel to him or someone in his family."

"But who? Only MI5 knew about Jamie. They kept tabs on me after I moved to Oxford."

"I don't know, but when I find out, there'll be hell to pay."

CB

David sat in an armchair, watching Miranda and the boy while they slept. The double bed didn't have room for three, unless they were very cozy. And they weren't that cozy yet. He propped his feet on a faded hassock, crossed his arms across his chest and tried to sleep, but failed. The gash in his side burned like fire, but at least it'd stopped oozing.

He'd actually stolen someone's only means of transportation and had very likely driven the rusting vehicle within an inch of its life before abandoning it at a car park. Once the present situation was behind them, he *would* find who it belonged to and make restitution, but still he suffered the pangs of guilt from being on the wrong side of the law.

Too much could still go wrong. Money wasn't the issue now. Keeping a low profile was.

CB

Awakened by an insistent, small hand patting her face, Randi yawned and rubbed the sleep from her eyes. "Mummy, Mummy. Wake up. DCI French says we can go to the seashore.

Please, Mummy, may we?"

She yawned again. "Wh-what?" Jamie's sweet face was right in hers, his expression anxious. "Your mum needs a shower first, okay. Can you wait that long?"

"No! I want to go now." He straightened up and put his hands on his hips. "And no makeup. That takes too long."

A bark of laughter came from the far side of the room. "A man after my own heart," David offered.

She sat up and swung her legs over the side of the bed, then looked down at her jeans in surprise. "I can't believe I slept in my clothes."

"You were exhausted. One minute you were talking at the speed of light, and the next you were sound asleep," he said, sounding a little guilty.

"I slept in mine, too," Jamie piped, "but he said I could keep them on until after we go to the beach."

"Oh, he did, did he?" She glanced over at David, wondering how bad she must look. She reached up and ran her hand through her red hair. Just as she feared, it stuck out in every direction.

"Just being practical."

"You're right." She stood and winced as the muscles in her back protested.

"Something wrong?"

"Nothing a hot shower won't cure," she replied, massaging the sore muscles.

"Hurry, Mummy. I want to look for shells."

"I don't suppose there's any coffee, is there? Sure would be nice to have some when I finish my shower. Hint. Hint." She glanced over at him, smiled and batted her eyelashes at him unashamedly.

David's face broke out with a broad smile. "All right, you femme fatale, coffee it is." He looked down at Jamie. "See here, young man, we must attend to your mother's abominable addiction to coffee. Are you up for a trip to the local *trattoria* before the beach?"

"Yes, sir." A puzzled expression crossed his face. He tugged on his elbow. "What's addiction?"

"It means your mother might be a tad grumpy until we can provide her with whatever her heart desires."

While his words were innocent enough, the same couldn't be said about the warmth in his gaze and the slow sensual smile pulling at the corner of his mouth. Randi took a deep breath.

Just what did he know about her heart's desires?

Regaining a bit of composure, she waved them away. "Get outta here, guys. You never know when I might get *grumpy.*"

"Come on, Jamie. Let's do as your mum says. We've had our warning."

Randi watched the pair leave and raced for the shower. Her heart's desires? If he only knew.

She adjusted the water until it was as hot as she could stand it and stepped inside the somewhat grungy shower stall. At least the water was hot and as the spray beat against her body, the stiffness in her shoulders and neck began to ease, but another more persistent ache between her thighs reasserted itself.

Her heart's desires? She leaned against the side of the stall. Her hand went unbidden to her moist feminine lips. Images of David's smile, the expression in his eyes as he knelt over her, the warm touch of his hands, the thrusting of his hips—she had to relieve the tension that grew and grew until she couldn't stand it any longer.

Release swept over her in wave after wave of pleasure and a moan ripped its way from her throat.

 C3

Randi hugged her knees and worked her bare toes into the warm sand. Trying to pinpoint the exact moment she'd fallen in love with David was a waste of time. She should've known it would happen. Damn! Why on earth had she allowed herself to skid down the slippery slope of friendship into this morass of sighs and erotic desires? The answer was only too obvious: her hold on reality was too fragile for comfort.

After all, they were still on the run. If she'd thought her six-month marriage to Stefan was a nightmare, being on the run from him was worse. After four or five nights—frankly she'd lost count—of sleeping in different places, sometimes driving all night, constantly on the move, always looking over their shoulders, she had to go and screw everything up by falling in love.

David would've been a lot better off to have turned them over to MI5 and washed his hands of them. On the other hand, she had the feeling that if he had, she might not be around to worry about anything. If not for him, her son might already be in the clutches of his father and the rest of that damned bunch. Not that she thought Stefan would harm Jamie, but the Kristoforus clan wasn't her idea of a proper family. If only she hadn't been so impulsive by marrying someone she barely knew. Experience, if nothing else, should have taught her something.

But no, here she was falling in love again—even if the very idea of having sex scared the living crap out of her. And at the same time, she could hardly wait for it to happen. Needed it to happen before she went nuts from just thinking about it.

Squinting and shading her eyes against the light of the brilliant Riviera sun, she scanned the beach. She watched Jamie dart back and forth, flirting with the breaking waves. Except for the two of them, the beach was deserted. How long it would stay that way, she had no idea.

"He's all right. I see him."

She jumped at the sound of David's voice. "You're back. I didn't hear you."

"You weren't paying attention."

"Sorry." He crouched on his haunches beside her so they were shoulder to shoulder. In spite of the heat, she shivered. "Sure you're not part Indian?" she asked, hoping he wouldn't notice her reaction.

He turned, his eyes shot with silver in the unremitting light of the sun, a puzzled expression across his handsome face. "I'm not sure what my ancestry has to do with your not paying attention to your surroundings, but I can assure you that I'm more British than the queen."

She rolled her eyes and sighed. "It's just an expression."

Honestly, he could be so literal at times.

She sprang to her feet and yelled, "Jamie! David's back. Let's go." Waiting for her son to obey, she kicked the sand off her feet and stuck them into her sandals, trying to act nonchalant. Even the glint of the sun shining on David's auburn hair did things to her heart rate. And some of those things she was better off not thinking about.

David frowned and folded his arms across his chest. "Must you announce to the entire Italian Riviera that we're here?" he asked quietly.

She grimaced and cringed. "Sorry."

"You *must* take our situation seriously."

"Of course, I do," she said. "I've seen first-hand what Stefan does when he gets pissed off," she whispered. "But we're the only people in sight for at least a mile."

Jamie chose that difficult moment to rush up the slight incline, his hands wet and caked with sand. "Look, I found a shell. May I keep it?"

She squatted down to Jamie's level. The long, spiral augur shell was flawless. "Sure, baby. It's beautiful. We'll keep it and put it with the rest of your collection at home."

If we ever get back home.

"Mummy!" Jamie huffed. "Please, I'm five." He held up five grimy fingers. "David says I'm not a baby anymore. Didn't you, sir?" Jamie gazed up at him with worshipful eyes.

A brief smile flitted across his face. "I believe I did."

"No fair! Y'all are ganging up on me. I don't have a chance." Not that she ever had. Jamie had stolen her heart from the moment of his birth. Now David had claimed a part of it—without half trying—but that was *her* problem. She'd already made up her mind it wouldn't be *his*.

"Why don't we return to the *pensione*? I've an idea where we should land next."

"*Land* as in another airplane?" She tried, but failed, to keep from whining. "I thought we were *driving* to Provençe."

"We are. It's an expression," he replied, handing her own words back to her. "Just teasing you a bit."

Randi swallowed the knot of panic in her throat. He

definitely knew how to push her buttons. "That's a relief," she managed with a forced smile.

She watched him reach down and scoop Jamie up into his arms, then over his shoulders. At six-feet two, he towered over her bare five-feet, two-inch height. Dressed in a black T-shirt and jeans, they suited him. His shoulders, broad and well-muscled, tapered down to a trim waist and slim hips.

Dear Heaven. The jeans fit his butt like they'd been laminated—and well-laminated, at that. She'd never had cause to pay much attention to men's butts until now. But she had to admit that on a scale of one to ten, his lean-muscled ass was an eleven.

He'd been the soul of discretion since the night he'd kissed her in Dijon. If she hadn't known better, she might've thought she'd dreamt it.

His focus on keeping them safe had slipped just a little that one crazy night, and if it hadn't been for Jamie's presence, it might've slipped a lot more.

From his vantage point high on David's shoulders, Jamie squealed, "See how tall I am, Mummy."

Overwhelmed with love for her son, she grinned up at him and waved. "So I see."

"Anyone starving?" David asked, giving her a decidedly hungry look.

Jamie raised his hand as if in school. "Me!"

Randi felt the blood rush to her face. She nodded and managed a, "Me, too." This new playful side of his would take some getting used to. Not that she minded a little confusion. It could be downright pleasant.

 og

After a satisfying lunch of pasta, antipasto, fresh fruit and the local cheese, the trio walked about, touring the city of San Remo.

"This is a lovely spot," David said as he stopped and gazed at the blue waters of the Mediterranean.

Miranda grinned up at him, her excitement evident from her sparkling green eyes to her inability to stand still.

"The *Côte d'Azur*. Wow! I never dreamed we'd end up here. It's beautiful. Stefan took me to Athens on our so-called honeymoon. We spent the night in a villa. I thought it would be so romantic." She bit her bottom lip and frowned.

Honeymoon.

The word hit him like a brick smashed into his solar plexus. His enjoyment of what until now had been a superb day, spoiled by a memory. He and Cassie had planned to honeymoon here in San Remo. He glanced up at the very hotel on Solaro Hill where they'd planned to stay. Damn it all, why had he chosen San Remo? Why not somewhere else? Why the same bloody city?

"David?" she touched his forearm. "Did I say something wrong?"

He shook his head. "No."

Miranda slapped her forehead with the palm of her hand. "Oh, no. I just remembered. I'm so sorry. Me and my big mouth, I—"

"It's all right. Not your fault," he rushed to reassure her. After all, she and Cassie had been flat mates. Of course, she would've known his and Cassie's honeymoon plan.

"What did you do, Mummy?"

He crouched down to Jamie's level. "Your mum didn't do anything, little one. Besides, we're getting tired. Are you ready to go back to our room?" he asked, anxious to shift the focus of conversation away from himself.

Jamie looked at his mother, then back at David, appearing to size them up. "Mm-hm, if you'll buy me *il cono di gelato*."

Miranda frowned. "What?"

"Your son is brilliant. He's already learned the words for ice cream cone. I'm quite amazed."

"Oh yeah? Well, I don't doubt my son's intelligence, but I have a feeling he's had some coaching?"

A smile tugged at his mouth. "A bit," he admitted.

"I thought so," she replied good-naturedly. "Okay, one *il cono* duh..." She faltered over the unfamiliar phrase.

"*Gelato*, Mummy!"

"Come on, let's go. We'll order *i coni di gelato* all around," he announced, determined not to spoil the evening for her and Jamie. He took the boy's small hand in his, then placed his free arm around her waist, pulling her close.

Her body tensed as if surprised, then relaxed again. In spite of her initial reaction, holding her felt right. In her gentle way, she was a healer. A balm for his soul.

The memories of Cassie would always be there in the back of his mind, but Miranda just might be his future...if they lived long enough.

Chapter Sixteen

The ice cream cone had hit the spot. Their next stop was at a pharmacy to buy butterfly bandages. If David wouldn't risk seeing a physician and getting stitches, she could at least stabilize his wound with those. However, the long walk back to their motel in the bright Riviera sun sapped every bit of Randi's energy. David's arm at her waist wasn't enough to keep her from collapsing into an exhausted heap on the bed.

And not even the lumpy bed could prevent her from falling fast asleep.

After an extra long siesta, she sat up and drew a deep breath of air, hot and stifling. She glanced across the room at David. He sat studying an unfolded map and appeared totally oblivious to the heat, even though there were tiny rivulets of perspiration running down his bare, well-muscled chest. Jamie sat beside him, just as intent on the map.

"Hi, guys."

David looked up from the map and smiled. "I see our sleeping beauty has awakened."

Our sleeping beauty.

Randi stifled a yawn, still a little bemused by David's calling her a sleeping beauty. "How's your cut? I never..."

The corner of David's mouth kicked up. "No problem. Your son is handier than you can imagine. Between the two of us, we managed."

"Mummy, I know where we're going!" Jamie exclaimed.

"Oh, and where is that, young man?"

Jamie jerked the map off David's knees and brought it over to her, nearly tripping over it in the process.

"Jamie, you should've asked first."

His eyes grew wide as he bit his lip in remorse. "I'm sorry." He looked over his shoulder at David. "I'm sorry, sir."

"No problem," David replied, throwing Randi an amused smile.

She frowned, hoping he would take the hint not to interfere.

"But your mum's right," he said, catching on. "It's best to ask first." *Okay?* he mouthed with a shrug of his broad shoulders.

She nodded. "Just remember in the future. Okay, son?

"Yes, ma'am." Jamie's eyes lit up. "David says we're going to take the A8 Expressway to Ste-Thérèse. And we're going to leave tonight." Jamie's voice rose with excitement.

"Tonight?" Why had he decided against spending another night before hitting the road again? But then she felt the lumpy bed boring into her butt... Maybe he was right after all.

"If that's all right? Actually, I thought we might leave around three in the morning. I'll settle up with the front desk and pack the rental car tonight."

"Why so early?"

"Less traffic, easier driving."

"So we're just going to drop in at breakfast? Does she know we're even coming?"

David grinned. "I was waiting for you to wake up from your beauty rest. We'll go out for dinner, and I'll call Mina then."

"Don't you think we should give her a little more warning? I mean, back home we have a tradition of Southern hospitality, but I wasn't aware the French did."

"Mina is British," he said, a tiny note of exasperation entering his voice, "and her husband is a jolly fellow and, from her letters, besotted. I promise you, we'll be welcomed with open arms."

"If you say so."

"I do," he replied, the easy grin returning to his face.

"Well, then, where're we going to dinner?"

"One of the *osterias* that the locals patronize."

"But I don't have anything to wear."

"Dear heaven," he muttered.

"What was that? Were you praying? At home we usually wait until dinner is in front of us before we say grace," she teased.

"You won't have to dress for dinner," he offered, his lips starting to twitch with a suppressed smile.

On a roll, Randi couldn't pass up the opportunity for another pun. "Well, I don't know about you Brits, but in the South we wear clothes whenever we go out to dinner."

He groaned, then declared, "You're impossible."

Jumping up from his chair, he closed the distance between them, pulling her into his arms from where she sat on the bed.

"Brat," he whispered in her ear just before he nipped the lobe.

A shiver zapped down her spine. The warmth of his breath on her neck, not to mention the thought of other places his teeth might nibble, just about did her in. She sighed. "Bite me." Then she remembered her young son was in the room. And that young son was staring at her with a puzzled expression on his young face.

She jumped back. "Uh—" She tried to make her mouth form words, but her tongue wasn't cooperating.

He released her, stepping back with a playful smile tugging at his soft lips. Lord, but she wanted to kiss him again and again. She took a deep breath. "I'm—uh—"

"Going to dress for dinner?" he suggested, his silver-gray eyes twinkling with merriment.

"Yeah, that's what I'm going to do."

"Mummy?"

"What, dear?"

"Why do you want him to bite you? Biting is rude."

Praying that the floor would open up and swallow her wasn't an option, so she did the next best thing. She fell back on an old standby. "You'll understand when you're older."

With her face burning as if she'd been out in the sun all day, she fled into the bathroom, shut the door behind her and broke down in a fit of giggles. Just let David answer Jamie's questions. It was all that man's fault for nipping her ear and reducing her into a puddle of passion in the first place. If the man only knew what he was doing to her, he might reconsider his teasing actions.

CXS

After Randi washed her flushed cheeks with tepid tap water, she reapplied her makeup. Turning her head from side to side, she groaned. Her spiked, red hair was a disaster. *Damn* if she didn't look like a punk rocker. All she needed was a nose ring and some black lipstick. She giggled, imagining David's expression if she had actually completed the look. Somehow the punk look just didn't suit her personality.

Pulling a T-shirt out of her bag, she sniffed it. *Clean.* But it was the last clean one she had. She hoped Mina's farmhouse had a washing machine, or she would go from game to gamey pretty quickly.

What day was it anyway? She'd lost track. It had been Friday when he first picked them up. Saturday night in Lille, Sunday night in Dijon. They flew from Zurich to Torino on Monday. They reached San Remo on Tuesday. That made today Wednesday? Hadn't there been a seventies movie like that?

She took a deep breath, preparing to face the guys. Hopefully her son had forgotten all about her ill-advised "bite me" remark. She couldn't stay in the bathroom all evening, now could she?

She opened the bathroom door with a spunky, "Are we ready?"

"Yes!" Jamie jumped up from his spot on the floor.

David offered his arm. "*Signora.*"

She placed her hand on his forearm, feeling the coiled strength he'd placed at her disposal.

Stop thinking like that. Then taking Jamie's hand in her other hand, she gave it a little squeeze. "Okay, guys. Let's have dinner."

The first thing she noticed when she stepped out into the early evening was the drop in temperature, a comfortable change from their room. Looking to the west, she realized the sun had already started to set, washing the sky with a remarkable display of vermilion, ochre and purple. The red tile roofed building on the far side of the cobble-stone street cast a long shadow, and the air was filled with the fragrance of flowers and the spicy scents of food cooking. Her mouth watered as she inhaled.

"I'm starving." She gazed up into his glittering eyes. "Lead on, MacDuff."

"And damned be he, who cries, hold enough," he completed.

"I should've known you'd know the rest of it. It's the only line I remember from *Macbeth*, other than 'out damned spot, out I say'."

"Shakespeare *is* our foremost British playwright."

"Mummy, you said a bad word."

"I'm sorry. Sometimes, I forget." Turning again to David, "So where is this 'asteria' of yours?

"*Os-teria*, not asteria."

"I stand corrected, good sir," she said, making a moue. "Languages were never my strong point."

"Well, we are agreed on that point at least."

Randi gave him a good-natured whack on his shoulder. "Lead us to the food, sir, or you shall pay dearly."

Inclining his head, he whispered in her ear, "What form of payment would you require?"

She looked up, a little surprised. "Starve me and find out." Flirting with him was still so new, she felt like a cotton-mouthed teenager.

CB

Randi walked through the arbor into the sidewalk dining area. At least a dozen locals were seated eating dinner and boisterously talking with one another, gesticulating broadly in the local dialect so rapidly, she couldn't make out a single, understandable syllable.

"Inside or out?" David asked.

The temperature had dropped. She shivered involuntarily and said, "Inside, if that's all right with you."

He nodded and opened the ancient, heavy door. "Watch your head," he warned, ducking his own under the low stone lintel.

She looked askance at the doorway. "I'm not that tall."

"Don't blame me if you bump it then," he said with a broad grin.

"I won't bump mine," Jamie added, stepping through the doorway easily.

She followed her son, eyeballing the lintel just in case. She cleared it, but only by a couple of inches.

"I warned you, didn't I?"

"Yeah, yeah."

The host, who Randi guessed was the owner, came forward to greet them. "*Buona sera, Signore et Signora*. Welcome to *La Dolce Vita*." He led them to a table in front of a window. "You are in luck tonight, for we have," he said, rattling off an unintelligible list of dishes.

"*Grazie*. We'll have that and," David said, spouting off a string of Italian, leaving Randi still wondering what the heck they were having for dinner.

The owner nodded, smiling all the time, then left them.

"Don't you want to know what we're having?"

"I'd rather be surprised."

"You may be afraid of flying, but at least you're not a picky eater."

"And if I were?" she asked, trying, but failing to arch a single eyebrow.

"Well, I should have to make you pay dearly."

Reflections from the flickering candlelight glittered in his eyes. "I think I've heard that phrase somewhere recently. You're repeating *me*," she teased.

The corner of his mouth twitched. "I must be slipping. I've always been known for my originality."

"Aren't you going to call your nanny?"

"Yes, I see a telephone on the back wall." He stood. "If you will excuse me?" he asked, bowing slightly.

"Of course," she replied, pleased and bemused by his old-fashioned courtesy. She watched him thread his way through the crowded room to the telephone, and reined in a sigh.

Handsome, kind and polite—a deadly combination as far as her heart was concerned. But once Stefan was recaptured, it would be over. She wouldn't see him again. He'd go back to London, and she and her son would go back to their neat cottage in Oxford.

Jamie's patting her forearm brought her back to reality.

"Why does David have a nanny? He's too old."

"He doesn't have one anymore, but his nanny from when he was a boy lives in Provence, and we're going to visit her tomorrow. You'll have fun there. She lives on a farm."

"With animals and everything?"

"I think so," she said, keeping an eye on David's back.

"Super! Do you think she'll let me milk a cow?"

"I wouldn't be at all surprised if she does." He was definitely talking to someone. He was too far away for her to hear the conversation, but his shoulders were moving, and he was nodding.

"What about chickens?"

"Oh, they probably have some of those, too," she said absent-mindedly, still trying to gauge whether or not the phone call was successful.

"Wizard! Do you think the chickens will try to peck me?"

"I don't know much about chickens. We'll have to check that out when we get there."

David hung up the receiver and turned around, then walked back to the table, beaming.

"Mission accomplished?"

"It's all settled. Mina was thrilled to hear from me and is willing to shelter us for the time being."

"That's very gracious of her, all things considered."

"She's a special person, but you'll see when you meet her."

Their discussion was interrupted by the waitress bringing the first course of their dinner. Randi looked down at her plate, knowing she absolutely could not turn her nose up at anything. Jamie was watching, and she was the adult. "All right, I'm surprised. What is it?"

David frowned, as if debating whether or not to tell her.

"Try it. You'll like it."

"It's not anything disgusting like escargot, is it?"

"No, of course not."

"Well, in Southern tradition, if it's fried, it must be good, right?"

"Of course. I'll tell you what everything is, after dinner," he said with a wolfish grin.

She speared one of the small batter-fried objects on her plate and bit into it. Hmm, not much flavor, a little on the rubbery side. Something from the sea?

Jamie looked at her anxiously. "Is it good?"

She nodded. What else could she do? She swallowed. And reached for her glass of wine.

"There's more." He chewed his own with relish.

Gamely she took another bite. "Go on, son. It's okay."

"Is it chicken?" Jamie asked.

"I don't think so," she told him in all honesty as she reached over to cut up his food.

Jamie gave the first bite a tentative jab with his fork and frowned.

"You remember the rule?" she reminded him. "You have to take at least one bite of everything."

Jamie glanced over at David. "Mummy has rules for everything," he announced.

David cleared his throat, his mouth twitching in a visible effort to rein in his reaction. "That's excellent. Your mum is quite right," he managed to say with a moderately straight face.

"All right." The boy grinned, held his nose and stuffed the batter-fried morsel into his small mouth.

"Jamie!" She reached for his hand. "You know better than that. Stop showing off and chew with your mouth closed."

"I'm sorry," she told David. "He's usually much better behaved."

He leaned back, his arms folded across his chest, grinning. "He's all boy," he replied, then applied himself to his dinner.

Jamie watched, his dark eyes wide. He ate another bite, too. "It's not so bad," he admitted. "I think I like it."

"It's pretty good."

If you like deep-fried rubber.

"Pace yourselves," he warned. "Long dinners are an Italian tradition."

He spoke the truth. Course after course followed: antipasto, pasta, the meat entrée with vegetables, cheese and finally dessert. Randi glanced over at Jamie, who'd declared he was full and fell asleep sometime between the cheese and the dessert course.

She took a sip of wine, watching David over the rim of her glass. The warmth in his eyes still shocked her. What was really going on behind them? She set down the glass. "It's been a long day."

"He's knackered. And did you truly like the calamari?"

"I liked the veal better," she confessed with a grin.

"Aren't you tired?"

"A little," she admitted.

Where's this conversation headed?

"I've enjoyed our day."

"Yes, San Remo is lovely."

"I mean, I've enjoyed spending the day with you and Jamie, especially you."

Her face grew hot as the blood rushed to it. She looked down at her plate, then back into his gray eyes, shining silver in the candlelit room. "I—uh," she stuttered, grasping for words. "I enjoyed it, too."

His gaze held hers. "Why was that so difficult to say?"

She shook her head. "I don't know. It just feels awkward, talking like this. I'm out of practice."

159

"Practice?"

"You know—dating, flirting, whatever it is we're doing."

"Me, too," he said. He reached for her hand and brushed his thumb across her knuckles. It took all her willpower not to jerk away.

"You don't seem awkward. No offense, but you're a very smooth operator."

"Is that so? What if I told you there hasn't been anyone since Cassie?"

"No one?"

"No one."

"I'm sorry," she murmured. Once again, the guilt of being alive and having wrecked the lives of two others overwhelmed her.

"Miranda, don't you see? This is a new beginning for me— for us."

"For us?" What was he suggesting? Was she reading things in his words?

"I know the circumstances are trying. We've been brought together again. You're still in danger from your ex, but after this is sorted out, do you think we might have a go at it?"

"At what?" He couldn't be suggesting what she thought he was...could he?

That's it. Make him spell it out.

That way she wouldn't misinterpret what he was saying.

"Ah, hell! You probably won't ever want to see me again when this is all over, will you?" he asked, a tentative smile on his lips.

An emotion akin to panic fought with desire in her mind.

"Why don't we wait 'til it *is* sorted out?" she hedged, refusing to admit her real emotions. Of course she wanted him, but could she ever take the man who was meant for her best friend?

His hesitant smile faded. Instantly she was sorry, sorrier than she could ever have imagined. "W-we're under a lot of pressure, to say the least. You might not want to see *me* when it's all over, and that would be perfectly understandable, too," she said, the words finally coming in a rush.

He continued stroking the back of her hand, saying nothing. If he didn't stop, she was going to jump across the table and land in his lap and give everyone in the *osteria* one hell of a show. Well, it was a nice fantasy. Her face grew warmer.

Damn it.

Why did she have to light up like a Christmas tree every time he touched her?

"I hope I'm the cause for your pink face," he said, trading his glum expression for a teasing grin.

"Sir, your arrogance knows no bounds." *Good Lord*, she sounded like some ditzy ingénue in a Regency romance.

"Methinks the lady doth protest too much." He released her hand and took a swallow from his cup of coffee.

Randi fidgeted with her spoon, swirling it around in a bowl of melted *gelato*. "Maybe I've learned caution."

He grinned, his gaze never leaving her face. "If anything, I've learned patience."

"Patience is good."

David frowned. "I can see I'm not making any headway with you. Are you ready to leave?"

"Mm hm." Truthfully she could've sat in the restaurant all night, just gazing at the man across from her. He was full of surprises, keeping her totally off-balance from one minute to the next.

He stood and removed his jacket from the back of the chair. "Here," he offered, placing the jacket over her shoulders. "You'll need this."

"Thank you." She snuggled in the warmth, conscious of his lingering male scent mingled with that of the soft leather.

Picking Jamie up carefully so as not to wake him, he told her, "You have a wonderful son. You should be quite proud of him."

"Thank you. I am."

Without further need for words, they walked back to their room. He laid the child down on the bed, then turned to her. "I'll settle up with the front desk. It's eleven now. I'll wake you at three."

"Okay."

He walked to the door, stopped and turned around. "Back in a few."

She watched him leave and let out a deep sigh as soon as the door closed. David couldn't be serious about their having a future—could he? He wasn't the type of man to say things he didn't mean. But still, why would he want a future with her?

Too many times, Stefan had told her how inadequate she was as a wife and as a woman. "I wouldn't need the extra stimulation of binding and punishing you if you were a *real* woman. A man needs a woman with big breasts or a great ass. You're built like a boy. No real man would ever be aroused by a body like yours." And then he'd beat her with his version of a rubber hose, the blows landing across her body, but never breaking the skin. The first time, she'd been stunned by his behavior, shocked by his dropping the charming facade he'd wooed her with. Then he'd fallen on her like a depraved animal forcing his brutal penis into each of her body openings. He'd bitten her breasts and thighs, leaving bruises that lasted for two weeks.

The first time, on their honeymoon, he convinced her to let him tie her up. Eager to please her new husband, she agreed. She clenched her teeth and bit back her cries and screams, but that only infuriated him more. After that, she learned to cry early on in his lovemaking. The sessions would be over sooner.

She would only disappoint David, too. Oh, he wouldn't mistreat her like Stefan had, but could she risk seeing the same disappointment in his eyes?

Stop it. Stefan was a brute and nothing she did would've satisfied his perverted ideas of marriage. It wouldn't be the same with David. It couldn't.

附

David unlocked the door and walked into their room. To his surprise, Miranda had taken up residence in the armchair. "I thought you'd be asleep."

"No, you take the bed. You haven't had a decent night's sleep in nearly a week. I had a long nap this afternoon."

He shook his head. "I can't sleep in the bed and know you're trying to sleep in a chair."

"It was good enough for you last night. It's good enough for me tonight. Women's Lib, you know."

"Sorry, I just can't."

She unwound from her cramped position and walked toward him, a guarded expression in her eyes.

"There is only one other solution," she suggested.

"Which is?"

"If we sleep like spoons, we'll all fit. And it's only for a few hours."

Like spoons? The very thought of her spooned in his arms did wonders for his heart rate. How in blazes would he ever think he would be able to sleep like that?

Slowly she slid into the middle portion of the bed, scooping a sleeping Jamie up in her arms, then patted behind her.

"Like this? You're insane. I can't sleep that close to you."

"Sure you can. Pretend like I'm your sister and we're on a camping trip."

"I don't have a sister and my imagination doesn't stretch that far."

"Come on," she said. "It won't be that bad. That way we can both get some rest."

Lord, how he wanted to lie next to her. And her eagerness certainly was baffling and encouraging at the same time. How would he ever manage to not embarrass the two of them? Perhaps, if he kept his clothes on, it would help. He sat on the side of the bed and kicked off his shoes.

"There's plenty of room," she said with a shy smile.

"Compared to what? A coffin?"

The woman had the temerity to snigger.

"I wasn't joking," he protested.

"Of course, you weren't."

"Grr." He turned around and into position directly behind her, who, for some unknown reason, decided to wriggle into his portion of the bed. "You're taking some of my space."

"No, just getting comfortable," she replied, giving a wiggle of her hips which connected with his groin.

He swore under his breath as his groin responded without his permission, straining against the confinement of his jeans. Lord, how he wanted her. She was actually teasing him. Why? Surely she had to know the effect she had on him.

"G'night."

He groaned. "Good night, Miranda."

His erection hardened further. Surely she had to be aware.

The sound of her breathing quickened. She was aware.

"Sorry," he muttered, his own heart beat hammering in his chest. Could she feel that too?

She twisted a bit and looked at him over her shoulder. "It's not your fault. The bed's so small and we're just so c-close. I'll go back to the chair." She tried to rise, but he restrained her.

"No," he rasped. "Stay, please. I want to feel your body next to mine. Wanting you is driving me crazy." He levered up on his elbow, leaned forward and touched her neck softly with his lips.

A sharp intake of breath.

"I won't hurt you. I would never—"

"I know." Her breath came in ragged gasps. "But we can't. Jamie."

"Come with me."

Ↄ

Randi eased from the bed, dazed by the heat of her body's response to David's. She placed her hand in his and followed him into the bathroom and shut the door behind them.

"Now," David said, lowering his lips to hers, and a blaze of desire ripped through her body weakening her knees. She backed away and gazed up into his eyes. The night light she'd thought to include for Jamie gave off just enough light for her to see the look of surprise on his face.

"Am I moving too fast?" David groaned. "We don't have to

do anything, but I'm dying of wanting you."

"I need to catch my breath." She clung to his body, her legs still limp as worn out fiddle strings. She trusted him, was already in love with him. Could she—should she—give into a single night of lust?

"I won't hurt you. I'm not Stefan."

"I know." She buried her face in his chest and inhaled his male scent. His erection was rigid and pressed firmly against her belly.

"I won't do anything you don't want me to do. You can go back to bed—I'll die—but you can."

She giggled. "No pressure?" She gazed up at him and smiled. "I wouldn't want to be responsible for your death." Her heart banged against her chest wall like a cymbalist gone mad. Was she dreaming? Was she really about to make love with David?

"Hardly that."

"Make love to me," she murmured and slipped her hands underneath his T-shirt.

Slowly he slipped her shirt over her head and then unhooked her bra. Her nipples beaded into nubs of excruciating pleasure. He cupped her breasts and rubbed her nipples between his thumbs and forefingers. A moan ripped from her throat.

"You're so beautiful...so desirable."

His lips moved to her neck and left a trail of kisses all the way to her throat. Her head fell back. He fastened on a nipple sucked gently. Pressure grew in her belly and threatened to explode.

He unzipped her jeans and eased his hand inside. Her breathing grew ragged as he touched her wet inner lips. She gasped. One finger, then two entered her. Even more pressure built as he began to massage her clitoris in easy round strokes with his thumb. She moved against his hand, faster and faster, then frantically.

She cried out, but he silenced her with his mouth against hers, his tongue battling with hers for possession. Wave after wave of pleasure coursed through her, each spasm of pleasure more intense than the one before.

Only his strong arms kept her trembling body from collapsing.

"Are you all right?"

"God, yes," she gasped. Again the thought she was dreaming crossed her mind. Had David really just brought her to climax with his mere touch?

His hard erection jutting against her brought her back to a vague semblance of reality. She splayed her hands against his chest, circled his flat male nipples, and traced a downward path to his flat abdomen, carefully avoiding his wound. Hastily she unfastened his belt and unzipped his pants. After slipping the jeans down over his butt, she grasped his penis in her hand marveling at the size and power of his erection. At the same time she, shimmied out of her jeans and kicked them aside.

Hindrance free, David hoisted her in his arms. She wrapped her legs around his waist as the head of his penis nudged at her outer lips. She wanted him inside her now before she exploded again.

"Mum! Mummy, where are you?"

"Oh, God," she gasped. "He never wakes up once he's asleep."

David groaned, then resolutely set her down. "To be continued, sweet Miranda."

"Mummy's coming." She turned to David who leaned against the wall. "I'm so sorry." She quickly pulled on her jeans and fastened them. She tiptoed and gave David a quick kiss.

"It's all right. Can't be helped."

Cß

Once Jamie had fallen back asleep, Miranda settled into David's arms. They slept like spoons, Jamie in his mother's arms and she in David's. At least Jamie and Miranda slept. He rested his head on the pillow next to hers and breathed in her intoxicating scent. Heady with desire, he couldn't sleep, but he discovered he could relax, experiencing a long-forgotten sense of peace.

When his watch alarm beeped at three A.M., he awakened

with a start and realized he'd slept after all. Was it possible he'd found the woman who could give him what he'd longed for? Love, family and, perhaps, forgiveness?

He lay there another few minutes, luxuriating in her sweet warmth. Finally, he shook himself out of his lassitude. He wouldn't feel safe until they were in Provençe and maybe not even then. Extricating his right arm from under her shoulder, he eased from the bed.

Miranda raised her head. "Time to go?"

"'Fraid so," he whispered.

Focus. He'd almost lost it that night, seduced by a soft, beguiling woman.

Chapter Seventeen

After crossing from Italy to France, David pushed the small car to its limits. Randi held her breath and hoped it wouldn't break down before they reached their destination.

They reached the outskirts of Sainte-Thérèse le Vieux. The sun breaking over the distant mountains washed the stone houses, rendering them into watercolor shades of pale pink and lavender. A picture postcard come to life, the village of Ste-Thérèse spread up a steep hill to the top of a small plateau, crowded with even more red-tiled roofs. Was the countryside really so beautiful or was her vision colored by the memories of making love with David?

"We there yet?" asked a sleepy voice from the back seat.

"I think we're almost there. It won't be much longer, will it?" She glanced over at David's drawn face. He looked so tired. It hurt to know the strain she'd put him through. Would they ever stop running? Would they ever find time to continue what had been interrupted?

ଓଃ

Thirty minutes later, Randi couldn't believe her eyes.

Good grief, it was Jane Marple in blue jeans, no less. Seventy-years-old if the woman was a day, but possessing the erect posture of a much younger woman. Mina's thin face was etched with wrinkles and tanned, but her wide smile welcomed them. She wore a large straw hat jammed down on her snowy-white hair. Her ice-blue eyes sparkled even as they appraised

Randi.

"Mina Pelletier, this is my friend, Miranda Raines," he said, then ruffled his fingers through Jamie's hair. "And this is her son, Master Jamie."

"I'm please to meet you, Mrs. Pelletier." Randi replied, before reminding her son about his manners with a gentle nudge. "Jamie."

"Yes, ma'am. I'm very pleased to make your acquaintance." Jamie even managed a stiff little bow.

"Miranda, I'm delighted to meet you and young Master James as well. His name is James, is it not?" the good woman asked.

"Yes, ma'am. James Michael."

"Please, come inside and meet my husband Jean-Luc. He's prepared a hearty breakfast, since Master David said you would be arriving quite early."

David's brow wrinkled at the "Master David". "Mina, none of that."

Mina turned around and faced the three of them. "Old habits are difficult to break." A tiny smile played about her mouth. "I suppose I could call you Detective Chief Inspector? That might be more appropriate?"

David gave an exaggerated sniff. "Please no formality. Chief Inspector will be more than sufficient."

Mina broke out into a great laugh. Her eyes twinkled with mischief. "You're a caution, you are. But you always were."

She led them into a large country kitchen. Terra cotta tiles covered the floor, while the walls were washed in a warm ochre pigment. A massive oak table, set for five with cobalt blue plates, occupied nearly half the room, while every cooking utensil Randi had ever seen—and a few she hadn't—hung from a wrought-iron rack overhead. Fragrant bunches of herbs hung from every hook not occupied by a pot.

A tall, robust man with grizzled hair and mustache stood in front of the iron stove, stirring something that smelled only this side of heaven in a large iron skillet. Randi's mouth watered in anticipation of the good food to come.

"Jean-Luc, our guests have arrived. Master David, his

friend *Madame* Raines, and Master James."

Jean-Luc whirled around, brandishing a meat fork in his left hand as he bowed over Randi's hand with the other, a smile spreading across his round face. *"Enchanté, Madame* Raines, *M'sieur* French and *le jeune homme. Pardon,* but I must finish the breakfast. My sausages, they will burn." Jean-Luc turned back to the stove, enthusiastically humming a somewhat atonal version of *La Marseillaise.*

"Please call me Randi."

"And no more, M'sieur Pelletier." He smacked his burly chest. "You mus' call me Jean-Luc."

"All right everyone, please be seated." Mina offered with a smile, "Would you prefer coffee or tea?"

"Tea," David replied.

"A cup of coffee would be just great. Thank you," Randi answered.

Jamie piped, "Tea, please."

"Oh, but I'm of the mind that you should have some milk, no?" Mina glanced at Randi for confirmation.

"Yes, he'll have milk."

"Mummy," Jamie whined, contorting his face into a mask of pure disdain. "Not milk."

"Don't Mummy me. You know you always drink milk."

"Yes, ma'am," he said, still pouting.

"Le petit déjeuner, it is served." Jean-Luc bustled around the table, heaping their plates with mounds of food.

CB

After an enormous breakfast of cheese, sausages, fruit, juice and flaky croissants fresh from the oven, all of which took nearly an hour to eat, Randi pushed back from the table with a groan.

"Are you all right?" Mina asked with a laugh. "I remember my first Provençal breakfast. I thought I had died and gone to heaven because I would surely never be able to leave the table."

"You certainly can't eat like this every day and stay as thin as you are," she protested to Mina, whose upright frame was as slender as any girl's.

"I eat like this every day. And I am a very fine figure of a man, no?" Jean-Luc asked in a booming voice.

"Oh, absolutely," Randi admitted, favoring Jean-Luc with a smile.

"And Da-veed, you must eat more. *Les femmes* like something to hold onto at night. Isn't that right, Ran-dee?"

"Now, *Monsieur* Pelletier, it isn't like that," she protested, feeling her face light up with the heat of a flush at Jean-Luc's insinuation.

"*Exactement!* Da-veed, put some meat on those long bones of yours, and *la belle* Ran-dee will..." He finished with a deep knowing chuckle.

"Jean-Luc, shush." Mina shot her husband a warning look.

"What shush? Oh—" Jean-Luc stopped short. Perhaps a well-aimed kick under the table had done the trick. Randi couldn't be sure.

"More preserves for your croissant, Randi?" Mina asked.

"No, thank you. I don't know when I've ever had such a wonderful breakfast. It was heaven." She heaved a sigh.

Thankfully Mina turned her attentions to David. "David was such a scamp." Reaching over, she ran her fingers through the top of his wavy hair. "Hmph! I believe you're in dire need of a trim, sir."

"We've been a little short on time," he admitted, his eyes sparkling with good humor. "Perhaps you'll do the honor as you did in our nursery."

"Indeed! If I do, I hope you have learned to sit still."

He feigned a look of horror. "Must you reveal all my boyish misdeeds?"

"Randi, I must tell you, he was incorrigible. Always the ringleader, too—even at the age of five."

"Now, Mama, you must not embarrass *M'sieur* French in front of his—uh, friends. Ja-mee, would you like to milk a cow? I have two in my barn and a cat with new kittens. I am sure I can find many things for you to do."

Jamie wiped a smear of butter from his upper lip, then clapped his hands. "May I, Mummy? Please?"

She nodded her permission. With a squeal Jamie flew from his chair and out the back door, following Jean-Luc.

Mina turned to Randi. "David has told me of your predicament. I shall be more than happy to look after your son if that is what you wish."

Randi hesitated, biting her lip before answering, "I'm not sure. Jamie's never spent a single night away from me."

"I do understand, but young James is just the right age. He'll be quite safe here. Ste- Thérèse is a very quiet village. The tourist season has wound down. As you can see, my husband and I live very simply. I've been in Provençe for the last fifteen years, but Jean-Luc was born here in this very house. Indeed, the entire village will rally 'round and protect your son if the need arises."

"Better if no one knows he's here." David leveled a glance at Mina.

"But by lunchtime, everyone in the village will know."

"Just like back home," Randi murmured, shrugging. "Small towns are pretty much the same everywhere." Not that Nashville was a small town, but somehow it retained the small town feel.

"An outsider wouldn't have a chance. A word in the right ears, you see? The older men in the village were Maquisards. You know of the Maquis?"

Randi nodded. "The French Underground?"

"Yes, exactly." Mina gave a smile of approval. "Their descendants are no less fierce. My Jean-Luc's papa was such a member as was Jean-Luc, though he was quite young. My husband has sons your age by his first wife. May she rest in peace. Your son will be protected with their very lives, if necessary."

Randi gulped and glanced at David, trying to gauge his thoughts. "Well?"

"Perhaps you could tell people he is your grandson?" David suggested.

"The story won't matter. As long as the village knows he's under our protection, no outsider will ever get to him."

172

"I-I guess so," Randi began, still not sure she could leave her son behind, no matter how well-protected he would be. Tears sprang to her eyes, but the slamming of the back door announced Jamie's return. Hastily she wiped her tears away.

"Mummy, look!" A tiny black kitten squirmed in Jamie's hands as he ran into the kitchen. "May I keep him? May I?"

"'Fraid not, son. He's much too small to take away from his mother. And if we took the kitten back to England, he'd have to stay in quarantine for a long time. He would be so sad away from his mother..." She faltered, realizing that was exactly what she was about to do: abandon her son to the care of strangers. Still, he had to be protected, and it was just for a little while.

Deciding she might as well get it over with, she summoned her courage. "Is there somewhere I can talk to Jamie, privately?"

"Of course, my dear." Mina stood and led Randi and Jamie into what appeared to be a small office. "I do a little writing, children's stories mostly," she explained. "I assure you, Master James will be well taken care of. Jean-Luc has grandchildren who visit, too." She rested a comforting hand on her shoulder.

"Thank you."

Mina nodded, took the kitten from Jamie, then left Randi alone with her son. She sat and wondered how to begin. Swallowing the knot in her throat, she then began, "Son, I need to talk to you about something."

Jamie's gaze narrowed, his brow wrinkling. "What is it, Mummy? You look sad."

"I am sad, but I want you to be very brave."

"I am brave. I'm a very big boy now, aren't I?"

"Yes, you are, but this is different. Mina and Jean-Luc are going to take care of you for me."

"Super! We'll have such fun," Jamie said, squirming with obvious excitement.

"What I mean is David and I are going to leave. For just a little while."

"Don't you like it here?"

"That's not it." She paused, wondering how to explain her absence without scaring her son. "You remember the bad men

173

who chased us?"

"Yes." His solemn gaze never left hers.

"Well, they're still after us, so David and I are going to lead them on a wild goose chase until the police can catch them. And you're too little to keep running around all over creation with us."

"But it's fun," he protested, his bottom lip stuck out in pout.

"You're missing school," she continued, struggling to keep her voice calm, "so Mina will help you with your studies while we're gone."

He frowned again and looked around. "I like it here. I could play with the kittens and learn to milk a cow."

"Right," she said, keeping her tone of voice bright and cheerful, but her heart was shattering. She forced herself to continue. "And as soon as the police catch the bad men, I'll come back and get you."

"David, too?"

"Yes, David, too."

"He'll take care of you, Mummy."

"Yes, I know."

Dropping his voice to a loud whisper, Jamie said, "Then you and David can get married."

"Darlin', I wouldn't count on that," she said, praying he wouldn't mention his bright ideas to David.

"We're going to leave this morning," she said, the words catching in her throat.

"I'll miss you, but don't worry. I'm going to have a good time here. I know it."

She sniffed. "I-I know you will." Hugging her son to her chest, she wondered how long before she would see him again, *if* she would see him again.

CB

When she'd had finally regained enough composure to face

David and the others, she stood and took Jamie by the hand. "Let's go tell David you're going to stay here with Mina and Jean-Luc."

Jamie gave a vigorous nod.

They found the others waiting in the living room. David spoke first. "Well?"

"I'm going to stay on the farm while you and Mummy lead the bad men on a goose chase," Jamie said, his young voice rising in excitement.

"And how is Mummy taking it?" David asked, raising a speculative brow in her direction.

"About as well as can be expected," she said with a sniff.

"Hmm." His expression grew soft. "He'll be fine. You'll see." He glanced at Jean-Luc, who nodded as something wordless passed between them. "Jean-Luc's son, Pierre, has a motorcycle he's willing to lend us, and he'll return the rental car to Aix."

"A motorcycle?" She groaned, unable to believe he'd found a new method of torturing her.

David frowned and leveled his gaze at her. "Don't tell me you're afraid of riding on motorcycles, too?"

"Only slightly less than airplanes," she told him with a touch of pique. Why was he always trying to find new ways to scare the absolute crap out of her? As if being chased by an ex with murder on his mind wasn't enough.

"You'll love it," he assured her with a wide smile that didn't reassure her at all.

"I'm sure. Not!" But she knew once he made up his mind, she might as well go along. "Okay, when do we leave?"

"Pierre arrived while you were talking with Jamie. He's giving the cycle a last-minute checkup. We'll leave as soon as he's finished."

Randi bent down and picked up her bag. "I'd better pull Jamie's clothes out, so he'll have something to wear." She looked at Mina. "I'm sorry. I haven't had time to launder the dirty stuff."

"Never you mind about that," Mina rushed to reassure her. "I've all the conveniences and plenty of time."

A tall burly man with Jean-Luc's same smile walked into

the living room. *"C'est finis."* He wiped his hands on the thighs of his jeans.

David cleared his throat. "We need to get on the road."

She nodded, took her son's hand, and walked outside. David and the Pelletiers followed behind.

Tears welled in her eyes again. She was going to blubber for sure. She put her arms around Mina's shoulders. "I don't know how to thank you for what you're doing. I'm so glad to have him somewhere safe."

Her shoulders shaking with barely suppressed sobs, Randi knelt down beside Jamie. Taking both his small hands in hers, she said, "You be a good boy now, son, and do whatever Mina and Jean-Luc say. We'll be back real soon. We'll call you tonight." She glanced up at David and was relieved by his nod.

Jamie's arms crept around her neck. "I'll be good, Mummy. Promise." He looked up at David. "You will take care of her, sir?"

David gave a solemn nod. "I will."

She kissed Jamie's forehead and thought her heart would surely break at the sound of her son's brave voice. Her little boy was a lot tougher than she was.

David pulled her gently to her feet. "It's time to go."

"Bye," Jamie said, waving as if he didn't have a care in the world.

"B-bye." She managed to get the words out, but her feet seemed rooted to the spot where she stood. David nudged her toward the motorcycle.

"Now, Miranda," he prompted, then slid his arm around her waist and led her away from the farm...and her son.

Chapter Eighteen

David let up on the gas and pulled over to the side of the road. He'd felt Miranda's shoulders shaking against his back. Booting the kickstand into position, he told her, "He's going to be all right, but I'm not sure about you." He stood and got off the motorcycle, pulling off his helmet at the same time. He turned around, then easing off her helmet, he hooked it over the backrest. He needed to see her face and judge her emotional state.

"Are you all right? Can you do this?"

"No, I-I'm not. You don't understand how much it hurts. I can't believe I just ran off and left my baby with strangers."

He put a comforting arm around her shoulders. "Mina's wonderful with children, and you saw how Jamie took to Jean-Luc. He won't even miss you."

Miranda blew her nose. "I know they're wonderful. I saw that right away, b-but he was so brave."

"He'll be fine, and you've done the best thing for him. Stefan will be looking for a couple and child, not a couple. And if he does find us, he won't find Jamie."

"You don't know that."

"It's only common sense. If we stay on the run long enough, Interpol will locate Stefan, then you and Jamie can go home."

"Why do I have this feeling it won't be that easy?" she asked with a sniff.

"Because nothing about this journey has been."

She looked over her shoulder and started sobbing again. It was then he remembered his own mother crying when he'd been sent off to school. Was he as hardhearted as his father had been? The situations were quite different, of course. Still he couldn't stand to be the reason for her misery. "All right. Stop your blubbering. We'll go back."

"Really?" She squealed and threw her arms around his neck. She kissed him full on the lips. "Thank you. Thank you."

Bemused, he kissed away the traces of her tears and held her close. Her trembling quieted as she gazed up at him. How could he have ever thought his plan would work? "It's against my better judgment, but yes, we might as well return." He took her helmet and eased it down over her head. "I can't drag a crybaby, motorcycle momma all over Europe, now can I?"

He threw his leg over the motorcycle, while re-fastening his helmet. "Hold on," he said. "I think we're in for one of those bumpy rides."

ა

The second they reached the farmhouse and David stopped the motorcycle, Randi jumped off. Ripping off her helmet, she tossed it in his direction, then ran into the farmhouse.

"Mina?" she called out. "Jamie?"

Hearing soft footsteps on the stone stairs, she turned around and saw Mina coming down.

"Miranda? Back already?" Mina looked down at her watch. "I gave you another fifteen minutes. Now I owe Jean-Luc a thousand francs."

"You knew we'd come back?"

"Most assuredly. In fact, I've prepared rooms for you both."

Mina glanced toward the stone stairway. "You're on the second storey. I'm afraid you and Jamie will have to share, unless..."

Mina paused and arched an eyebrow toward David, who'd just entered the house.

"Sharing is fine." Randi said, then added in a rush, "That's not an issue."

David raised a quizzical eyebrow. "What's *not an issue?*"

"Just never you mind," she said, feeling the heat spread up her neck. Whenever his warm gaze settled on her, she remembered the taste of his lips on hers. And the feel of his hands.

Mina cleared her throat, jerking Randi back to reality. "I just told Miranda she'll have to share a room with Jamie, but—"

The clamor of running feet announced the entrance of one young boy, fresh from the barn. "Mummy!" Jamie shouted as he rushed up and threw his arms around his mother's waist. "I knew you wouldn't leave me for long. I'm so glad you came back."

"*Sacre bleu!*" came the gruff tones of Jean-Luc, who followed Jamie into the house. "I cannot keep the comings and goings straight in this old head of mine. If you keep this up, I will be forced to write it down." He followed his pronouncement with a deep belly laugh.

Jean-Luc tapped his watch. "You owe me, Madame." He held out his hand, rubbing thumb and first two fingers together.

Mina waved him away.

"Humph! Yes, I shall win the other wager, too," he said with a smirk.

"Jean-Luc," Mina warned, shaking her head.

Puzzled, Randi looked at David, who merely grinned in response. The realization hit her. Mina and her husband had a bet on how soon she and David would—

The blood rushed to her face—so hotly it must be blazing red. She glanced at David. A twitch of a smile tugged at the corner of his mouth, and his lips parted, revealing white, even teeth.

"What wager would that be?" he asked, his expression as innocent as a choirboy's.

Randi's mouth turned dry as cotton. She couldn't speak, too lost in the memory of his kiss. Instead she shivered. Dear heaven. Her feelings must be *so* obvious. Mina, Jean-Luc and even David could read her as easily as a London tabloid.

"Jean-Luc," Mina warned again, this time elbowing her husband in his ample paunch.

David stepped up behind Randi. His warmth surrounded her as did the smell of his leather jacket until she her head swam. Distraction—she had to create one—not be one. "Jamie," she cried, "did you really miss me?"

"I didn't have time. Jean-Luc—he said it was all right to call him Jean-Luc—it is all right, isn't it, Mummy?"

"Yes, dear." She tried to move toward her son, but one of David's arms wrapped around her waist. She gasped, but then relaxed against the warmth of his body.

"Your mum doesn't like riding a motorcycle any more than she likes flying. Nothing would do but for me to bring her back."

"Mummy, you're such a silly. I'd like a motorcycle ride. May I?"

Still in his strong grasp, she felt him nod. All in all, she decided, it was a good thing he had hold of her. Her knees were trembling like she'd actually ridden the motorcycle all day instead of a mere fifteen minutes.

"Yes, as soon as your mum and I are settled. A day or two, all right?"

"*Oui!*" Jamie announced, then looked up at Jean-Luc. "Did I say it correctly?"

"*Mais, oui,*" Jean-Luc agreed with a vigorous nod.

♋

Across the English Channel, Brinks stared at his boss, Deputy Minister Charles Moreland. "I've had no word from him. Not since he called from Naples."

"While our records show he was actually in Torino. Why did he lie? How did you manage to warn him? We dispatched two operatives to bring him in with the woman and child. They're both in hospital."

"I didn't warn him. I told you he'd become suspicious if I asked too many questions. Mind you, he's not a bloody novice."

Moreland slammed his hands down on the desk. "Thank

you for reminding me. This is not good for your career, you know. I don't see advancement in your future."

"Is that all, sir?"

"You bloody well know it is," Moreland replied, dismissing Brinks with an irritated wave.

Brinks turned and left his superior's office. Career advancement wasn't the first thing on his mind. Staying alive was.

Perhaps an incognito trip to the States or South America would be in order quite soon. Timing was of the essence if he were to stay ahead of the treacherous Deputy Minister. And he had to warn David. But how?

Chapter Nineteen

After dinner on the flagstone terrace, Randi helped Mina clear away the dishes and load the dishwasher.

"I'm glad you came back," Mina said. "Jamie would've been quite all right, but I'm not sure *you* would have."

Randi stopped in the middle of folding a towel. She shook her head. "No, I was a wreck. I don't think we went ten kilometers on that bike, and I bawled like a baby the whole time."

Mina smiled and placed her strong arm around her shoulder. "You are losing that pinched look you had when you first came to us."

"That bad, huh?"

"Not bad, but still it was there."

"I do feel safe here," Randi admitted.

"You must relax because David will protect you and your son. It is very obvious to these old eyes how important the two of you are to him."

Mina's words gladdened Randi's heart, but surely the older woman was exaggerating. "He's been absolutely wonderful, but..."

"Time will tell, my dear. Be patient." Mina removed the towel from Randi's trembling hands. "Let's go outside and enjoy this nice fall evening. The men shouldn't have all the fun."

ﾃﾃ

On the terrace Randi eased down into a lounge chair and watched David and Jamie wrestle in the grass. A sensation of pure contentment stole over her and wrapped her in easy comfort.

She turned to Mina. "Dinner was wonderful, Mina. Thank you for having us. For everything."

"It is my privilege. I'm so glad that David thought of us. So rarely do we have visitors from the U.K.—at least none we are so happy to see." Mina turned to her husband. "Jean-Luc, why don't you play some music for us?"

Randi's ears pricked. "Music? Oh, yes, please."

Jean-Luc grumbled, but with good nature, "She doesn't want to talk to me, so she asks me to play. I am wise to her tricks." The older man hauled his cumbersome self out of his chair and ambled into the house, returning a moment later with an old violin.

David turned to Randi, a wide grin spread across his handsome face. "Did you know Miranda plays?"

"*Bon!*" Jean-Luc declared. "You will play for us, Ran-dee?"

"Yes, but you must go first. I warn you I'm very rusty."

Jean-Luc drew the bow across the strings, then frowned at the sound. "Just a little adjustment." He tightened the E string and drew the bow again. "*Parfait!*" he pronounced, and then launched into an old folk tune which Randi immediately recognized as *Sur le Pont d'Avignon*.

After the rollicking tune which had young Jamie up on his feet, dancing, Jean-Luc paused and extended the violin toward Randi. "Now you must play us something from your country, *s'il vous plaît.*"

Randi nodded her assent and took the violin from Jean-Luc's gnarled hands. "I'll play you our state song." She drew the bow across the violin, the melodic strains of *The Tennessee Waltz* filling the night air.

After she completed the waltz, Jean-Luc stood and clapped. "*Bien*, Ran-dee! *C'est bon.*"

"Mummy, play *Rocky Top*. Jean-Luc, you'll like that one. It's bouncy."

Randi looked from Mina to Jean-Luc to David whose eyes

were actually closed. It was the first time she'd seen the taut lines of tension erased from his lean face.

"*Rocky Top, Tennessee* it is," she said with a nod, then launched into the sprightly tune. Jamie sang, charmingly off key, "Once I had a girl on Rocky Top," then fell to humming when he didn't know the words, but intoned, "Rocky Top, Tennessee," during the chorus.

Randi lost herself in the energy and rhythm of the country tune, until it came to an end.

"*Encore, encore!*" Jean-Luc prompted.

"Something classical, dear?" Mina suggested. "I believe David told me that you play with chamber groups as well."

"All right." Soon the lyrical strains of the second movement of Beethoven's Violin Concerto rose through the valley, soaring into the night. Swept up in the mood and imagery of the music, Randi became the violin, the music. When the last note faded, she heard a collective sigh of appreciation.

"That was simply lovely, dear," Mina told her, pulling her sweater tighter around her shoulders. "Why don't we go in? It's getting too cool for these old bones. Besides, I think your son has fallen asleep."

Randi nodded. "He's been conditioned. Whenever he has trouble going to sleep, I play for him until he does."

⅋

Randi tapped on David's door. She heard sounds of his moving about through the door, then it opened. Apparently he'd been getting ready for bed. His shirt was unbuttoned and pulled out of his jeans. Her breath caught in her throat when she caught sight of his broad, muscular chest and washboard abs. She felt his arms surround her, pulling her into his strong embrace.

"You played beautifully," he murmured in a voice so soft and seductive it sent ripples of desire to the pit of her belly.

"Thank you," she said, as he maneuvered her into his bedroom and kicked the door shut behind him.

"It's paid a few bills," she quipped before she could stop

herself. Lord, why was she so nervous? David would never hurt her, not physically anyway.

"Is Jamie asleep?"

"Yes, he's all tucked in."

"Have you come to tuck *me* in?"

She bit her lip and tilted her head to the side. "You're a big boy. Do you need to be tucked in?"

"I might do." He closed the short distance between them, his gaze never leaving her eyes. "Depends on who's doing the tucking."

"And would it be presumptuous to assume the *who* would be me?" she asked, trying to keep her tone light so he wouldn't know how scared she really was. She was just no good at sex.

Stefan had told her so countless times.

"No, you'd be right on target."

His lips brushed across the top on her head. "Miranda, will you stay with me tonight?"

She pulled back and looked up into his warm gray eyes and swallowed hard before answering, "Yes."

Oh Lord! Had she really said yes?

His lips, warm and demanding, descended against hers. Every bone in her body liquefied with the heat of his kiss. He wanted her. The reason didn't matter. She wanted him, too.

Together they fell backward onto the bed, his hands skimming under her sweater and caressing her breasts though her bra. His kisses were hungry and demanding. She opened her mouth to his. His tongue swept into her mouth. He tasted of the strong French coffee he'd had at dinner.

One expert twist, then his hands, warm and gentle, were all over her again. The memories of their earlier bathroom tryst flooded back. Too late to stop, even if she'd wanted. And she didn't. Her ex had never been this kind or gentle. Forcing the bad memories and fears far, far away, she gave her trust again to David.

Suddenly they both were tugging at her sweater. Over her head it went along with her bra, tossed somewhere. He rolled her nipples between his thumbs, then applied his lips and teeth, raking them ever so tenderly, teasing them into taut buds of screaming sensation. An unfamiliar heat spread down her belly and centered between her thighs.

She gasped, "Oh." Hands shaking, she slipped his T-shirt over his head, taking care not to disturb his bandage. She gazed into his eyes and saw the passion and desire burning there. She shivered. Her fingers splayed over his chest. His flat male nipples drew into tight nubs. She kissed one, then the other.

He let out a groan and her name, soft as a sigh. He pressed against her, his rigid erection straining against the confinement of his jeans. His hands worked at the button and zipper of her jeans, easing them apart. She raised her hips, allowing him to slip her jeans and panties down over her hips.

She kicked off the jeans, giving him access. He quickly found the warmth between her legs, his caress gentle, yet urgent.

"You're lovely," he told her, kissing her inner thigh. Shivers ran through her, fanning the heat of her desire into a blaze.

He pulled away. "No, don't go," she protested as he stood.

Glancing down at his jeans, he grinned. "I'm not going anywhere." He unzipped and shucked his jeans in record time.

He stood before her, his lean-muscled body tense. More excited than ever, she reached out and touched him, marveling at the texture of his arousal—rigid steel covered in the softest of silken skin.

"Easy," he gasped, his lips claiming hers again.

Their bodies matched, warm skin to warm skin, lips to lips.

Again, his fingers were at her feminine core. Two entered her while his thumb circled the sensitive spot above. Delicious waves of heat spiraled up from her center, setting her entire body ablaze.

"You're so beautiful." Kneeling between her thighs, he kissed her, circling the sensitive part of her body with his tongue. The fire grew and spread until, swept along, she lost all control and cried his name.

Before she could come down, he thrust into her. She felt the flames again and arched to meet his challenge.

He set the pace, furious and fast. She clasped her legs

around his waist, arching against him, matching him thrust for thrust. Together they ignited and blazed and spiraled into oblivion.

Afterwards, they lay spent from their exertions. "So sweet," David murmured against her neck. She brushed back a damp curl from his forehead and snuggled deeper into his embrace.

Soon his regular breathing told her he'd fallen asleep.

Sheltered in his strong arms, her eyelids grew heavy. Her thoughts drifted to what she'd known before. Stefan had used sex as a weapon and punishment for her many so-called failings. But this man, this precious David, had treated her body as if it were a treasure to be enjoyed and shared.

Chapter Twenty

The next morning, David awoke before Miranda. From the amount of light in the room, he estimated it was early, not quite six. She was still asleep, spooned into his arms. The heat her body generated aroused him more than he'd ever thought possible.

Her womanly scent intoxicated him.

She had loved him with everything she had, tentatively at first. He wondered how any man worthy of the name could've abused her the way her ex-husband had. He would bring Kristoforus to justice again. This time they'd better lock the man up and toss away the key so he'd never harm another woman.

Especially this woman.

As he eased from the bed, the old urge for a cigarette overcame him. He'd quit smoking years before. After Cassie's death, he'd resumed the habit very briefly. Then, finally, he'd gone cold turkey.

Why? Was it the old craving or was it deeper? He pulled on his jeans, zipped them and padded barefoot downstairs.

Jean-Luc was bound to have left a pack lying around somewhere.

Ah, he spied a pack of Galoisies. He liberated one of the strong smokes and, still barefoot, walked outside.

He stood on the flagstone patio, his feet cold from the damp on the pavers. He took a deep drag, but the harsh burn in his throat made him throw it down. It sizzled, then fizzled in the dew-dampened grass.

Making love with Miranda had been incredible, and it was time he moved on with his life. If he and Cassie's places had been reversed, he wouldn't have wanted her to forego love and companionship only to mourn him for the rest of her life.

Then why feel so guilty? Because his absolute arrogance had contributed to Cassie's death. Yes, Kristoforus had set the bomb, but try as he might, David couldn't deny his own responsibility in challenging Miranda's ex without thinking of the possible consequences.

ଔ

When Randi awoke, she sensed David's absence before she opened her eyes. She'd slept so soundly she hadn't felt him leave. "David?"

She pulled the sheet tighter around her; the old uncertainties emerged. Was he sorry he'd made love with her? Was she really as bad in bed as Stefan had always told her? Had she made a horrible mistake?

Well, why on earth had she expected anything different? She was hopeless as a woman. She was a good mother, but a sexpot she wasn't. And now David knew the truth. Just as well. She'd get over him. It was just a roll in the hay.

A sob racked through her. No, it wasn't—not for her. But she'd put on a happy face and let him know she had no expectations.

Might as well take a shower. Not that she wanted to wash off David's touch. To the contrary, she wanted to remember every fevered stroke of his hands. Even the taste of his kisses. Those memories would keep her fantasies fired for a long, long time.

ଔ

David eased into the bedroom and shut the door behind him. Miranda was nowhere to be seen but he heard the shower running and then it stopped. She emerged from the lavatory,

189

Marie-Nicole Ryan

her fresh-from-the-bath scent reaching him before she spoke.

"You're back," she said with her gaze downcast. She tugged shyly at her towel.

He watched her start at his presence...and was undone. She wore a bath towel, barely fastened about her waist. Her perfect pink-tipped breasts were bare for his eyes alone. He was hard before her towel slipped slowly to the floor.

Her hair, still damp, was brushed back from her face, the face of the woman he loved. His breath came in ragged gasps. He struggled for control, but gave up. Her skin, dewy from the shower, beckoned him. He reached out. He had to touch her.

He had to touch her before he could enjoy her warmth. He slowly closed the distance between them, reaching for her body. He shivered in anticipation...and he wasn't disappointed. He caressed her loveliness, tracing the line from her ear lobe to her shoulder.

So smooth. So wonderful. He could never get enough of touching her. The simple act of touching Miranda...his woman. His touch claimed her, made her his once more, for all time.

Slipping her arms through his, she pressed the entire delicious length of her lithe body against his, then breathed a sigh, light as the touch of a butterfly's wing. "David."

Perhaps in an attempt to regain control, he said, "I should shower."

"Don't. I love your man scent," she said, nuzzling his shoulder and splaying her hands across the muscles of his back. His arousal grew to an excruciating level. Every cell in his body screamed for completion.

"Jamie? Is he up yet?" he tried to protest.

"We'll be very quiet," she promised, placing one delectable finger across his lips. Her wide green eyes promised even more. He kissed her finger, nibbled it, then slid her hand down to his groin, while he ravaged her sweet lips.

"Careful," he warned, the second she touched him, fearing a total loss of control.

"Shh." He stopped her words with his lips. She parted her lips for him and slowly rubbed her pelvis against his erection. Powerless before her surprising aggression, he stepped out of his jeans and nudged her down on the bed.

Her pale skin, the glitter in her eyes, green as the finest jade, drew him and captured his heart. Her legs snaked around his waist leaving her feminine warmth vulnerable. In one sure stroke he thrust home and plumbed the depths of her heated welcome.

He struggled for control as her muscles grasped and released, grasped and released, until any idea of control was lost. He rode his love as if his life depended on it. She arched against him, thrusting and giving him everything.

Selfishly he slaked his thirst, mindless of her pleasure. No games, no control. Technique be damned! He soared, spiraled, and then crashed over the edge into a glorious shower of pyrotechnic sensations. She grasped his head, her fingers twining through his hair. He thrust again and took her with him, her need as great as his.

Heaven could not be any better than the one he found lying in her arms. "I love you," he whispered.

"I love you. I still can't quite believe all this." She sniffed, then added, "I never believed I...deserved this much love."

He rubbed his thumb over her eyebrow. She was so precious to him, but her words wounded him. What had he done to earn her trust and love? Did *he* deserve this much love?

Her fingers trembled as she caressed his cheek and her eyes grew more luminous with unshed tears. "I-I don't have any expectations. This doesn't have to be anymore than it is right now." She pressed a kiss into his palm, her lips warm and soft against his palm.

He looked down at the floor, then back at her. "I want to apologize for last night and now. I'm not usually so—uh, greedy."

Randi pulled away. "Think nothing of it," she managed to say in what she hoped was her most nonchalant manner. What was the matter with her? Why was she acting so weird? Was he sorry they'd made love, after all? He'd said the words. Was he already regretting them? "I guess we got a little carried away. Are you all right?"

At that moment, an even worse thought occurred. He was about to dump her because she hadn't measured up in bed, again.

"Yes," he murmured, gazing into her eyes. "I-I—" he broke off as if not knowing what else to say.

"You don't have to say anything. It just happened. It was just one of those things." Good Lord, she sounded like she was getting ready to break out in a song. "You don't owe me anything. I don't have any expectations."

Oh, yes, I do. I want to spend every night for the rest of my life doing exactly what we did last night.

"Please stop. I wanted it to happen. I've wanted you for days."

"I didn't mean to take advantage of you."

"Take advantage?" He sat on the bed beside her and pulled her into his arms. "You sweet, bloody, little fool," he said, punctuating each word with a kiss. "I took advantage of you and your kind heart, your generous nature."

"But—"

"But, nothing. I'm a cad."

"Well, since you put it like that, I guess you are," she sassed, her spirits lifting. "Poor little Randi, so easy to take advantage of. Whatever must she do now that she's a fallen woman?"

"Staying in bed with me all day would be a nice start."

"What? And allow you to take advantage again? The horror of it all!"

If only he would.

He kissed the tip of her nose. "And if I were to encourage you? Render you powerless with my kisses?"

"You can't, because I'm starving. Get that lecherous grin off your face. You are *not* my idea of breakfast."

"No?"

"No." She gazed up into his eyes. "You're more like dessert."

"I see."

"You know, I was thinking. Maybe this wasn't a mistake, after all," she murmured into his shoulder. "Maybe we could have dessert first."

"It could prove habit-forming."

"Should we try it again to see if it is?"

"Mind you, purely for scientific interest?" he suggested.

"Oh," she moaned. "I do love it when you talk technical."

"Percentages, margin of error, coefficient." His gray eyes darkened as he grinned.

"Oh, yes."

He gripped her shoulders and covered her body with his. Murmuring between kisses, he continued, "End result. Blind study."

He kissed her senseless until she couldn't hear a single word.

ଔ

Much later, their legs still entwined, Randi poked David in the chest and giggled. "You know, your feet are like ice."

"My feet are cold?" David kissed the tip of her nose. "Maybe. But there are other parts of me that make up for it."

"You really think so?"

"I'm sure of it."

She slid her hand down his flat stomach to the patch below, then lower. "I swear and declare, sir, you are quite warm," she said, exaggerating her Southern drawl.

"Have I ever told you how much I love your Southern Belle accent?" he said with a growl, then nibbled her ear lobe.

The newly familiar thrill coursed through her. "Tell me again."

ଔ

Stefan strode into his father's office and slammed his fist on his father's desk. "Why the bloody hell can't your contacts locate them? It's been a week."

"I won't have you yelling in this manner," Alexander told him coldly. "Control yourself, or I will never give you any responsibility in the organization."

"To hell with the organization. I want my son. My son! Do you hear me?"

His father's voice became cold as the grave. "I'm not deaf. You lost them in Zurich. They must have flown out of there, and you were at the airport. Why didn't *you* find them? Can't you remember what your ex-wife looks like?"

"There were thousands of people in the bloody airport. Besides, she must've worn a disguise."

"At any rate, we wait," his father decreed.

Stefan spun on his heel. "I'll find them. I just need to get the detective's bloody attention," he muttered under his breath. "Why didn't I think of it before?"

"Stefan! Leave this to me!"

"I've left it to you long enough. Now it's my turn!"

Chapter Twenty-One

At the old oak dining table, Randi sipped her coffee. Through the window she watched Jean-Luc huff and puff up the drive, carrying a newspaper. He wore a worried expression on his usually smiling face. She glanced over at Mina. "Something's wrong."

"What can it be?"

"Minette, Ran-dee," Jean-Luc called as he came in the front door.

Randi missed the rest of his words, since they were all in French, but Mina's face turned pale.

Jean-Luc shoved the paper at Randi. "*Désolé*," he said shaking his grizzled head.

She set down her cup of coffee. A knot formed in her stomach before she read the headlines, actually she could just make out a couple of words of French. *Anglais*—English, *Mort*—dead. The photo of a bombed car. Who was it? "Mina?"

Taking the paper, Mina scanned it. "Oh, dear, Lord Middlebury has been killed by a car bomb," she said, her hands shaking. "And David's brother was in the car as well. He was injured and isn't expected to survive, either."

Shock and disbelief knocked the air from Randi's lungs. Her knees buckled, and she sank into the nearest chair. "Oh, my God. Stefan. He's done it again."

"You really think your ex-husband did this?" Mina asked.

"Yes! Car bombs seem to be his favorite solution to all problems. But why? Why would he kill David's father?"

"To make David surface..." Mina paused, "...because he can't find *you*."

The grim reality of Mina's words hit her like a punch to the gut.

The clap of the back door slamming shut forced her to focus as David walked into the house, carrying a shotgun and two pheasants slung over his shoulder. "What's happened? I saw Jean-Luc rushing up the hill as if the very devil were on his heels."

"Maybe we'd better go upstairs," she suggested, wishing she didn't have to break the news.

David looked from Mina to Jean-Luc and back to Randi, the muscles in his face tightening. "What's going on?"

"Come on." She turned and walked up the stone steps to the second level, leaving him no choice but to follow.

Once inside his room, she handed him the newspaper. "It's very bad. Your father. I'm so sorry." She watched his face while his expression changed from one of puzzlement to one of disbelief.

"Dead? He's really dead. I can't comprehend it."

"There's more. Your brother was hurt in the explosion. The paper says he's critical."

"T-Terry? No!" He sank down on the bed, his eyes tracking the rest of the story. "Blown up by a car bomb. Both of them? Why were they together? Terry didn't get along with Father any better than I did."

"D-do you think Stefan...?"

She couldn't bear to say what she already thought. The explosion had to be Stefan's doing. It wasn't the first time. But why would he kill David's father?

Why not her own? Because David's family was closer? Maybe she'd better call and warn her parents.

"I wouldn't be at all surprised."

"But why?"

Please don't let this be my fault, she prayed, but she already knew the answer. It *was*.

"To get at me. So I'll surface."

"If your brother dies, will you *have* to be the Earl of Middlebury? Or isn't that how it works?"

He nodded. "I never wanted the title. And certainly not like this," he said, raking his hand through his hair. "All I ever wanted to be is exactly what I am—a copper. My brother—we always knew the title, everything would be his."

"I'm so sorry. I've brought you nothing but pain and death." She emitted a harsh, bitter laugh. "I'm not just trouble, I'm a disaster. Two, maybe three people you've loved are dead because of me."

David paced about the room, his face a study in despair and anger. "You know, I never loved my father. I hated the way he treated my mother. I'll always hold him responsible for her death. I'm not sorry he's gone, and I'll not waste one second of my life mourning him."

"Tell me about him." Her natural impulse was to put her arms around him and comfort him, but she hesitated, fearing he might reject her overture. Instead she took his hand and led him to the bed. "Sit," she commanded softly, then sat beside him.

"My mother drank. She was a lovely creature, a truly gentle woman, who never said an unkind word to anyone. In the beginning, I suppose she loved him. I don't really know why he married her," he said, then added bitterly, "except she was talented and intelligent—the very things for which he came to scorn her. Did I ever tell you she was a musician, too?"

"No."

"She was a fine pianist, of whom everyone said could've had a professional career, but she met and married my father. He wouldn't hear of her continuing to play. He started by belittling her whenever she did. After he started hitting her, she quit playing and started drinking instead.

"She wasn't a falling-down drunk. She just sat in a quiet corner and, with great determination, drank herself to death. She died when I was seventeen."

In spite of her previous determination, her arms slid around his shoulders. "I'm so sorry." He didn't resist her embrace. In fact, he seemed totally oblivious of it.

"I was away..." he said, swallowing before he continued,

"...at school when she died. My father didn't even tell me she died until after her funeral. I wasn't able to say my farewells, so I ran away from school. I came home. My lord father had marked her grave with a simple headstone engraved with only her name and the years of her birth and death. Not even a 'loving wife' or 'beloved mother' to mark her passing. He made more fuss over his hunting dogs than my mother."

Her heart broke as she listened. Truly, the death of David's father was no great loss—not to a man who'd never recovered from his mother's death.

"I'll make some tea." She started to stand, but David caught her by the hand and pulled her back down on the bed beside him.

"Don't leave me," he murmured, his breath warm on her neck. "Everyone I love leaves me."

Still sitting beside him, she put her arms around him and held him for as long as he would allow.

Standing, he announced, "I have to go."

She rose and ran to his side. "G-go?"

"Terry's still alive. I have to go to him."

Suddenly aware of how selfish she'd sounded, she said, "Of course, you should. Jamie and I are safe here with Mina and Jean-Luc." At least she hoped they would be. But she had no right to keep him from his dying brother. None at all.

"It's very likely this is a stratagem to make me come out of hiding and leave the two of you unprotected."

"Then you really think Stefan is responsible, too?"

"It's likely. His *modus operandi*, you know."

"Yeah, I know." Guilt and grief by association wracked through her. "I'm so sorry. I..." Words failed her. How could she ever make up for all the pain she'd brought this one brave man?

Damn it! She couldn't, not in a million lifetimes.

"Stop!" He spun around and grabbed her shoulders, his body trembling with rage. "This is *not* your fault. Stop acting the bloody martyr. Every vile thing your ex-husband has done has been his choice. Not yours!"

She'd never seen David so close to losing it, but better than anyone, she understood the reason for his pain and frustration.

An expression of utter dismay flashed across his face. He stepped back and dropped his still shaking hands to his sides. Clenching his hands into fists, he struggled for control.

"Oh, God. Miranda, I'm sorry. Did I hurt you? I'm no better than my father."

Randi shook her head and stepped toward him. "David, I'm fine." She reached out and touched his forearms, stroking downward to the backs of his strong hands. "Do you want me to come with you?"

"No. That would make it too easy for him. You have to stay here. I can't risk losing you and Jamie, too."

"But you shouldn't be alone at a time like this."

"Stay with your son. He needs you even more than I do." David relaxed his rigid stance. He turned away and grabbed his bag, jamming it with clothes and shaving gear.

He glanced around, his expression desperate. "Passports?"

Randi spied the small leather folders. "There," she pointed at the bureau, "right under your nose."

He snatched the documents and one of the credit cards. "I'm leaving the other card for you. You might need it," he told her with a shrug of his broad shoulders and headed for the door.

Randi followed him downstairs. Mina and Jean-Luc both rose from their seats. "We're so sorry for your loss," Mina murmured.

"Thank you. Jean-Luc, if you will drive me to town, I'll make arrangements from there. I don't want anything traced back here."

"*Certainement, mon ami,*" the older man replied with a vigorous nod.

David turned to her, his expression unreadable and his eyes a flat lead-gray. Feeling awkward and unsure of what response to make, she settled for a feeble smile. "Well—uh, be careful."

David swept her into his arms, his gray eyes now warm with emotion. "Jean-Luc and Pierre will watch out for you and Jamie while I'm gone."

She nodded. "I know." Now, if only David had someone to

watch out for him.

He leaned down and planted a kiss on her forehead. "Mind you, behave yourself. Don't give Jean-Luc too much trouble."

Tears started welling up in her eyes. "I won't." She sniffed, then rubbed away her tears.

A smiled quirked at the corner of his mouth. He turned to Jean-Luc. "If she becomes bored, you might take her skydiving. She loves airplanes."

Randi's mouth dropped open. Both Mina and Jean-Luc laughed, having already heard David's *very* exaggerated stories about her fear of flying.

"You jerk," she murmured, cuffing him gently on the shoulder.

Jamie burst into the house along with Jean-Luc's son Pierre. "Are we moving again?" he asked with a long face.

David knelt down to Jamie's level. "I have to go home to London for a few days, but you and your mum will stay here with Mina and Jean-Luc. Is that all right?"

Jamie nodded, his face wreathed in a wide smile. "Yes. I love it here. I want to stay forever."

"Now, will you promise to be a very good boy and take care of your mum for me while I'm away?"

"Yes, sir. I will." Jamie looked up at his mother, giving her a speculative grin. "Does that mean I'm in charge?"

David laughed. "Not exactly, but you will look after her all the same?"

"Yes, sir." The boy straightened his shoulders before adding, "But it would be much easier if I were in charge."

In his most conspiratorial manner, David told him, "Your mum has already promised to be on her best behavior. I don't think she'll give you much trouble."

Jamie gave a single nod. "All right."

David stood and gazed into Randi's eyes. "I have your promise?"

"Yeah, I'll be good," she told him, her heart filling with love and her mind with fear.

"All right then."

The warmth she saw in his gaze made her knees wobbly.

Breaking eye contact, he turned to Jean-Luc. "I hate long good-byes. Jean-Luc?"

"Oui, M'sieur Da-veed."

He picked up his bag, casting one lingering glance as if memorizing her face.

Randi watched the two men hop into Jean-Luc's farm truck. As she waved them on their way, she wondered if she'd ever see him again. No, she couldn't bear the thought of anything happening to him.

He'll be all right. He'll be all right.

It would be her mantra until she saw him again.

Chapter Twenty-Two

Never in his wildest imaginings had David ever expected to sit at his brother's deathbed. Making the decision to turn off life support wasn't something he'd ever expected to do either. He took Terry's flaccid hand between his, marveling that the strong hand of his older brother was now so pale and lifeless. Unable to think of anything else to do, he stroked it. "I don't want the damned title, Terry. I never did. It's not fair. You were supposed to succeed Father, not me." Bitterness toward his father welled up in his throat. "The very thought of my inheriting everything is bound to set him spinning in his exalted tomb, you know.

"I've fallen in love. I know, I never thought it would happen, again, even if you did tell me it would. Her name's Miranda. I'm sorry there wasn't time for you to meet her, but she's a lovely woman. A good mother. You would like her. She's a lot like Mum was before we went off to school. And she's very sexy in a quiet way, as if she isn't aware of it. And her little boy's a right cracker—such a brave lad. A heart like a lion, he has.

"As soon as I find the right time and the right words, I'm going to ask her to marry me. I don't know if she'll have me, but I can't let her go without finding out. She's the only good thing that's happened in the last six years."

His brother made no response to David's long oration, not that he expected one. "I love you. I wish you could hear me. The doctors and nurse assure me you can't. Th-they say it's time to let you go. It's the hardest thing I've ever had to do, old man."

"DCI French?" The ward sister in her dark blue uniform touched him on the shoulder. "Doctor's on his way."

David nodded. "Another minute, please."

"Of course, sir." Sister backed away, leaving him alone again.

"I guess it really is time." He swallowed, then stood and kissed his brother on the cheek. "Say hello to Mum for me. Tell her I miss her."

"Chief Inspector French." The burly surgeon walked into the glass-walled cubicle.

David gave an abbreviated nod. "Mr. Farnon."

"Are you ready?"

He hesitated, still not sure he could continue. "I guess."

"It's for the best. Your brother has no brain activity. It's only his heart that's pumping, and it won't once the respirator is disconnected."

"I understand." Resignation, bitter and unwelcome, settled on him, the weight nearly unbearable. All of this because he'd made the fatal mistake of underestimating Stefan Kristoforus. How arrogant he'd been. Again.

"Need more time to say your farewells?"

He shook his head. "I've said them."

The surgeon nodded, then reached for the ventilator and shut off its whoosh-whoosh.

He continued holding his brother's hand between his and watched the monitors. First it seemed as if the heart rate sped up.

"V-tach," the surgeon announced.

The spiky tracing evolved into an irregular and wavy line.

"V-fib," the ward sister said.

Then a straight line. "Asystole," Farnon announced, then glanced down at his watch. "Time of death, 6:02 A.M."

The ward sister stepped forward. "Excuse me, if it's all right with you, your Lordship, we'll need to prepare the body. You'll need to sign some papers at the desk."

"All right." He released his brother's hand. *Your Lordship.* It hit him. Two words and his life would never be the same.

Heart heavy, he walked to the nurses' station. "I need to sign some papers."

"Yes, your Lordship," the unit assistant slid the papers

toward him.

He scrawled his name. "A telephone?"

The unit assistant pointed. "On the left. If you'd prefer some privacy, there's a lounge at the end of the hall."

"Thank you." He lumbered down the hall, plagued by a profound weariness. Only the deaths of his mother and Cassie had affected him so.

Damn it! He'd had enough of death and losing the people he loved.

Kristoforus, you will pay. You will pay.

ॐ

Randi hung up the phone, a lump forming in her throat. She turned to face Mina and Jean-Luc. Mina appeared to be holding her breath. "David's brother just passed away. They shut off the machines a few minutes ago."

Collapsing on the nearest chair, Mina's eyes filled with tears. "Poor Master Terence," she said, giving a small sigh, "was calmer than Master David, but he was still an affectionate child. Amazing, really, when one considers their father. He was a cold, critical man, never satisfied with any of the boys' accomplishments."

Randi took a ragged breath. "I wish I were with him. He sounded so alone."

"I'm sure he knows you're with him in his heart. You are, aren't you? I know he's very fond of you—more than fond if I were to hazard a guess."

Her face heated under Mina's knowing gaze. "I-I'm not sure if that's true or not. I certainly care for *him*. He's such a strong man and a good one, but he has every reason in the world to hate me."

"Oh, my dear, surely not," Mina protested, shaking her head in disbelief.

"I'm responsible for his fiancée's death."

"How can that be?"

"Do you know how we met?"

Mina shook her head. "No, dear, why don't you tell me."

"My mother and I had come to England on an antique buying trip, and I met Stefan. He swept me off my feet. He was so handsome. We married soon after we met, and it was a big mistake—the stupidest thing I've ever done. He used me as a punching bag...and worse. After six months, I managed to escape him. I was looking for a job when I met Cassie in her bookstore and—well, to make a long story short—she invited me to move into her flat. But soon after that, Stefan found me and started stalking me, making threats."

"How horrible that must've been for you."

"Yes, I'd just found out I was going to have Jamie. I hadn't even told Cassie yet. David was at our flat one night, visiting Cassie—they'd just gotten engaged—when Stefan showed up very angry. David stood up to him and wouldn't let him near me, so he and my ex got into a shoving match. Later, David looked Stefan up and threatened him with the police, if he didn't leave me alone."

"Good for him."

"No, it was awful, because Stefan came after David, but killed Cassie by mistake. So you see, it is my fault she's dead. Now David's told me more than once he doesn't hold me responsible, but I still hold myself responsible. And now, his father and brother are added to the list. I've wrecked David's entire life. How can he ever forgive me?"

"You poor thing," Mina murmured. "I'd no idea you'd been through so much."

"David is..." The words wouldn't come. If she felt overwhelmed by loneliness when surrounded by good and kind people, how must he feel right now?

"There, there," Mina placed a motherly arm around Randi's shoulder. "Everything will be all right. Master David—I mean, His Lordship—will set everything to rights."

Digging a tissue from her pocket, Randi blew her nose. "I don't know if anyone can ever do that."

Chapter Twenty-Three

David clenched his teeth. Being dressed down by Chief Superintendent Goodacre was never pleasant, and like any bitter medicine, it was better if one swallowed it in one gulp.

"You've had the entire department in an uproar. Quite a disadvantage since we didn't know where the bloody hell you were for a week. For seven days, you didn't report in. It's unconscionable, whatever your reasons," the Chief Superintendent blustered.

"They were excellent, I assure you."

"Enough cheek. I expected more of someone of your background and rank than to go haring off with a woman and child on a bloody vacation."

"Hardly a vacation, Chief Superintendent. My assignment was to protect Miranda Raines from her ex-husband. I did."

"And where is the good woman?"

"I'll not reveal her location, but she and the boy are safe."

Goodacre's face turned beet red, as if a fit of apoplexy were imminent. "I order you to tell me!" he shouted.

Crossing his arms across his chest, he replied quite calmly, "Sorry, Gov."

"I'll have you stripped of your rank, my boy."

"Doesn't matter. Miranda Raines Peyton and her son are under my protection, and there they shall stay until I am certain they're no longer in danger from leaks in this or the MI6 office."

"Leaks? What bloody leaks?"

"The ones that have kept Stefan Kristoforus dogging us for the last week. He showed up at my house minutes after I took her there. To do that he had to have had inside information as to her whereabouts and followed us from her cottage. Do you realize how close we came to losing her and the boy?"

"You're too close to the situation. I shouldn't have assigned you after all."

"Far too late now. Now if you will allow me, I have a father and brother to bury."

"You're off the case. Take some downtime. Sort out your family responsibilities, then let me know when you decide."

"Decide what?"

"When you will leave the Force...officially, that is?"

"Leave the Force? Are you dismissing me?"

"Of course not, but your circumstances... You can't deny that they've changed. You've a title now. I suppose I should address you properly."

"I've no intention of resigning this case or my position. If you want to fire me, do it. Otherwise, title or no, I'm a copper for life, sir."

Chief Superintendent Goodacre's mouth dropped open.

David spun on his heel and strode from the office.

C7

Randi clutched the telephone, her lifeline to the man on the other end.

"I can't talk long," David told her. "I'm having the devil of a time getting out of London."

"I thought you said it would only take a couple of days."

"The Yard and MI6 are both on my case regarding your whereabouts. They even have someone shadowing me."

"What?"

"It's for my protection, they tell me, but I don't believe them—not for a minute. They've even threatened to place me under protective custody if I don't cooperate. I've managed to give them the slip long enough to make this call. At least, I think I have."

"Oh, no!" She paused, took a deep breath before suggesting, "Well, maybe that would be better. At least you'd be safe."

"No, something's off. I haven't been able to contact Brinks either. On assignment in Malta, they say, but I'm not sure I buy it."

"Well, we're fine here."

"Nothing suspicious? No strangers in the village?"

"No, Jean-Luc has made sure of that each day when he goes into Ste-Thérèse."

"Good." David sighed. "See here, I need to ring off before they spot me and check the call log."

"All right. Take care." *I love you, David,* she told him mentally, since she couldn't bring herself to actually say the words.

"I miss you. It won't be much longer."

"I miss you, too." She sighed as she hung up the phone.

He misses me.

Mina looked up from her needlepoint. "David?"

"Yes."

"You look troubled. What's wrong?"

"He's having trouble with the authorities. They don't want him to leave England."

"Oh dear," Mina replied, her needle piercing the mesh of her needlepoint piece. "It's like that, is it?"

"'Fraid so."

"You must have faith in his Lordship. He brought the three of you here, didn't he? I'm sure he'll return when you least expect him."

Randi heaved a sigh. "I know you're right, but I'm scared for him." She took another ragged breath. "I'd never forgive myself if anything happened to him because of me."

"Miranda, you must trust him. He's a professional. He won't take any unnecessary risks."

"B-but—"

The older woman set her handwork aside. Reaching over, she patted Randi's knee. "He's in love with you, dear. He'll come back."

Leaning back, she shook her head in disbelief. "I don't understand it. Why would he love someone like me?"

"Like you? Well, what's wrong with you, my girl? Nothing I can see."

"You mean, other than the fact that I've ruined his life? Well, it's just that Cassie was so beautiful. Perfect."

"But my dear, you're very pretty. Lovely skin, eyes and hair. You underrate yourself."

"All I know is, in high school, my brothers' friends always treated me like a kid or, worse yet, like another one of the guys. I guess that's why Stefan was able to sweep me off my feet the way he did. I didn't have any basis for comparison. He was handsome and exciting, so I thought I was in love."

"What did your mother say?"

"Oh, she tried to warn me, said it was all happening too fast. But, of course, I wouldn't listen. That's one of the reasons I didn't go back to the States. I didn't want to hear *I told you so* every time I turned around."

"Surely, she wouldn't be that trying."

"Don't get me wrong. I love my mother. She's a really great lady, but she's *never* wrong if you know what I mean?"

Mina nodded and resumed her needlework. "My own mother was a bit like that, too." She held up the piece of needlepoint. "What do you think? It's for a fire screen."

Welcoming the change in subject, Randi nodded her approval. "It's lovely. I've seen examples of them in some of the restored plantations in Virginia."

"Well, I thought one would look nice by the hearth. I discovered a frame for it the last time I went antiquing. It's a very old French piece. Jean-Luc had to do a bit of restoration before I could consider using it, even as a decorative item."

"I've always loved old things. I guess I get that from my mother."

"She's in antiques, I believe you said."

"Yeah, she used to drag me around to flea markets and

antique stores. My brothers were always playing football and baseball, but I had a lot of fun with my mom. I don't know how she managed. She never missed a single one of their games or any of my recitals."

"She does sound like quite a lady. I think you must take after her."

"Thank you. You know, talking about her makes me miss her and my brothers and my dad, too."

"What does your father do?"

"He's a doctor, internal medicine."

"A busy man, I'm sure."

"Yeah, but he never quite approved of my being a musician. He can be pretty pompous. I think it must come from having nurses trailing him around, jumping on command, you know. He told me that if I were going to be a musician, I should go to Juilliard or Eastman and pursue a concert career."

"And you didn't?"

"No, I went to Blair School of Music at Vanderbilt, right there in Nashville. That wasn't good enough for Daddy, and when I told him I wanted to play country music, he nearly had a stroke."

"He wanted what he thought was best for you."

"But he got over it, sort of," she said with a laugh.

"I'm sure he's very proud of you."

"Oh yeah, having his daughter marry an international arms dealer and murderer was right up there at the top of his list."

"How did he react?"

Randi grimaced. "After Cassie was killed, he came to London. He yelled. He stomped around the flat and threatened to have me committed to an institution, but finally he went back home. When I told him I was expecting, he ordered me to have an abortion. Bad genes and all that. Finally, he agreed that if I wanted to have the 'spawn of the devil', maybe I ought to stay in England. Those were his exact words."

"Oh dear. And how does your father feel now?"

"He's never even seen Jamie." She stood and walked over to the window. She smiled at the sight of her son *assisting* Jean-Luc's youngest son, Pierre, with cleaning the pool and preparing it for winter.

She turned back to Mina. "Mother comes over twice a year on buying trips, and she's crazy about Jamie. But not Daddy. She says he's softened, but his pride won't let him make the first move. I guess when all this is over, I'll go home. Maybe that's where I belong anyway."

"I wouldn't be so quick to run away, dear. You may find another reason to stay."

Randi bit her lip and gave Mina a sheepish look. "David?" She shook her head. "I don't think I'm right for him. This is just one of those 'ships that pass in the night' deals."

"I think you do yourself and His Lordship an injustice."

Mina applied herself to her needlework and added, "But time will tell."

"I get it. You and Jean-Luc have another bet going, right?"

"My dear, really."

The very idea of the staid Mina and her jovial spouse wagering on her relationship with David gave her a fit of the giggles. "You two—"

A high-pitched shriek shattered the quiet afternoon, followed by a splash.

"*Madame, Madame*, the boy..." Pierre shouted.

Randi sprinted for the back door in time to see Pierre dive headfirst into the pool.

Time slowed, like molasses in winter, then stood still. She tried to move, but her legs wouldn't cooperate. She opened her mouth, but no sound would come.

Then time shifted into a sickening fast forward. Suddenly she found herself at the edge of the pool, standing over the unmoving body of her son. Pierre knelt over Jamie, giving him mouth-to-mouth resuscitation. She dropped to her knees on the opposite side.

"Jamie," she whimpered, feeling Mina's arm slip around her shoulder. "Why isn't he responding?"

Between giving puffs of air, Pierre gasped, "Hit his head."

Jamie's body jerked. He coughed and water rolled out of his mouth. "Mum," he croaked.

Chapter Twenty-Four

Mina returned from phoning the local pharmacist. "He said since Jamie's inoculations were up to date, we should check his temperature throughout the night and for the next forty-eight hours. If he doesn't show a rise, he should be all right."

Randi sat in an old rocker with Jamie cradled in her arms. "Thank heavens. I think he's ready for a nap. Aren't you, sweetheart?"

Jamie gave a drowsy nod. "Yes, Mummy."

"Excuse me while I settle him down." And settle herself down, too. The close call had unnerved her more than she wanted to admit.

"Of course, my dear. Do let me know if you need anything."

"That's all right. He just needs a little nap." She cuddled Jamie to her chest, combed back his damp bangs and took him to his room. "Here, let's get you out of your wet things before you get sick."

Later that afternoon she made another routine check on Jamie. He'd slept most of the day since his tumble into the pool. Mina had read poor Pierre the riot act for not keeping closer watch.

She came back from Jamie's room, carrying the thermometer. "It's only two-tenths of a degree," she said. "That's not bad, is it? I still don't understand degrees Centigrade. Give me a good old Fahrenheit thermometer anytime. Anyway, it's probably all the excitement. I'll check it again in another hour, just to make sure it doesn't go any higher."

"Does he feel warm?"

Randi shrugged. "Just a little. I took off the extra blanket. That should help." She flopped down on an old tapestry-covered chair. Shutting her eyes, she rested her face in her hands, wishing she could go home like E.T. or Dorothy.

"How about a cuppa?" Mina offered. "You look as if you're about ready to pass out."

"Thank you. That would be great."

CB

For the next few minutes, Mina busied herself with making the tea. Then she heard Jamie come down the stairs, whining in a plaintive voice, "Mummy, I'm hot."

Randi jumped up and grabbed the boy in her arms. "He's burning up."

Mina snatched the tympanic thermometer and inserted it carefully into Jamie's ear. They waited. Fifteen seconds later, the thermometer beeped and in unison the women gasped at the digital readout: Thirty-eight, point nine C.

Randi's eyes grew wide. "I can feel his chest rattling when he breathes. I think he has pneumonia. What'll we do? Where can we take him?" she asked, her look of desperation growing.

"Come on, I'll drive," Mina offered as they rushed from the farmhouse toward an old green Peugeot. "We'll have to take him into Aix. It's the closest medical center."

CB

Randi sat in the passenger seat, holding her son, while Mina, who boasted of having learned her driving skills at the ripe old age of sixty-five, drove as if the streets of Ste-Thérèse were on the route of the Grand Prix. "Go faster," Randi urged. After his initial outburst when she'd had mentioned the word hospital, Jamie had lapsed into unconsciousness.

As soon as Mina pulled the car to a screeching halt at the emergency entrance, Randi leapt from the car and ran inside with Jamie's limp body in her arms.

"My son. Someone must see him immediately," she demanded of the first person she saw. "*Parlez-vous anglais?*" exhausted her command of French. At least Mina could interpret.

The receptionist sighed. "Madame, you must fill out these forms, and then wait over there, *s'il vous plaît.*" She nodded toward a row of chairs, already filled to capacity.

"No, I mean *now*. Are you blind? He's unconscious!" Randi shouted, desperate to have him seen by a doctor.

"You'll have to wait just like everyone else, *madame.*"

"No, I won't!" She'd never seen Jamie so ill. Frantically she turned to Mina. "Make her understand!"

"*Le docteur, s'il vous plaît!*" Mina demanded, in perfect French and with attitude.

A tall, graying man walked down the hall toward her. "What's going on here?"

Randi rushed past the receptionist. "My son. He's unconscious. Please help him," she begged and then broke into tears.

"Come with me," he said. "Nurse, room one!" he shouted.

Randi hurried down the hall after the physician. He continued to question her. Thank heaven he could speak English.

"How long has he been this way? What was his temperature the last time you checked it? Has he been anywhere unusual?"

"About half an hour. First, it was thirty-seven point six, then fifteen minutes later it was thirty-eight point nine. I think it's even higher now. He fell in the pool this afternoon and had to be resuscitated," she blurted out, answering all the doctor's questions without stopping to take a breath.

"A swimming pool?" he asked looking over the frames of his gold-rimmed glasses. The nurse had taken Jamie from her and was in the process of checking his temperature again.

"The house where we're staying has a pool out back. They were getting it ready for winter when he fell in. I think. I'm not really sure. I was in the house." Even to her ears, her excuses sounded feeble, as if she weren't capable of caring for her son.

Obviously she wasn't, or he wouldn't be sick right now.

"Well, he's obviously aspirated something, but if the pool is chlorinated properly, he should be all right, but one never knows, *madame*."

"Forty point nine," the nurse announced. "Cooling blanket?" she asked and received a curt nod in the affirmative.

"Oh, my God." Randi's knees grew weak. Her stomach lurched and nausea threatened at the thought of losing her baby.

"Is he allergic to any medications? Do allergies run in the family? I want to treat him with a broad-spectrum antibiotic, as well as one with a narrower spectrum to cover all the possibilities."

"No, no allergies...in either family. My husband is dead—car accident," she lied, "but he was never sick while we were married."

The doctor raised an eyebrow. "We need to lower his temperature quickly," he explained. "It's too high, and we can't risk brain damage by waiting for drugs to take effect. That's the purpose of the cooling blanket."

Randi nodded. "I understand."

A second nurse entered the examination room, walked toward Randi, placing a comforting hand on her shoulder. "Now, *madame*," she explained in English, "your son he is in good hands. You were right to bring him so—so quickly. We're going to take very good care of him. I want you to wait outside. Once he's stabilized, we'll move him to a room. You'll be able to stay with him then."

"I don't want to leave him." Randi planted her feet apart and folded her arms.

"But *madame*, you must. As you see, this is a small room. You'll just be in the way, no? You don't want to delay his treatment?"

Randi's determination wavered in the face of common sense. "No, of course not." She allowed the nurse to lead her from the room and down the hall, giving Jamie a long glance over her shoulder.

Mina jumped up. "How is he?"

Tears streaming, she fell into Mina's arms. "Oh, Mina, he's so sick. His temperature's even higher."

∞

David paced back and forth in the small hotel room. He'd managed to give his police shadow the slip. Billing the call to one of his fake credit cards, he punched in Mina and Jean-Luc's number. At some point he would make restitution for his fraudulent credit card usage. Still, it went against his grain, skating on the wrong side of the law. But protecting Miranda and her son was more important than breaking a law or two.

He desperately needed to hear the sound of her voice. She had a way of centering him, settling him. Funeral preparations were taking an inordinate amount of time to arrange. It might be another week before he could find his way clear to return to Provençe...and Miranda.

Dodging his police shadow and keeping on the lookout for Stefan or his brothers was tedious to the extreme. Why at least one of the clan hadn't traced him to his brother's hospital was curious as well. Had they drawn him away from France merely in order to leave Miranda and Jamie vulnerable to attack.

More anxious than ever, he waited. The phone rang six, seven, eight— Finally! Jean-Luc answered, *"Allô?"*

"Bonjour, Jean-Luc. It's David. May I speak with Miranda?"

"Oh, *mon Dieu,* Da-veed. The little one, *il est dans l'hôpital!"*

"What is it, serious?" Stupid question. Of course it was, or he wouldn't be in hospital.

"The little one, he hit his head, fell in the pool. He's critical, *mon ami.* Can you come?"

"Of course, as soon as I can catch a flight."

"He's at *L'hôpital St-Michel* in Aix."

"How's Miranda holding up?"

"Very worried. *Il est trés* sick boy."

"All right. Tell her I'm on my way."

"Bien!"

"Au revoir, Jean-Luc." He hung up the telephone. As cold-

blooded as it might seem, his father and brother were beyond caring when their services would take place. Jamie was ill, and Miranda needed him. The funeral arrangements would have to wait.

CB

Stefan paced back and forth. Just a little more time and a little more luck, and it would all come together. His cell phone shrilled. His hand shook as he pulled it from his pocket. "Yeah?"

"Stefan? Theo."

"It's about time. Have something for me?"

"Xander found the forger the detective used in Dijon. After a bit of *persuasion*, he gave up the two names DCI French is using."

"So? What are they?"

"Edward Jameson and Gaston Girard."

"Finally, we can run a trace on them." The telephone grew sweaty in his hands. He would find his son. "Have Xander check the airlines and the trains. He has to move around the country somehow."

"We've already had a hit. He made a call to a village in Provençe from the Claremont Arms."

"I knew we'd find him." Stefan licked his lips. "Where's Xander now?"

"Still in Dijon."

"And you?"

"Hanging out at the mortuary, waiting for him to show and complete funeral arrangements."

"All right. Tell Xander to head for Provençe, just in case we miss French at the Claremont. What was the name of that village?"

"Ste-Thérèse."

"All right. Meet me at the Claremont. Maybe we can catch him before he leaves the country."

Chapter Twenty-Five

Randi paced back and forth in the Emergency Ward waiting area, while they were stabilizing Jamie in the exam room. It seemed like they'd been in there for hours, but her watch told her it'd only been fifteen minutes. The receptionist had even given up trying to persuade her to sit and have a cup of coffee.

All she could think about was her son. He'd become ill so quickly, and his fever was dangerously high. How could such a tiny boy survive such an ordeal? She walked quickly down the hall, her shoes squeaking against the tile floors. Peering through the small window into the exam room, all she could see was his dark head and one thin arm, attached to plastic tubing. A plastic bag containing some type of intravenous fluid was running into his vein. The rest of his body was wrapped and covered by a rubber-appearing apparatus that looked like a large, flat mat.

That must be the cooling blanket. She wondered how it worked. Well, hell, as long as it worked, it didn't matter *how*.

The doctor turned and saw her. He walked toward her, not smiling. His grim expression froze the blood in her veins. She stepped away from the door as the physician exited. "I'm sorry, I didn't introduce myself earlier," he said. "I'm Dr. Marc Chalfant."

"Miranda Peyton, and this is my son Jamie. I'm very grateful for your quick attention," she murmured, giving him her hand.

The doctor took Randi's hand and held it for a brief moment, telling her, "We've done an x-ray picture of his chest, and it appears that your son has an aspiration pneumonia.

There are diffuse patches of infiltrate throughout his chest. His tumble into the pool has resulted in his illness."

"An aspiration pneumonia?" she asked, confused by the medical terminology. *Why do doctors have to use such complicated language?*

"Yes, unlike bacterial or viral pneumonias which are caused by an organism or virus, Jamie's illness is the result of aspirating water into his lungs. Antibiotics are of no use in treating an aspiration pneumonia like this except in preventing the occurrence of secondary infections."

"Wh-what are you saying? You can't help him?" Her spirits plummeted. She'd been so hopeful that she'd gotten him to the hospital quickly—and in time.

"It will be touch and go. We will give him the oxygen, breathing treatments and intravenous fluids. We will monitor and support him in every way, but ultimately, it is your son who will have to fight off this assault."

Fear knifed like an arrow into her heart. Jamie was her heart, her life. "He could die?" she managed to ask, dreading the awful answer.

"He could, but I think that, given his youth and good health before this episode, he should survive." The doctor looked at her kindly. Maybe it was pity she saw in his eyes. "You must not give up, no. *We're* not. We're going to fight with the young boy every step of the way, I assure you."

"Thank you. I'm not sure I'll make it if my son doesn't." She peeped over Dr. Chalfant's shoulder and asked, "May I see him?"

"Soon. We're preparing to move him. His temperature is coming down, but I feel that he belongs in our intensive care unit. Our nurses can keep a much closer watch on him there. As soon as we have him settled, I'll allow you a few minutes with him. After that, the visiting hours will have to be observed. They are frequent, but of short duration. We have the very comfortable parents' lounge where you may stay in between visits. There are even some sleeping facilities, if you are uncomfortable leaving."

"Thank you! I couldn't possibly leave, not now."

"*Certainement, Madame.* Peyton," he replied.

Randi watched as the two nurses brought a small stretcher and lifted Jamie onto it, trailing tubes and an intravenous pump.

Finally, when all the equipment was in its appropriate place, the nurse wheeled Jamie from the small exam room into the hall.

She looked at her son's small, pale face. Her heart thudded with fear for him, but she sniffed, wiped her tears, and followed quietly behind the entourage as they made their way to the elevator which would take them to the pediatric ICU.

Prayers learnt long ago passed through her mind and across her lips.

ॐ

The night shift was well into the dead zone—the time when normal people were asleep, but the demands of duty required vigilance. Randi paced back and forth in the family lounge outside the intensive care unit. She drained the last dregs of coffee from the paper cup, crumpled it and tossed it into the trash. In the far corner, a coffee vending machine spewed forth more bitter cups of coffee good for only one thing—staying awake.

Afraid to go to sleep, afraid Jamie would take a turn for the worse and need her. How could she sleep while, in the next room, her child fought for his life?

Fragile. Life and her son.

"Hold on, baby. Please don't let him die," she beseeched the universe and anyone else who might lend an ear to a mother's prayer.

At the sound of Randi's voice, Mina, who had fallen asleep on a couch, stirred, sat up and rubbed her eyes. "Is it the little one?"

"No, just me. Sorry." She walked over to Mina and sat beside her. "I'm so grateful that you're here," she told her, "but you should be home in bed."

"I wouldn't think of leaving you to face this alone. Not that I've done you any good, falling asleep like this," the older woman remarked wryly. "Here, you must take my cell phone. If David calls the farm, Jean-Luc will give him my number."

Randi took the phone and placed it in her purse. "Don't be silly. But I'm glad you're here because I don't know what I'd do without you."

"What time is it?"

"It's nearly one. He's no better, but no worse. 'Stable for the time being' is all the nurses will tell me."

She turned her head from side to side, stretching the muscles in her neck. It seemed that every last one of them had tightened until her neck and shoulders had excruciating pinpoints of pain that literally burned and danced across her shoulders.

"Poor thing," Mina murmured. "Here let me give you a massage."

"Okay, but then I'll give you one. That couch isn't very good for sleeping, is it?"

"I've slept on worse," Mina replied with a grin. "Never mind about these old bones."

As Mina's strong hands kneaded her shoulders and neck, Randi's head nodded once, twice. She was unable to keep her eyes open another minute. Her eyes snapped open, her few second's respite interrupted by the shrilling of Mina's cell phone. Blearily she fumbled for her purse and pulled the offending instrument from it. "Hello?" she answered, repressing a yawn.

"Miranda, it's David. I'm at the airport. How's Jamie?"

"Stable. That's all they'll tell me."

"My plane leaves in ten minutes. I just wanted to you know I'm on my way."

"B-but you have your father and brother's funerals. They should come first," she argued, even though she wanted nothing more than to see him and feel the comfort of his arms around her. "Mina's here with me. I'll be fine."

"I said I'm on my way."

Through the telephone she heard the airport address system announcing, "Last call for Flight—"

"That's my flight. See you soon, luv." He hung up before

she could protest.

Mina smiled. "His Lordship's coming?"

"Yes." She breathed a sigh of relief. "He's at the airport."

The door of the parents' lounge opened, and Randi looked up sharply. "Dr. Chalfant, I thought you'd gone for the night."

He walked toward her, his face solemn.

Oh, God, what if—? She couldn't bear to finish the thought.

"They called me back," he said with obvious hesitation. "I'm afraid your son is worse."

"No!" What little strength she'd had deserted her abruptly.

Mina caught her before she could fall. Together, the physician and Mina supported her until she regained a semblance of strength and self-control.

"I'm all right," she insisted, pushing them away. "Tell me about Jamie."

"He's having more difficulty breathing and clearing the fluid from his lungs. The extra work of breathing is stressing his heart, making it beat too fast. He needs a tube down his throat to help him breathe. We'll sedate him, too, so that he won't fight the tube. It will be much easier to suction the secretions from his lungs, as well. It's only a temporary measure, designed to rest his heart as well as his lungs."

"Then do it," Randi said decisively. "What are you waiting for?"

Dr. Chalfant gave a weak smile. "Just your permission—"

The public address system on night mode, interrupted his explanation. "*Docteur Chalfant, à Services d'Urgences Pédiatriques.*"

Randi looked toward the door. "That's where Jamie is, isn't it?"

On his way out the door, Dr. Chalfant replied with a grim, "Yes."

Chapter Twenty-Six

After landing at the airport and jumping in the first available taxi, David strode rapidly down the semi-dark hall of the children's ward at *L'hôpital St-Michel*, his quick steps echoing along a nearly deserted hall. His concern for Jamie was real, but two-fold. Not only had he come to care deeply for Miranda and her small son, but he also feared her reaction if the unthinkable happened. Jean-Luc had sounded so grave on the telephone.

At night, the hospital seemed to have a different rhythm. The hall lights were dim. Fewer personnel rushed about. The pace was slower. He'd managed to convince the night guard that he was fairly harmless and had been directed to the intensive care ward for children.

He peeked through the small square window in the door to the parents' lounge and saw Miranda talking to Mina. Her fidgety movements proved an accurate indicator of her state of nerves. As quietly as he could, he opened the door.

She jumped up and ran to him. "You shouldn't have come. Your family..." She ran her hands through her hair, another sign she was upset.

"And I told you I was coming. How is he?"

Heaving a deep sigh, she shook her head. "When the door opened, I thought maybe you were the doctor. He's been with Jamie for the last hour. They haven't told me anything." Her green eyes grew large with worry and fear.

"I'm sure they're doing everything possible for him." He tried to soothe her by enfolding her in a hug. "Why don't you sit down while I see what I can find out?"

She shook her head. "No, I'm going, too. Maybe they'll let me see him this time."

"Let's go. Now stay positive. Stay focused. He *will* get better."

She attempted a smile. "I hope you're right. I'm sort of glad you came," she admitted. "But you shouldn't have. Your place is with the rest of your family."

He sat on a sofa, pulling her chair next to him. "Why don't you tell me everything that's happened? That will give the doctor a little more time to help Jamie."

She complied, detailing the downward spiral of her son's illness. She'd just told him about Jamie's being placed on the ventilator, when the night nurse entered the lounge.

Miranda grabbed David's hand. "Yes?"

"*Mme.* Peyton, Dr. Chalfant said it's time to call a priest. You did indicate your son is Anglican, didn't you?"

"Yes, but I don't know anyone here. We're visiting." Then the importance of the nurse's words must've dawned on Miranda. Her face turned pale. Her eyes widened as she jumped up. "A priest? Jamie needs a priest? He's dying? That's what you're telling me, isn't it?"

"Get any priest," David ordered. This couldn't be happening. They could *not* be losing that precious boy.

"I shall have to call one, *m'sieur.*"

"Do it."

Miranda grabbed the nurse's arm. "I have to see him. I have to see him now."

The nurse nodded. "Follow me."

He kept a supporting arm around her waist while Mina assisted her on the other side. Together they led her down the hall to Jamie's bedside.

On entering the sector where Jamie lay, a sense of déjà vu hit David. Only days before he'd seen his brother attached to the same lines and tubes. Now it was Jamie who was ill-to-death. The boy lay motionless with a tube down his throat while a machine breathed for him and multiple intravenous lines pumped medication into his tiny veins. How his small body managed to survive the assault of the miracles of medicine,

David couldn't imagine.

The doctor walked toward them, extending his hands to Miranda. "I'm sorry, *Madame*. Peyton. I'm not sure we can save him."

Tears running down her cheeks, she turned to the doctor, fixing him with her unwavering gaze. "He can't die. You *have* to save him. He's all I have," she told the physician fiercely.

"The next few hours will tell us."

"Then I have to stay with him." She stared up at the tall, graying doctor as if daring him to disagree.

"*Oui, madame*, you may stay." Dr. Chalfant turned to a nurse and asked her to bring a chair.

"Thank you," she said, sitting down by her son's bed. She took his small hand into hers and kissed the back of it.

"You're going to get better, or I'll know the reason why, young man. It's not nice to scare your Mama like this. Of course, I don't mind the horrible coffee in the waiting room, but we're all so worried about you. David and Mina are here. So you'd just better get busy and wake up. You hear me?"

David's eyes stung as he listened to her nonsensical chatter. She was the bravest woman he'd ever known. She was barely holding herself together, but she was for her son.

CƷ

"Heathrow!" Stefan barked, then swore under his breath as he settled back into the taxi. He and Theo had missed French at his hotel. Already checked out, indeed. After a generous gratuity, the doorman had disclosed the inspector's destination.

He and Theo would follow on the next flight to France and meet Xander. Together they would retrieve his son. The question remained: why had the inspector returned to France in such a rush? Something was wrong with either Randi or his son. If she had allowed something to happen to his son and heir...

Stupid cow. All she had to do was let his family take care of the boy. But no, she'd kept his son's existence secret from everyone. And for that, he would never forgive her.

ℂℨ

Randi stood at the window in Jamie's cubicle and watched the morning sun as it crept over a growth of old oaks, illuminating the morning sky with bright red streaks. Hope dawned in her heart, as well. In spite of her worst fears, the crisis had passed.

Her son had made it through the night.

She felt, rather than heard, David at her side and turned to him. "See, he's better."

"*You* look totally exhausted. When are you going to get some sleep? What about some coffee or tea?"

"Just coffee, thanks."

"Has the doctor been here?" David asked.

"He was wonderful. He stayed the rest of the night." She smiled, but felt the tears well in her eyes. "After the priest came, Jamie started to improve. His breathing, his color—everything."

Just then the door to intensive care opened. She turned and saw the physician and a new nurse enter. They walked into Jamie's cubicle, Dr. Chalfant looking a little rumpled, but with a wide smile on his craggy face.

"*Madame* Peyton," Dr. Chalfant said, "I've seen your son's latest laboratory studies, and I think it's time to reduce his sedation and start weaning him off the ventilator. If all goes well, he should be breathing on his own by midmorning."

"That's wonderful. May I stay?" she asked, anxious to hold him in her arms without all the tubes. And never let him go.

The doctor smiled. "Just until he's awake and knows you're here, but then *you* need to get some rest."

ℂℨ

Randi rushed into the parents' lounge. Mina sat up, her white hair sticking out in spikes from where she'd slept. "What's wrong?" she asked blearily. "Is he worse?"

"No, he's so much better." She rushed over to the sofa and gave the older woman a ferocious hug. "He's waking up and even breathing on his own now. They're going to let me back in once he's finished a breathing treatment."

"That's wonderful, dear. Now if you don't mind, I'm going to go home and get some real sleep." Mina stood and stretched and twisted her spare frame. "Somehow, this sofa's body and mine don't match," she said with a wry grin. "You have my number, dear. Keep the cell phone and if you need me, just call, and I'll come back."

Randi beamed at the older woman. "I will, but please get some sleep. David's gone to bring me some breakfast and more coffee. I'll manage."

"All right then. I'm off. You two take care of our little lad, and I'll come back this evening."

Randi watched Mina gather her handbag and slip her feet into well-worn tennis shoes. Gratitude surged through her, gratitude for having the good fortune to have found such a good friend. She wrapped her arms around the older woman's thin shoulders. "Thank you so much. I'm sorry we've been so much trouble, but I don't know what we would've done without you."

"My dear, you would've been fine. You know, you're a very strong woman. His Lordship is very fortunate to have found you."

Shaking her head in disbelief, Randi said, "I think the jury's still out on that."

"But you love him, don't you?"

Randi hesitated, then admitted, "Yes."

"Then you'll work it out together."

"Maybe." Dear Mina possessed the heart of a true romantic, but she couldn't possibly be right—that they'd "work it out together". There was no future with David, in spite of the fact they'd made love. Once all the action and excitement were over, she and Jamie would go back to their old lives of school and music. Suddenly the thought of going home to their sunny little cottage sent a sucking sensation of loneliness through her body. Now why was that?

Answer: because they'd be alone again without David. He'd become such a part of her life—their lives—so quickly, it hurt to imagine life without him.

CŚ

Jamie pushed away the mask. "I don't like this thing. It smells bad."

The nurse gave him with a stern look. Yes, she was mean; she wouldn't let his mummy come back.

"Finish your breathing treatment, and you may see your *maman*."

"I want my mummy now!" he declared.

"You must be quiet. There are other sick children in here besides you."

"Don't care. I want my mum!" he yelled. He still had a big needle in his arm. He didn't care if there were other sick kids. He wanted his mum to hear him. That's why he was yelling. Didn't the nurse know anything?

"All right, young man. I'll get your *maman*, but you have to be quiet. Do you understand me?"

"*Oui, madame*."

"Oh, you are a very smart young man. You know a little French, *n'est-ce pas*?"

"A little," he admitted grudgingly; however, he didn't think the nurse was very smart. He never had to yell at his mum. His mum was smart because she always knew what he needed.

"Mummy!" he squealed as soon as he saw her coming through the door.

"Good morning, big fellow. I see you're not behaving yourself." Then she hugged him until he thought he'd break, but it was still a real good hug.

"I'm ready to go home. I don't like it here." He folded his arms across his chest. "Ouch," he said, then pulled at the needle. "Take this out, please. It hurts."

His mummy shook her head. She could be pretty stubborn, too. "No, they're giving you medicine through the needle. I had one when you were born. It wasn't so bad."

He had an idea. "Then you may have this one."

Mummy laughed and shook her head. "I'm afraid it doesn't work that way, son. I'm not sick. It's your medicine and your needle, but I'll bet that it won't be too long before the nurse here takes it out. Maybe tomorrow or the next day."

He looked at the nurse. "Well?"

The nurse got a funny look on her face, like she was going to laugh. She had better not laugh at him.

"That's right. If you keep on doing so well, I'm sure the doctor will have us take out that needle in a day or two."

"Can't I just drink that stuff?"

"'Fraid not, son." She stroked the hair back from his forehead. "Here in the hospital, the doctor is the boss. The nurses carry out his orders when he's not here, and he wants you to have the fluids and the medicine."

"You're mean. You won't let me have my way, no matter how many good ideas I come up with." He looked around the big room. There were other kids in beds just like his. He waved to one of them. "She's sick?"

"Yes, Jamie, she is."

"She's got needles, too?"

"Yes."

"Well, I guess I'm tougher than any old girl. I'll keep my needle." He'd show that old nurse, too. "I'm fine," he declared and nodded.

Chapter Twenty-Seven

By the time Stefan, Theo and Xander reached the village of Ste-Thérèse, it was six in the morning. Stefan was amazed that people were actually moving about the narrow cobblestone streets. The bakery was open, and some of the villagers had already lined up to buy their daily loaves. The yeasty aroma of fresh-baked bread was tempting. He couldn't remember the last time he'd eaten.

"I think we're going to look suspicious," Theo said, "if we just show up and start asking questions. The tourist season is over."

Stefan waved aside his brother's concern. "Doesn't matter. We're just looking for a good place to stay. We heard about a farmhouse that some of our friends used, but don't remember exactly where. We're here for some good food and wine—" He slapped his knee. "And truffles. Yes, it's truffle season."

"Not bad, little brother," Xander muttered. "Now let's find out where Randi and your boy are. I'm sick of this dinky-arsed village and its inhabitants already."

"But if they help us find my son, they'll be worth it."

"To you maybe," Xander said with a grunt.

"To all the family. My son is the only male heir of this generation. He will inherit our worldwide business interests. Xander, your wife is barren, and Theo's wife has had four girls in four years," he said, not giving a damn if he insulted his brothers. "I am the only one with a son. It is *my son* who will carry on the Kristoforus bloodline, and who will eventually inherit everything, but he must be taught. The earlier, the better."

Xander muttered an expletive. "You think too highly of a kid you've never seen. He may not have the stomach for it."

"That's why I said the earlier the better. He'll come to the business just like we did."

"Who's to say one of my daughters won't head the business?" Theo protested.

"You'd allow one of your precious little girls to sully their hands with arms dealing and terrorists?" Stefan asked. "I don't think so. That's not our way, and you know it."

"Keep your voice down, you idiot," Xander ordered.

"Get in the queue," Stefan ordered. "I could do with a bite to eat. One thing the French can do is bake a good loaf of bread."

Xander sputtered, "Who put you in charge?"

"This is my son and my operation. If you don't like it, turn your ass around and run home to Father."

03

According to the doctor and the critical care staff, Jamie's recovery had been spectacular. After a breathing treatment, he was moved to a private room before David returned with Randi's breakfast. She opened a carton of milk, inserted a straw, then handed it to her son. "Here you go."

"Mm. I'm thirsty." Jamie sucked on the straw, then set the carton down on his breakfast tray. "I want some real food. I don't much like mushy stuff."

"You're feeling pretty feisty this morning, aren't you?"

"Yes, ma'am, I want to go home," he said, beating his spoon against the side of his bowl of hot cereal.

"The doctor says you need to keep taking the medicines in your arm for another day, then we'll see. Jean-Luc says the cows are waiting for you to milk them," she said, trying to distract him.

"Not the farm. I mean our real home. When can we go home?"

"Not yet. The farm is our vacation spot, right?"

At that moment David walked into Jamie's room, carrying a mysterious package which sent a tantalizing aroma wafting through the air. "Do I hear sounds of rebellion? Is someone ready to go home?"

"Rebellion, yes." She sniffed the air. "And just what do you have in *le package*?" she asked, pointing at the fragrant bundle.

"Coffee, juice and some fresh croissants from the *boulangerie* down the street."

"You are a man after my own heart." She grabbed for the bag of goodies.

"Indeed, I am," he replied, holding it high above her head.

As she reached for the croissants, David swept her into an embrace. "You must say thank you properly, or you shan't have any breakfast."

She stopped struggling, composing her face into as humble an expression as she could manage. Glancing down at the floor, she said in her meekest tone, "Thank you so much, Chief Inspector French. I humbly request but a crumb or two from the feast you have so thoughtfully provided."

David took a moment to consider. "I could do."

He looked over at Jamie. "Do you think I should let your mum have some breakfast?"

"Not unless I may have some, too. I hate porridge," the boy said, pulling a frown.

"I think he's quite improved."

"That's for sure."

"All right." David brought the sack down to the level of her nose. "Smell how fresh they are," he teased, keeping them just out of reach.

"Still warm, too," she said, making another grab for them, but missing. Frustrated and dying of near-starvation, she huffed, "All right already."

David grinned. "Brought some coffee, too."

"Now I know you have an ulterior motive," she accused him, pouting, hands on her hips.

"Miranda, please sit down. I will prepare our breakfast. Young James, you shall have some, too. I must say you look a thousand times better than you did last night."

"A thousand times?" Jamie asked, his dark eyes wide. "That's a lot."

"Yes, indeed."

αβ

Stefan watched in disbelief as Theo trudged out of the bakery, his arms filled with bread and pastries. He dug in the bag and shoved a sugary confection in Stefan's face. "Here, have something to eat. Maybe it will improve your disposition."

"Fool!" Stefan spat, but his mouth betrayed him by watering for the sweets. "You're making a scene," he said, brushing the powdered sugar off the front of his tailored suit.

"Making a scene?" Theo muttered. "Keep a low profile? A village this small, you think we can do that? We don't exactly look like tourists in our three-piece suits."

Waving his brother's protests aside, Stefan continued, "We need to find out where the Pelletiers live."

Xander drifted out of the bakery, carefully carrying three cups of coffee. "We need to talk privately," he said.

"What's wrong with the car?" Stefan asked. Xander walked around like he had something stuck up his ass.

Once inside the car, Stefan whirled around and demanded, "What is it? What's wrong?"

"I picked up on a bit of local gossip. Your son is in the hospital."

"What?"

"If I'm not mistaken, *le jeune anglais* they called him, was rushed to St. Michel's Hospital in Aix yesterday."

"What's wrong with him?"

"Pneumonia or an accident of some sort."

Stefan's heart sank. He'd come so far, too far, to lose his son now to a stupid accident. "I'll kill her," he muttered under his breath. "I'm going to the hospital. Xander, you and Theo stay here. Find the Pelletier farm. We might need to hold out there."

⋄

Theo leered at the buxom woman who served his espresso. "*Merci, madame.* Perhaps you could tell us of a place with rooms to let? We are thinking of hunting for truffles. It is the season, right?"

"*Oui, M'sieur.*"

"So you do know someone? I think my cousin stayed with the—what was their name—oh yes, the Pelletiers—last year during the truffle season. He had a great time. All that fresh air and the magnificent truffles, of course."

"The Pelletiers? Why yes, I know them, but are you sure? M. Pelletier is not exactly known for his hospitality. He's an irascible old devil. I've never known him or his wife to take in paying guests."

"Old, you say? No, the one my cousin told me about was quite young and lived north of the village."

"No, M. Pelletier lives to the southeast, about five kilometers on the A21."

After she left, Theo leaned across the table and spoke under his breath. "See how easy it is to obtain information? She never knew what I was about."

"Fine, we know where the Pelletier farm is, but what should we do about it? There are only two of us."

"An old man and his woman. Shouldn't be much trouble. We'll take them in hand and wait for the detective to show up and take him by surprise. Then we'll wait for Stefan. He's running this show after all. It's his brat."

"Doesn't feel natural, letting him take the lead. I remember when we used to make him cry by breaking his favorite toys."

Theo grunted. "Let's go. I've had enough of this espresso crap. It needs some *raki.*"

⋄

Jean-Luc set down the receiver and looked over at his son Pierre. "*Merde!*"

"What?"

"Strangers at the bakery, then at the café, asking for a place to stay. Told Emil's wife that he'd heard the Pelletier's had rooms for hire, asking for directions. They want to hunt for truffles!" He laughed and held his belly.

Pierre's face turned pale, but he jumped up, ready to spring into action. "So this is it. They've traced Ran-dee and the boy to us."

Jean-Luc hoisted himself out of his chair, the sense of excitement building. "Call Robèrt. Tell him to alert the others. We'll show them how the Maquis welcomed intruders!" It had been a long time since he'd felt so alive. His juices were flowing. His heart beat a little faster.

Damn! It felt good!

&

Stefan jumped out of the rental car and gazed up at the *L'hôpital St-Michel*, his heart pumping with trepidation. Finally, he would meet his son. It was obvious his ex-wife was incapable of caring for the boy. Dragging a child all over the continent until he succumbed to a serious illness. It only made sense that he should take the boy and let his family see to his well-being and education.

He took advantage of a commotion at the end of the hall and slipped into a linen room. Relieved to find it empty, he stripped off his jacket, vest and slacks. He wadded them up and stuffed them into a hamper, then pulled on a pair of blue scrubs. He would feel less conspicuous attired like the rest of the staff.

He went from floor to floor, trying to find anything which would tell him where his son was, or even if it was his son who was a patient. On the fifth floor, he lurked at the end of a darkened hall until the nurses' station emptied. He seized the opportunity to check the computer. He touched the keyboard.

Ah, wonderful. It hadn't been signed off. Quickly he entered Kristoforus. *Searching*, it said, then *Name not found*. He entered the assumed name, Peyton. Ah ha! *Peyton, James M., Services d'urgences Pédiatriques, numéro 12.*

Now all he had to do was find wherever the hell the children's ward was.

Footsteps.

He abandoned the computer and headed for the first exit sign and up another flight. After walking down the hall, he found what he needed. Through sheer luck, rather than by design, he spied a sign with an arrow pointing to *Services d'urgences Pédiatriques.*

He walked past the door. His son must be very ill. Unlike the wards he'd left, this unit was occupied by many nurses, all of whom looked wide-awake. He peered through the small square window, hoping he could see his son in bed twelve.

Bed twelve was empty. Had his son been moved? What if? Grasping at straws, he remembered seeing the chapel on the ground floor. Since he could do nothing else, he would wait there, formulate a plan, and...and pray for his son.

He took the elevator to the ground floor, then walked toward the chapel. He opened the door and slipped inside. It wasn't a chapel of his particular faith, but it was a holy place, and it would do.

C

"There's no taxi, *m'sieur.* You'll have to walk. It's not far, only five kilometers."

"That far?" Theo asked. "You're sure there's no taxi?"

The waitress huffed. "Didn't I just say there was no taxi? Are you deaf and stupid?" The rest of her sentiments followed in such rapid Provençal that Theo wasn't quite sure what she said.

"Witch. What did she say?" he asked Xander.

Xander laughed. "I'm not sure, but I think she insulted our mother."

"Bloody cheek, I call it. Whatever. Let's get on with it."

Theo looked down at his Savile Row, three-piece suit and expensive handmade Italian shoes. He gave an exaggerated sigh. "I supposed there's no help for it. I'm afraid we're a trifle conspicuous."

"Don't look much like tourists, do we?"

"S'pose not."

"Lead on, you dimwit."

"Age first, however that goes."

"Now which way did she say?"

"Southeast."

"Well, the sun's over there, so southeast should be..." Xander turned and pointed forty-five degrees, "...that way."

☙

Forty-five minutes later, Theo huffed and puffed as he made his way to the top of what had to be the eighth interminable hill. "Bloody hills! Don't look like much until one starts walking up the buggers. I've had it. How much farther, do you think?"

"Don't know, but a bicycle wouldn't be bad about now."

"In your shape?" Theo bent over and laughed. "Hah! You'd have a coronary before you rode a kilometer."

"At least I'm not carrying a fifty-kilo tire around my middle."

"Go on. Mind you, I'm feeling a bit knackered myself."

Rounding the next curve, they came upon a flock of sheep. The pungent odor of at least fifty of the blighters nearly overwhelmed Theo as he tried to wend his way through them. "Come on, come on," he yelled, waving his hands in the air. He was rewarded by a single-finger salute from the shepherd, who muttered and spit on the ground.

Xander snorted. "Guess we know what that means. Insulted our mum, too."

"If I thought he really was, I'd show him what for."

"And he'd probably take his stick to you, too."

"I'd like to see him try it. I'll take my nine mil against his stick any day." Theo patted his underarm holster.

Finally, the flock crossed into the field across the road.

"Don't you think we need a game plan?" Xander asked.

"O'course we do. What do you say we continue pretending to be tourists and ask them to put us up for the night?"

"And if they don't want to, nimrod?"

"Then we'll encourage them at bit." Theo patted his gun again.

"Hmph. Sounds like a plan. Shall we get on with it?" His brother smiled. Sometimes he scared even Theo.

 C3

An hour later, Theo stopped and brushed the dust from his previously pristine suit. "Ruined. It's simply ruined. Yours is, too. Make yourself presentable!"

Xander complied, grousing, "This is the worst idea you've ever had."

"I've ever had? This was Stefan's idea."

"No, I meant walking. I think the woman at the café lied. Even a one-horse village has a taxi or can get one from the next village."

"I don't know what's supposed to be so hot about this area. Dust, sheep, grapevines. It sucks."

"Come on. It can't be much farther. Around the curve, there's another farmhouse. Go see what the name is on the mailbox."

Xander sat beside the road and wiped the sweat from his forehead. "Check it yourself. I need to rest."

"Gamoto!" Theo exploded. "You're a sorry sod if there ever was one."

"I'm thirsty. Maybe we could get a drink of water at the next place, even if it isn't the one we're looking for."

"You always were a whiny brat."

Five minutes later, they huffed and puffed up the road to the Pelletiers' farmhouse. "Damn good thing," Xander blew. "I couldn't have gone another step."

"Well, I hope the two old coots here aren't in better shape

than you are, or our little mission is in deep trouble. Stefan will be very disappointed."

"Yeah, yeah, screw Stefan," Xander muttered. "This was a bad idea from the start."

Theo gave a quick look around. No barking dogs. Nothing. It was too quiet.

The door opened. Theo's mouth dropped in amazement as a rotund old man stepped out—armed with a long gun. *"Arrêtez!"*

"See here, *Monsieur* Pelletier, is it? Your place was recommended to us by the fellow running the café."

"Fermez la bouche! I know who you are."

"Well, then," Theo attempted, "good. We'd like a room, and we want some truffle hunting."

"We *all* know who you are!" the farmer bellowed as five armed men stepped out from each side of the farmhouse.

Xander turned to Theo. "Like the Frenchies say, *Merde!*"

"Shut up, you idiot!"

&#x3;

Randi sat by her son's bed, the soft purring of the IV pump the only sound. She thanked her lucky stars that he'd had such a good morning after nearly dying the night before. His rapid recovery stunned her, as it had the doctor, but he attributed it to Jamie's youth and prior good health.

Reaching over, she smoothed the sheet covering his small frame. The sound of his regular breathing filled her heart with joy. She'd never been so scared in all her life. The thought of what she would do if she lost him still had her in its grip.

"Why don't you at least take a nap while he takes his?" David asked from his chair across the room. "I'll be here."

She shook her head. "I'm really not all that sleepy," she said, then stifled a yawn with the back of her hand.

"Of course not. You're so alert you're ready to slide from your chair."

"It's just one more day," she said. "The doctor said he might actually go home tomorrow, if he continues to improve."

David stood, then walked toward her. "That's wonderful, but, luv, you're dead on your feet," he whispered, leaning over her.

She smiled up at him. His closeness sent a delicious blend of heat and chills through her at the same time. "Then why don't you go find me another cup of coffee at the nurses' station or the cafeteria?"

"I'll get you that cup of coffee, but before I do, I'd like to go on record and state you are without a doubt the most stubborn human being I've ever known."

"He's my baby. I came too close to losing him." She leaned her head against David's strong chest. He smelled of fresh croissants and coffee and his leather jacket.

"I know," he said, pressing a kiss on her forehead.

Sighing, she watched him walk from the room, admiring his straight back and wide shoulders. She still found it difficult to believe that he'd left London and rushed back to Provençe—just to be with her and Jamie. He was a very thoughtful man indeed. A keeper, her Gran would've called him.

If only she *could* keep him.

She heard the door open. "You're back already?" she asked without looking up. "Forget something?"

"Just my son. It's been longer than you think, Randi."

Chapter Twenty-Eight

"Stefan," Randi gasped. "Wh-what are you doing here? How—?"

"How did I find you? You always were a little on the slow side, Randi. We traced your hero detective's phone call from London." He shut the door behind him. He towered over her, his face red with rage. Fists clenched at his sides. "Damn it! Why didn't you tell me I had a son? Why keep him from my family?"

"Why?" Randi stood, ready to fight if necessary. "You have to ask? Because you're a murderer, and the rest of your family is worse. Why on earth would I want my son to have anything to do with you?"

"Then why didn't you take him back to America?"

"I-I don't know. I mean, I don't have to explain my actions to you. The police and Interpol are looking everywhere for you."

"It won't matter. As soon as I have my son, I'll disappear. My family can arrange it, you know."

"Well, yeah. After all murder and mayhem are their daily activities. I'm sure a mere disappearance won't cause them too much trouble," she told him, placing her body between him and Jamie. She would *not* let this monster take her son.

Stall for time. David should be back any minute. She gave what she hoped was a surreptitious glance around the room for something to bonk him on the head with. The damned urinal was plastic. And the chair was too heavy.

"Don't try anything stupid, Randi. You don't have to get hurt. Just stand aside."

"No! You can't take him. He's attached to that machine."

Stefan took a step closer. "A few tubes. That's nothing."

"Nothing! Are you *stupid*? He nearly died last night. He's not going anywhere with you!" She'd claw his eyes out if she had to, but he wasn't taking her son—*her* son, damn it—anywhere.

David, where the hell are you?

"As charming a picture as you present, I'm here for my son. Maybe I'll kill you anyway, you stupid whiney bitch. You deserve it."

"Big deal," she bluffed, sounding a lot more confident than she felt.

"So?" Stefan shrugged. "Get out of my way."

"Over my dead body."

Turning his palms upward, he smiled. "As you wish." Taking another step toward her, he pulled a gun from his coat pocket.

She took a deep breath. "Look, Stefan," she stalled. "There's no need to get violent. Just wait a couple of days 'til Jamie's stronger. Then we'll talk about custody and visitation. You're right. I shouldn't have kept him from your family."

"Custody and visitation? Are you nuts? I can't go to court. I'll take my son, and I'll take him *now*."

"Shh—you'll wake him."

"That's fine. Wake him up. And take that tube out of his arm."

"I-I don't know how. I'll have to call a nurse."

"Bloody hell! Get out of my way. I'll do it."

She raised her chin a defiant notch. "No."

Stefan's sudden rush took her by surprise. With a fierce shove he knocked her to the floor, stepped over her and advanced on Jamie.

"No!" she rasped, then wrapped her arms around Stefan's legs. He tried to kick her loose, but she held on with all her might.

She heard Jamie whimper, "Mummy?" but she couldn't let go.

Her efforts paid off.

"Bitch!" Stefan yelled as he lost his balance and fell on top of her with a loud grunt. His gun skittered across the floor and underneath the bed, out of reach.

"Mummy?" came Jamie's worried voice.

Her teeth already latched onto Stefan's calf, she grunted.

Stefan colored the air with a medley of Greek and English expletives, some so foul they made Randi sick at her stomach.

The door flew open, slamming against the wall. "Bloody hell!" David took a flying leap and tackled Stefan. "Miranda, let go. I have him."

David pulled Stefan out of her grasp. She struggled to her feet, then back down on her knees, scrambling under the bed for Stefan's gun.

Stefan kicked, knocking David to his knees.

"Mummy!"

"It'll be all right, son. We're going to take care of the bad man." Biding her time, Randi swung the gun butt at her ex-husband's head. She connected.

Stefan collapsed in a heap at her feet.

And stayed down, thank goodness.

"Give me the gun," David ordered and held out his hand.

Hands trembling, she handed the gun over, then ran to Jamie's bedside. She gathered her son, now wide awake and terrified, in her arms. "It's all right. It's all right," she crooned. "I won't let the bad man hurt you."

Looking over at David, she cried, "No, don't!"

Chapter Twenty-Nine

David stood over Stefan. First, images of Cassie's fiery death, then his father's flooded his mind. Images of Terry hooked up to machines. David's hand trembled. His trigger finger twitched. All he had to do was—

"David, no!"

Then he felt Miranda's hand on his shoulder. "No, you can't."

A nurse ran into the room. *"Mon Dieu!* What is this? Put the gun down, *m'sieur, s'il vous plaît.* I will call *les agents de police."*

"Call them, please," Miranda begged the nurse, who ran from the room. "David, wait. Please."

"Give me one reason why I shouldn't."

"I'll give you two. You're not like *him*...and he's Jamie's father," she whispered in his ear. "How can I ever explain how I stood by while you killed his father?"

His shoulders sagged, then straightened.

At David's feet, Kristoforus emitted a low groan, quickly followed by an expression of pure spite. "You always were a soft-hearted bitch," he told Miranda. "I'd rather die than go back to prison."

"Only too happy to oblige," David muttered, once again placing the barrel on Stefan's forehead.

"David..."

"So that's how it is, is it? What's the matter, *Randi?* Does he give it to you the way you like it? Did she tell you, Chief Inspector? She likes a bit of rough."

A film of red clouded David's vision. An overwhelming desire to take his prisoner and slowly tear off body parts seemed to make a lot of sense. "You bloody bastard, how dare you talk about her that way!"

Hatred and disgust overran his innate sense of caution. Unable to do what he really wanted, he pistol-whipped his prisoner. The disgusting piece of slime collapsed against the wall. "Find me something to tie him up with while he's unconscious."

Miranda opened the bedside table and pulled out a wide roll of adhesive tape. Just right for Stefan's foul mouth. "Will this do?"

"Admirably."

He bent down and set about taping Stefan's hands and feet together. "There, that should do it."

"Thank you. I know he deserved a lot worse, but I just didn't know how I would ever..." Her voice faded. "It's going to be hard enough, as it is. But it won't be today."

David stood and pulled her into his arms and pressed a kiss on top of her head. "It'll be all right."

A groan from Stefan alerted them that he'd regained consciousness. "I should've known you'd fall for him, you round-heeled cow."

"More tape," David ordered. "I'll not listen to any more of his venom." Miranda left his embrace and resumed her place at Jamie's side.

"You are so eff-ing stupid, you don't even know how I got out of prison or how I traced you so easily."

"And *you're* so eff-ing stupid you don't know that none of it matters. You're going back into custody as quickly as we can extradite you back to the U.K."

"Oh, no? Then you need to check with your superiors. All it took to get me out was crossing the right palms with silver. Your precious Met. is riddled with bad coppers. I almost got what I wanted this time. Next time, I will."

"Next time? There won't be a next time." David bluffed, "I already know about the leaks. Plugging them is next on the agenda."

"My father and brothers will take care of you. No mistakes this time."

"Shut your eff-ing mouth!" Before he could stop himself, he backhanded Kristoforus, then slapped a piece of tape across the man's mouth.

From down the hall, he heard the police approaching. He rose and really looked at Miranda for the first time. All the color had drained from her face as she stood with a protective arm around her wide-eyed, silent son.

"Sorry. Forgot myself. Are both of you all right?"

She nodded.

"Mummy, who was that man?"

"Just a very bad man who wanted to hurt me." Okay, so it wasn't the complete truth, but it certainly wasn't a lie, either.

⚃

After David and Randi explained the entire situation and the French police had taken Stefan away, Randi sat and rocked Jamie in her arms. Too much excitement for one little boy.

"Mummy," Jamie said, patting her cheek.

"Yes, baby? What is it?"

"Is the bad man gone for good?"

"Yes, he is."

"David took him away for us?"

"Well, the police took him away, and David went with them."

"I want to go home."

"Sounds like a great idea," Dr. Chalfant said from the doorway.

"Really? I mean, he's ready to go, so soon?"

"I'll listen to his lungs, and if they sound as good as he looks, I'll release him into your care. I'm afraid there's too much excitement here."

"I think the excitement is over. Thank heaven."

The physician gave her a curious smile.

"It's a long story," she told him.

"*Certainement.* Now then, young man, I want to listen to those lungs of yours." The doctor placed the stethoscope on Jamie's chest and listened intently. "Unbelievable! His lungs are much improved, not one-hundred percent yet, but excellent. Little one, you are on your way to recovery."

"May I go home now? Please. Please."

"Absolutely." The doctor turned to Randi. "Now if all goes well, I'll want to see him again in a week. Try to keep him quiet, but if you have any questions at all or his temperature should go back up, I want you to bring him back to the hospital immediately."

"Of course."

"Then I'll write his discharge order and leave the prescriptions I want him to take on the chart. Make sure he takes all of them and check his temperature every four hours for the next week."

"I will, doctor."

"Nothing that tastes bad, please," Jamie opined from his bed.

Dr. Chalfant laughed. "I'll see what I can do about that, *mon ami. Madame Peyton,* I trust everything else is in order?"

"It is now."

"*Au revoir, madame.*"

"Good-bye and thank you so much for everything. He was so sick and—"

"It is my job, and I am glad your son is so strong and healthy. *Au revoir,* Jamie."

"*Au revoir,* Dr. Chalfant."

CB

As their rental car reached the outskirts of Ste-Thérèse, Randi turned to David. "I barely remember the ride to the hospital. It seemed to take forever."

"I wish I could've been here. I know you were frightened."

"I don't remember the ride at all, sir."

"Just as well. You know how your mum gets when she's worried about you?"

"Yes, sir. She gets all hyper."

David laughed. "That's a pretty good description."

"I'll thank you two to stop discussing me as if I'm not in the car."

"Yes, ma'am."

The off-key wailing of a siren sliced through the air. Jamie held his hands over his ears; she felt like doing the same. David pulled over to the side, allowing the police vehicle to pass, then tromped on the gas.

"You think there's something wrong at the farm, don't you?"

"Wouldn't be at all surprised. Stefan may have been alone at the hospital, but I doubt he was acting entirely on his own."

"Oh Lord, David, if something's happened to Mina or Jean-Luc, I'll never forgive myself." Truly she wouldn't. She had too many deaths on her conscience as it was—Cassie and David's father and brother.

The rental car rattled around the curve and barreled up the drive leading to the house. David burst out laughing. Jean-Luc, his son Pierre, and at least ten other men had Stefan's brothers surrounded. "I don't think you have to worry about Mina or Jean-Luc. I think the welcoming party proved quite sufficient."

Cos

For what she hoped was the last time for a long time, Randi zipped up Jamie and her single piece of luggage. "Well, that's it, then," she said, handing the bag to David.

"You're sure you have everything?"

"Even if I don't, I don't care. I'm so anxious to get back home that I'd get on an airplane all naked."

"Would you? Now that's something I'd dearly love to see."

Would you? Then why haven't you? David had been distant since they'd brought Jamie home. Well, what had she expected after all? Basically they'd had a one-night stand, and now the deal was over. He could go back to being a copper and an earl, for Pete's sake. And she could go back to her normal, and now it seemed, very boring, life.

"What's wrong?" he asked. "You look a little down."

"Nothing," she said, shrugging. "Adrenaline rush is over, I guess."

"You're sure?"

She stamped her foot. "Quit questioning every comment I make."

"But—"

"But nothing. Let's get out of here."

"All right. But we must say our farewells."

"I know that. Do you think I was brought up in a barn? You probably do! I don't know about you, but I have a train to catch." Randi flounced down the hall, leaving him holding her bag. Good enough for him.

Bloody cheeky bastard!

Good Lord, she was starting to swear like a Brit. Maybe she needed a trip home to the States before she lost touch with her roots entirely.

ᙢ

What did I do? David asked himself. He'd never understand women, even if he lived to be the father of one. And Miranda Raines was the most mystifying one of all. Trying to be considerate, he'd given her some space. A great deal had happened between them, and yet he still felt as if he had unfinished business with Cassie. He wanted to go to her grave one more time. He needed to say a final farewell before he asked Miranda the big question.

There were funeral arrangements to complete, and he also needed to straighten things out on the job. And with his old friend Brinks. Stefan had alluded to leaks. Was his old friend one of them? He had to find out before he could place Miranda in harm's way again. His arrogance was at the root of all that had happened. This was not the time to leave any threads untied.

Chapter Thirty

England, a week later

David met Brinks in the small park where they'd played as children. "I see you're back from Malta. What do you have to say for yourself? They traced me through you, didn't they?"

"See here, Davey. Before you damn me for a traitor, the secure line was monitored, after all. The Deputy Minister called me in and raked me over the carpet. I out-and-out lied or they would've caught up with you sooner than they did. I tried to warn you, but everything I said and did was under surveillance."

"Why? That's what I don't understand."

"Why? The DM has ties to the Kristoforus family, I think. Money-laundering is my guess. He resigned. And, in fact, he's quite disappeared."

David reached into his jacket pocket. "Here's a check for the amount I took from your account. Still, I couldn't have protected them without your help."

"At least that part worked?"

"Yes."

"Do I detect a hint of something between you two?"

"If everything goes right."

"Good show. You've had a difficult time since Cass—"

He cut Brinks off. "Quite."

"New life and all that?"

"Depends on her."

"Always," Brinks said, then laughed. "An invitation to the wedding?"

"Of course." David thrust his hand at his old friend. "You were in a dicey spot. You did the best you could. I understand."

CB

David braced his Chief Superintendent in the man's own office. "I've heard there were leaks. I'd like an explanation."

"You're quite right. There was a leak at MI6, quite high up."

"And it was?"

"Can't say officially, but the Deputy Minister has retired. Retired to parts unknown, don't you know?"

"But why?"

"Had to do with money and a shady connection to the Kristoforus family. Apparently, he'd been in their employ for years."

"And...?"

"We'll find him. Shouldn't take long. Stefan and his brothers will be in the nick for quite a while. The brothers are jokes, but Stefan will never get out. The old man—he had a cerebral hemorrhage when they told him the boys were all in jail. I understand he'll be urinating through a tube and eating baby food for the rest of his life. The rest of their crew will web into new organizations, but the Kristoforus family is finished."

"Miranda and her son. You used them as bait, didn't you, Gov?"

"Bait! Good Lord, man. What an idea."

Sickened, but certain he'd pegged it correctly, David spun on his heel. He'd played into the Gov's hands. He turned back.

"You may have my resignation. I don't have the stomach for the deception and the lies."

"David, don't be rash."

"You may address me as Your Lordship."

CB

David prevailed on Miranda's generous nature to accompany him to his father and brother's memorial services, but he had another mission in mind when he stopped at the gate of the Wheeler estate cemetery. Generations of Cassie's family were buried there, some marked by simple headstones, others in the mausoleum.

"I'll wait here," she told him, handing him the small bouquet of roses.

"All right, I won't be long."

The trees surrounding the Wheeler mausoleum were a brilliant blaze of orange and gold. The muted tones of the old oaks softened the effect of what had turned out to be a beautiful fall day.

No rain, unbelievable, but true.

He strode down the path and found his way to Cassie's grave. He knelt beside it and laid the posy of roses on the headstone. The dates of Cassie's birth and death stood out as freshly as if they had been carved the day before.

He swallowed, not sure he could bring himself to say the words he'd come to say. Closing his eyes for a moment, he envisioned Cassie's easy smile, her snapping brown eyes and the love that shone there.

"Cassie," he began, "I know I've been lax in visiting. You know how it is. Things come up. Work. Mostly work. The thing is...I've fallen in love with Miranda. She has a fine son. She never had the chance to tell you he was on the way." He swallowed before continuing, "I'm going to ask her to marry me tonight.

"So much has happened. Father's dead. Terry, too. I had a chance to kill the man who murdered you, but I couldn't do it. Stefan's the father of Miranda's little boy, but I'm going to adopt him. That's about it. I guess I'd better go. I'll never forget you. Miranda won't, either. You brought us together in a way."

He stood, brushed the tears from his eyes, turned and walked away.

Life is for the living.

But he would never forget the high price those he loved had paid.

CR

Randi waited in the car. She would say her own farewell to Cassie, but not now. Somehow she couldn't face the prospect. While she waited, she listened to a bird singing its mournful song. Unfamiliar, but fitting.

Hearing footsteps, she looked up and smiled at David through the open window.

He leaned his elbows on the doorframe. "You'll sit in the family pew with me?"

"I-I don't think I should. I'm not family."

"Hang it all. I want you by my side."

"But your family..." she protested with a shake of her head, "...you should be with them. They need you now."

"What family? My father and brother are dead. Other than Terry's fiancée and my aunt and cousins, there's no one." He shrugged. "I want you. I need you."

Tears threatened to well up in her eyes. "Of course, I'll be with you, but good Lord, David, this title thing is a little much."

"Forget about my title. I need you."

"But doesn't your family blame me? They should. I would if I were in their shoes."

"They'll love you as I do."

She glanced away from his penetrating gaze. She couldn't bear the earnest expression in his eyes.

He loved her. Yes, he'd said the words in the throes of passion. But how could he? She, who had usurped the life Cassie should've had. Her life and her man. David never would've given her a second glance if it hadn't been for Stefan and his car bomb.

David murmured, "Miranda, look at me. Don't turn away."

"It's too soon. You're very vulnerable right now. You've just lost two members of your family, and you're confusing your feelings for Cassie with what you feel for me."

"Bloody hell, I don't need you to be my shrink."

"I'm not trying to psychoanalyze you. I'm just trying to point out some of the realities of our situation."

"Why don't you just shrink-wrap me? I'm sad over my brother's death, of course. But I would never confuse what I felt for Cassie with what I feel for you."

"But you and Cassie would've had children by now, if Stefan hadn't killed her, and I'd be back in the States—probably."

David glanced down at his watch. "We don't have time to hash this over. Are you coming with me or not?"

"I said I would."

He opened the car door, then slid in and settled beside her. Her heart skipped a beat when he reached over and covered her hand with his. She grew strength from his warmth. Perhaps he even grew strength from hers. He'd lost so much. Going to his father and brother's services was the least she could do for the man who'd protected her and her son.

"Thank you," he said, his voice roughened with emotion. "Your being here means a great deal to me."

She swallowed the knot forming in her throat. He wanted more from her than she could ever give. He deserved better. He deserved someone who could love him without reservation, without guilt.

ℭ

The memorial service lasted an hour. Randi thought she bore the surprised looks from David's relatives with as much grace as possible. She didn't fit in with this high-nosed bunch. She knew it. His relations all knew it, too. The limousine pulled up in front of Wyndswept House, the French family estate. Managing to keep her mouth from dropping open, she took his hand as he assisted her from the limo. Her shoes slipped in the fine pea gravel of the circular drive, but his steadying hand in the small of her back kept her from falling flat on her butt.

Man, wouldn't the relatives have loved that?

Aware that every eyeball in the place was turned in her direction, she felt her face heat up. "David, I mean, my Lord

Middlebury." She attempted a smile, then muttered under her breath, "What am I supposed to call you, anyway?"

He extended his arm. "Just call me David like always. I'm still the same man you shared your bed with. Have you forgotten already?"

"No," she gulped. Good Lord, how could he say such things and still maintain such an innocent expression?

"Come. I want you to meet one of my cousins." David smiled and nodded as they walked past the other guests. He stopped in front of a young woman, who was nearly as tall as he. "Miranda, I want you to meet my cousin Hillary."

"*Lady* Hillary, you wretch," she corrected, her tone teasing, then glanced down at Randi. "How charming you are, dear. I'm so pleased to meet David's assignment. Now if you will excuse me, I must simply greet an old school chum of mine."

"That went well," Randi muttered, her tone tinged with sarcasm. "Just what I expected. She hated me."

"Actually, it did go rather well," he said with a wry smile. "Hillary's a veritable tiger when it suits her."

"Well, I still feel like she had a little nibble. Maybe she'll come back for the main course later."

"I certainly hope not. It wouldn't do for me to have to rescue her from you, since I know exactly how ferocious you are."

The butler announced dinner.

"Let's go in. You're seated on my right."

"Thank you, my lord," she said, attempting a curtsey.

"Stop that nonsense. I refuse to have you stand on ceremony. We've shared too much for you to act so silly about my title."

03

The bereavement dinner had gone well enough. Certain she hadn't used the wrong fork or anything, it had been all Randi could do to keep her eyes off David. Charming and witty, he'd kept the continual, if somewhat subdued, conversation flowing at their end of the table, always including her, making her a part of it all. This new side of him, as charming as it was, gave her pause. It brought home even more how she didn't fit with the people she saw around her. Was it her imagination, or were they all looking at her with a trace of amusement? No, maybe she was just insecure.

At the far end of the table, Lady Hillary rose. "Ladies, please join me in the salon while the gentlemen have their brandy."

Reluctantly, Randi stood. She'd rather stay with the guys, but she'd better adhere to convention. No point in making waves.

"I'll see you in a few," David murmured, giving her an encouraging smile.

What else could she do? She nodded in agreement, then followed the other women into the salon.

Lady Hillary paused at the doorway, waiting. "Quaint old custom, don't you think—the men and women separating after dinner. Why don't you accompany me to the ladies', and we'll have a little chat?"

Randi's stomach sank. "A little chat" certainly had an ominous sound to it. She already had a pretty good idea what Lady Hillary wanted to chat about and wasn't looking forward to it.

David's elegant cousin peered into the mirror, arranged a curl to perfection, then turned to Randi. "So, Miranda dear, when are you and your young son returning to America?"

Randi smiled to herself. *Here it comes—the bum's rush, the old heave ho.* "I haven't given it much thought."

"No? Obviously your child has no future here. Considering who and what his father is."

"My son has done nothing wrong. I don't see that who or what Jamie's father is has anything to do with his future."

"Oh, yes, that's so American of you. Seriously, don't you think you would be more comfortable with your family in— Tennessee, is it?"

"Nashville."

"Yes, country music and all that. I believe David said you're a musician—a fiddle player?" Hillary asked, her tone arch and condescending.

"Violin or fiddle. I play whatever style the gig calls for, but since I've been in England I've played mostly the classics."

Lady Hillary, apparently satisfied with her appearance, continued, "But I'm sure you must miss your family a great deal?"

That did it. Placing her hands on her hips, Randi couldn't hold back. "Look, if you're trying to be subtle, you're a wash at it. Why don't you just come out and say what you're dying to say? It'll save time."

"All right. I'll be frank."

"By all means."

"You don't belong here. David is no longer a mere detective, but a peer of the realm. He needs to marry someone of his own class with a similar lineage."

"And not a common little baggage from across the pond? Is that what you mean?"

"Well, I wouldn't have put it so crudely, but yes, that's exactly what I mean."

"Save your breath. I'm not after David. He saved my life and the life of my son. I'm here because he wanted me here. I'm grateful, but I'm not looking for another husband. The first one was quite enough."

"I should say."

"Is there anything else?"

"Why, yes, now that you mention it. I'll be happy to make your excuses. Will a sudden migraine suffice?"

"Migraine? I don't have headaches. What I have right now is a major pain in the ass."

"Well, I never."

"Really? How fortunate for you." Randi squared her shoulders and raised her chin a notch. "I think I've seen enough of how things are done in your class. You can look down your long nose at me if you want to, but I can assure you, no one would ever treat a guest this way in Nashville."

She didn't wait for Hillary's response. She'd just burned a major bridge and might as well leave the party and David, too, for that matter. The worst part of it—

Hillary was right. Randi didn't belong.

☙

David swallowed the last sip of coffee from his cup. "Shall we join the ladies? I think we've tarried long enough."

He stood, anxious to see Miranda. She'd been nervous through dinner, whether it was he or the unfamiliar situation he wasn't sure. He led the men into the salon, but saw no sign of her. He turned to Hillary. "Where's Miranda?"

She gave him a wolfish smile that made his stomach churn. "Why I believe she left, Cous."

"Left, but—"

Damn! What had his cousin said or done to make Miranda rush off without saying good-bye.

"Well, there's no accounting for her manners. The least she could've done was bid good-night to her host. After all, it's not every day someone of her class is welcomed into polite society."

"Come off it, Hillary. I was going to ask her to marry me tonight." He fumbled for the box in his pocket. "I've the ring and everything."

"Well, then," Hillary said with a broad smile, "her departure has saved you from making a terrible mistake."

He gritted his teeth. "Pardon?"

"I mean, she just isn't suitable for someone of your lineage and rank. And I think she understood that fact."

"What utter rot! This is the twenty-first century, not the Victorian Age."

"Good breeding always tells. You can't get around that."

"If that's true, then I'm fairly certain someone made an unfortunate error in your branch of the family tree."

"David! I believe you meant to insult me."

"Thank heavens, you've just enough intelligence to realize my intent!" He spun on his heel, turning his back on the other mourners.

A telephone, damn it. He must call Miranda and apologize for his cousin's boorish behavior. And there was a wedding proposal to arrange.

He strode into the library, grabbed the phone and punched in her number.

No answer. Finally, her voice mail picked up. "Miranda, David here. I'm not sure what Hillary said to you, but you mustn't pay her any mind. We need to talk." He paused. Damned if he was going to propose by telephone! "Please call me when you get in. Bye."

Chapter Thirty-One

The telephone rang. And rang.

Randi sat on the sofa, holding her breath. Willing the incessant ringing to stop, she let out a sigh of relief when finally it did.

Ever since her headlong escape from Wyndswept House, she'd spent the night listening to the telephone ring and wrestling with her emotions. Deep down inside she knew David's cousin was right, in spite of his numerous phone messages. Randi Raines from Nashville, Tennessee, had no place in his new life as the earl of Middlebury. When he'd just been a detective, she'd entertained visions of what their life together might be like...possibly.

Jamie certainly worshipped the man she'd fallen in love with. It didn't matter that she'd made a mistake the first time with Stefan. This time she knew the measure of the man she loved. He was brave, resourceful and made her feel things she'd never felt before.

The telephone rang again.

Instinctively, she reached for the receiver, but stopped herself just in time. Tears rolled down her cheeks. Would he never give up? She had.

Scrambling from the sofa, she yanked the cord from its connector. "There!" she said, wiping her hands in satisfaction.

But she could still hear it ringing in the kitchen.

"A plan," she said aloud. "I need to make a plan."

ભ

The next morning, David was in the midst of reviewing estate records when the butler tapped on the open library door. He looked up at the familiar tall, gray-bearded man. "Yes, Fields?"

"Ms. Raines to see you, Your Lordship. Are you at home?"

"She's here? Now?" He'd just eaten breakfast and it sat like a stone in his stomach. Miranda hadn't returned his calls from the night before, and he hadn't wanted to call too early this morning.

"Yes, my Lord."

"Of course, I'm at home. Show her in."

The butler nodded, then left David to his thoughts. Seeing her face-to-face would be the ideal thing. He would ask her to marry him right then and there.

"Ms. Raines, my lord."

"Thank you." David rose and walked to her side, ready to sweep her into his arms, but something in her manner made him hesitate. "I'm so glad you've come. I've something important to discuss with you." He motioned for her to sit.

She sat in the chair in front of his desk, nervously brushing the skirt of her gray suit. "I'm sorry for showing up so early and all, but I just wanted you to know that I—uh, I just wanted to tell you, I've made up my mind about what I'm going to do."

"And?"

"I'm moving back to the States."

"You are?" Taking a deep breath, David sank into his chair. Moving back? How could she?

"I-I miss my family."

"I see." He stalled for time, drumming his fingers on the desk. He hadn't expected her to just up and leave. How could he have misjudged her feelings? Why had he ever thought she'd stay and marry him? "When?" he managed to get out the bitter word.

"As soon as I make arrangements to sell my house. I've an appointment with an estate agent in twenty minutes."

"Please call me if there's anything I can do to assist you."

Fool! Ask her to stay. Damn it all, she doesn't want to stay. What's the point?

"Jamie should get to know my side of the family. That way he won't be so..." Words appeared to fail her.

"If you're sure, then I guess that's best." Of their own accord, his hands fumbled with the papers on his desk. At least she wouldn't be able to tell how shaken he was by her sudden news.

"W-well, that's all I came to say. I can see you're busy."

"No, you don't have to leave. Stay," he said, grasping at a straw. "Cook will serve a brunch. I—"

"No, I mean, thanks, but I do have that appointment, so I guess I'd better get going." She gripped her purse, as if she were afraid it would fly from her grasp. She jumped up, apparently ready to run away from him, as well.

"Wait." He rose from his seat. "I'll see you to the door."

Giving a tight, little smile, she shook her head. "That's okay. I can find my way out."

"But I want to." He stumbled over his words, trying to find the right response. "Only good manners, after all."

Bugger!

Whatever made him say that? He walked beside her, struggling against an uncontrollable urge to sweep her into his arms and carry her up the stairs to his bedroom.

If she wanted him—no, she *wanted* him. But if she *loved* him, she wouldn't consider leaving. And because he loved her, he must let her go.

The walk through the long hall ended too soon. They stopped at the front door. He had one last chance to stop her if he could just summon his courage and abandon his pride.

She looked up at him, her crystal green eyes brimming with unshed tears.

"Don't go," he murmured, finally able to say something.

"I have to. G'bye, David." He reached for her, but she slipped away, avoiding his grasp. "I'm late. Gotta go."

"Promise you'll call before you leave."

A nod was her only response.

He watched her run to the taxi, the lifeblood draining from him. Powerless to stop her, he watched as the taxi drove away.

Marie-Nicole Ryan

"Bloody hell!" he yelled, slamming his fist into the door frame. Sharp twinges shot from his hand to his elbow, but it didn't begin to compare with the agony ripping through his gut.

Once again, he'd lost the woman he loved. How could he have been so blasted stupid? How could he have just let her go?

C3

A week after her meeting with David, Randi looked around her sweet little cottage. Jamie sat on the bare floor, rolling a small truck around as if he'd lost his last friend in the world.

Everything was settled. The cottage was in the hands of a real estate agent. A few pieces of furniture would stay with the house. The antiques had already been packed and picked up, ready for shipment home.

Home. Funny, but Nashville didn't seem like home anymore. Her heart was here like Jamie's. The man she loved was here, but that was going nowhere. She didn't fit in with his life. No point in going over it again and again.

She pulled the zipper closed on the last of their luggage, then glanced at her watch. Unable to put off calling David any longer. She'd promised she'd call him before she left, and she would keep her promise...just barely.

She picked up the cell phone, which seemed to weigh a ton. Slowly, she punched in the number for his office in Scotland Yard, her finger trembling over each button.

It rang.

"DCI French here."

She'd hoped that he'd be out or too busy. "David, this is—"

"Miranda, I'm so glad you called."

"Well, I did say I'd call before I left. We're leaving for the airport now."

"Now? What's your flight number?"

"American Airlines, flight two-oh-four." Silently she prayed, attempting to keep her voice normal and business-like. "Our plane leaves in three hours, but I need to be there at least two hours before it leaves."

"But—"

Seconds from losing control, she forced the words, "Anyway, our cab's here. I've got to go. Good-bye." Without waiting for a response, she snapped shut the cell phone and disintegrated into tears.

Jamie tugged on her sleeve. "Mummy, do we have to go? I don't want to go to America. I-I want to stay here."

She collapsed on the floor beside her son, giving him a bear hug. "I know, sweetheart, but it's for the best. You have lots of cousins, and your grandmother and grandfather will be there. They'll be so excited to see you. You'll love Nashville. It's b-beautiful."

௸

David slammed down the telephone, greatly tempted to throw it across the room, but an earl wasn't supposed to behave in such a manner and certainly not in his office.

"Hell!" David threw it across the room anyway.

Just "Good-bye". After all they'd been through.

He glanced at his watch. Three hours, and she would be on her way to America and out of his life forever. He'd never see her again. Never hear her soft Southern drawl again. Never touch her silken skin again.

Damn it. The last week—the waiting for her to contact him had been interminable. He'd consoled himself by thinking she *would* call. He'd changed his mind about resigning the Force; she could jolly well change hers about leaving. But she hadn't.

It was time he faced the truth. Could he live without her?

And his final answer was yes, he could, but he'd be damned if he *would*.

Chapter Thirty-Two

David slammed on the brakes. But the sickening crunch of his passenger door and the window glass smacking against the side of his head told him he'd been too late.

Hesitating just long enough for his head to clear, he jumped out of the Jag, then ran around to the passenger side. "You bloody idiot! See what you've done!" he yelled at the other driver.

"Come on, mate. It's not so bad. Just a little ding."

"I'm on my way to the airport. I don't have time for this."

"Oy! Ain't that just too bad. I've got me some damage, too. You ought to watch where you're driving that bloody motor." The man drew up his fists. "We can settle this right now."

"You're right. We certainly can." He pulled out his warrant card. "I'll haul your sorry posterior down to the nearest station."

The punk backed up. "Now. Don't have to get violent."

A police constable, walking his beat, entered into the fray. "All right, you two. Just tell me what happened."

"See here, constable. I'm on the force, and I'm in a hurry," David protested, desperate to get on his way.

The constable eyed David's identification. "Now, now, Chief Inspector French. Exceptions can't be made, sir. Surely, you realize that. How would it appear? I've me forms to complete."

"I don't care how it appears. You can reach me at the Yard later. Right now, I have to reach the airport before a certain flight departs."

The constable's eyebrows raised a notch. "A fleeing felon, sir? That's different."

"You're just going to let him leave? Look at me car!" the punk objected.

"Police business, after all," the constable offered.

"Thank you, Constable." David spun around and jumped into his car. He glanced at the clock on the dashboard. He was running out of time. Miranda's flight was due to leave in thirty minutes. Bloody hell!

☙

Tickets and baggage checks in one hand, Randi held tight to Jamie's small hand with her other.

"Are you still afraid of flying, Mummy?"

Flying? Flying was the last thing on her mind. "Not this time. We're going home, Jamie."

"But I want our old home. I miss my mates."

"You'll make new friends."

He jerked his hand from hers, folding his arms across his chest. "No, I won't go," he said, lifting his chin.

Not now. Of all times for her son to turn into a sullen brat. Her heart was breaking, and he was probably going to scream all the way across the Atlantic. "Stop it," she ordered, grabbing his hand in hers. "Why are you acting like this?"

"I wanted David to be my dad. Now he'll never marry us."

A soft snicker sounded behind Randi. Turning around, she glared at the elderly onlooker. "Mind your own business," she mouthed.

"Perhaps you ought to listen to the lad. Forgive me for saying so, but you don't seem too happy about leaving."

"I'm not," she admitted, wishing the busybody would just go away.

"Then why're you going against your heart, dearie?"

"Because it's the best thing for everybody."

"Are you sure?"

Was she sure? Well, she'd thought she was.

"You're not sure, are you? I can see it in your face. I'm

thinking there's someone else going to be just as upset as you are right now."

"Yes, Mummy. David loves you. He loves me."

"See there. The lad knows what's what."

Overhead the loud speaker announced, "Flight two-oh-four boarding at gate twenty-east."

She choked back her tears and doubts. "That's our flight. Come on, son."

♋

David ran down the concourse, checking his watch again and again. He simply had to stop her from leaving. No eff-ing way could he live without Miranda. Too bad he hadn't realized it an hour earlier. Damn traffic. A fender-bender with an irate punk who'd tried to punch his lights out. Questions and forms? Bloody hell!

He couldn't help it. He'd lied. He'd straighten everything out tomorrow. First he had to stop Miranda from boarding that flight.

Over the PA system, he heard, "Final call for American Airlines flight two-oh-four for New York, now boarding at gate twenty-east."

Flight two-oh-four. That was her flight. He would make it after all.

But a frantic cry stopped him in his tracks. "Stop, thief!"

Glancing around, he spied an elderly woman who'd been knocked to the ground. "Help. He took my purse. It has my passport and all my cash."

Over her shoulder, he spotted a tall, slender male running for all he was worth, a woman's shoulder bag in hand.

What else could he do? Torn between desire and duty, he sprinted after the purse snatcher, maneuvering his way through the crowd.

♋

After turning the thief over to the airport authorities, David ran to the gate. Lord, what if he was too late? "Flight two-oh-four?" he gasped.

"I'm sorry, sir," the attendant replied. "That flight has departed."

Each word, a spike in his heart. He'd missed her. All because he couldn't bear to see an old woman weeping in distress. Once again, he had to be the eff-ing hero. Now the woman he loved was bloody well on her way back to the States.

He slumped over the counter. Time to think. Catch his breath. Regroup.

Damn it! He'd follow her. Bring her back. He'd bloody well marry her, if she'd have him. Dear God. What if she still didn't want him? Hell, he'd cross that bridge when he came to it.

First things first. He had his passport. All he needed was a plane ticket.

"Your next flight to the States?" he asked the attendant. He felt a gentle tug at his sleeve and heard the sweetest sound in the world, a soft Southern voice.

"David."

He spun around and saw her, her green eyes brimming with tears, standing with Jamie at her side. "I can't believe it!" Sweeping her into his arms, he crushed his lips against hers for a hungry, bruising kiss.

Life was good. Hell, it was superb. "I thought I'd lost you."

She gave him a sheepish grin, then drawled, "You know how I hate flyin'."

"Lord, yes, I know. And thank heaven for it."

"What about me? Don't I deserve a hug, too?" Jamie asked.

He stopped kissing Miranda long enough to declare, "Absolutely!" then bent down and swept up Jamie with his left arm, keeping his right one tight, very tight, around the woman he loved. "I'm not giving you another chance to leave me."

"Are you sure? I mean, I'm not a blue-blood. Your family— I'm just a fiddle player from Nashville, Tennessee." A tiny frown crossed her face. "I mean—uh, I didn't mean to assume."

"Of course, I want you to marry me. As for my family,

they'll come to love you like I do." David set Jamie down, then dropped to his knees in front of her and her son. "James Michael Peyton, will you give me your blessing? May I ask for your mother's hand in marriage?"

Jamie's eyes grew wide. "Will you be my father then?"

"I most certainly will."

"Then you have my blessing, sir." Jamie looked up at his mother. "Did I say it right, Mummy?" Then he whispered, "Do you want to marry him?"

"Young fellow, I'm supposed to ask your mum that question myself."

"Oops." Jamie's brown eyes twinkled as he placed his hand over his mouth in a vain attempt to keep from smiling.

Miranda cleared her throat. "We're standing here in the middle of the airport. People are watching."

"Then I best get on with it." He glanced around and grinned at the onlookers. "The lady says 'get on with it', so I shall."

Taking her hand in his, David inhaled deeply and pressed a kiss across her knuckles. "Miranda, my love. Will you do me the extreme honor of becoming my wife, forever and always loving me, bearing my children and keeping my feet warm at night?" He held his breath, and it seemed that his heart stopped.

At least he thought it might. She could still say no.

"Yes, David. I will marry you, love you forever and always, bear your children..." she paused with a wide grin, "...and keep your feet warm at night." She motioned for him to rise. "You do realize you're on your knees in the middle of Heathrow?"

He sprang to his feet, knowing he had a silly grin plastered over his face. He gathered Miranda and Jamie to his chest once again, feeling whole for the first time in his life.

Applause rang out. "Good show, old man. Bloody good show!" Men clapped him on the back. And more than one woman wiped away a tear.

"Congratulations!"

"First time I've ever seen a proposal in the middle of an airport."

David walked along in a daze. He had won the love of a brave and good woman, not to mention the approval of her child. The future was not the one he'd planned so many years before, but far more satisfying for the trials they'd been through together. Indeed, there was a great deal to be said for finding love on the run.

An insistent voice brought him back to reality.

"Where's the ring, Mummy? Isn't he supposed to give you a ring?"

"Quite right. I see I've been somewhat remiss in the proprieties." He removed the Middlebury crest ring from his finger and slipped it onto the third finger of her left hand. "I'm afraid this will have to do until I retrieve the one I meant to give you earlier."

"Earlier?"

"Yes, after the funeral, but you ran away."

Tears fell unchecked down her cheeks. "I love you, David." Though her tears kept falling, she giggled. "Not because you're going to give me a ring. I mean, you don't have to—"

"Of course, I do. The countess of Middlebury will have a mighty fine diamond, which will surely feel shame that it cannot outshine your beautiful eyes."

"Once you get started, you just don't know when to stop, do you?" She tiptoed and kissed him softly on the lips, effectively stopping his attack of purple prose and giving his heart a jolt he wouldn't soon forget. He took a deep breath and marveled. All the flowers of Grasse couldn't compare with the sweet freshness of her scent.

He had to be the luckiest man in the world. In his arms he possessed everything he'd ever wanted—a woman he loved and who loved him and his soon-to-be adopted son—a real family.

Epilogue

Kinsey Green, East Anglia

In the honeymoon suite of the East Anglia Inn, Miranda Raines French, countess of Middlebury, lay naked and shameless in her husband's warm embrace. She rolled over and gazed into her David's silver-gray eyes. She'd never seen them so warm or so full of love, and all for her. His sensual mouth pulled into a smile. Her body, still languid and warm from their loving, instinctively moved closer to his.

"Good morning," she murmured, barely breathing. Slipping her arms around his neck and her feet between his, she told him, "Your feet are warm, my lord."

His smile grew wider. "My lady, every bit of me is warm. Good morning, luv. No bad dreams?"

"No, no bad dreams."

"Good." He placed a kiss on the tip on her nose and began to make love to her all over again. Her last coherent thought as she opened her body to his—no matter what the future held she could face it as long as she was with this warm and loving man. Together they'd already braved the worst that life had offered...together.

The end...or was it just the beginning?

About the Author

Romantic suspense author, Marie-Nicole Ryan, has had a life-long love affair with books. Like a lot of people, she thought she'd write a book some day. Since time passed so quickly (when you're supposed to be having fun), she found herself well into middle age and still no book—as long as you don't count the hundred pages of one she typed on an old portable Smith-Corona typewriter back in the late Seventies.

Love on the Run was her first book published (2002), and it was the realization of a long-held dream. Although she spent most of her life working as an RN, she also found time to earn an associate degree in interior design, something that comes in handy when it's time to visualize a room. And since she can't resist placing her characters in jeopardy, her medical experience isn't wasted either.

Since that first book, she's published three more books. *Too Good to Be True* is her first release at Samhain Publishing, Ltd., and she has three more contracted for release this fall and in 2008.

To learn more about Marie-Nicole Ryan, please visit http://marienicoleryan.com. Send an email to marienicoleryan@yahoo.com or join her Yahoo! group to keep track of her latest releases and contest news. Send an e-mail to Marie-NicoleRyanNews-subscribe@yahoo.com.

GREAT
CHEAP
FUN

Discover eBooks!

THE FASTEST WAY TO GET THE HOTTEST NAMES

Get your favorite authors on your favorite reader, long before they're out in print! Ebooks from Samhain go wherever you go, and work with whatever you carry—Palm, PDF, Mobi, and more.

CPSIA information can be obtained at www.ICGtesting.com
224750LV00001B/49/P